ANONYMITY

BY

RACHEL MARTIN

ANONYMITY

This book is a work of fiction. Names, characters, businesses, organizations, places, events and incidents either are the product of the author's imagination or are used fictitiously. Any resemblance to actual persons, living or dead, events, or locales is entirely coincidental.

For information contact:

Garnet Moon Publishing

http://www.garnetmoonpublishing.com

ISBN: 978-1-7360791-0-2 (paperback)

Cover Illustration by Damonza

First Edition: 2020

10 9 8 7 6 5 4 3 2 1

SWIM!

Preposterous as it sounds, it wasn't the first time my life hanged by the strength of my hands around a smooth tree root. *I do hope it's the last.*

As I swing, twisting and flailing by sweaty palms, the answer I need, *and fast* to—*do I trust the Doc*—materializes in a flash of memory.

My father had taught me to cliff dive among crocs, *hardly the coddling sort.* Pop's bad judgment should've taught me *not* to jump. Given the only valuable skill he'd instilled was to pierce the water so harmoniously at its entry that it would chase me downward, in lieu of splashing out of protest . . . I'm going to bet on me.

Doc is screaming overhead for me to grab his hand as I plant my feet against the black shale of the hillside. Muscles locked and loaded for action, in one motion—I explode off the side of the cliff, releasing the root at the peak of my swing. From my toes to fingertips, I'm aligned with perfection as I perform the dive that dad had taught me . . . *only in reverse.*

Plunging into the ferocious current, I'm shocked back to reality by the bite of the frigid, icy depths filling every orifice! Doc was right about its threat, *but I haven't come this far to fail now!*

Shoes intact, *the point of going feet first,* my soles slam against a rock's edge under the obsidian depths. Instinctually, as I push against it and torpedo toward the surface, I'm met by a liquid barricade. *Keep calm Merlot.*

Mimicking a sea creature, I hold my limbs against my sides, slithering underwater with the tide. Systematically, I inch closer to the open air with each full body movement— remaining submerged deep enough to leave the water's surface undisturbed. *I've got to get as much distance out of this breath as humanly possible.* My willpower is beckoning to me . . . "You're out of his sight by now!"

Fatigued and oxygen starved, I capsize, a human buoy, inhaling a dizzying lungful of sweet air. My audible gasp echoes as if in an empty cathedral. *This is in an oddly quiet setting*?

Treading water, my eyes adjust to the darkness, and I squint to locate the distance to land. Shadows of a thick tree line loom nearby—*or are they merely whispering "come hither lies" to my optimism?* Ignoring the grain of doubt that blooms in my gut, I feel sure I can make it to shore soon . . . or perhaps I'll swim a bit further to be sure. A good head start is imperative.

Minutes into a peaceful swim, I find myself easing into the waltz of the narrowing ravine . . . until finally, I'm treading water again—but this time with ease. *Wait, why is it slowing to this lackadaisical pace?*

I fill my lungs again and descend, a human measuring stick, exploring the depth below my naked frolic. *It's deeper all right.*

As I come up to survey my surroundings, a colossal opal moon emerges before me, spanning the width between forestry on either side of the channel. A vulnerable speck in its presence, I imagine the only thing separating us are the jewels of light twinkling off playful liquid, revealing the velocity of its flow.

For the first time in a month, I exhale a calm breath, appreciating the moment of freedom I feel. *Surely,* this moon is a gift from the universe—a positive sign of what is to come.

In all the glory before me, a horizon on the river's edge serves as the backdrop for this showy spectacle . . .

Wait, horizon? That means . . . oh no—*a waterfall!*
Waterfalls are beautiful *unhappy* endings!

3

ABOUT THE AUTHOR

ANONYMITY, an Adult Suspense Thriller, is Rachel Martin's debut novel. Her protagonist is finally released to fulfill his plans of calculated debauchery, in much the same way that Rachel has freed herself to pursue her desire of becoming a published novelist. Along Rachel's professional career, she has embarked upon many creative "side" endeavors. She describes these as "patching the hole in a dam", or "being handed a glass of water in the desert". They quenched a need to exercise her creative muscles, but weren't passion-igniting in the way that unloading her imagination in story form is. An unapologetic daydreamer, Rachel's inspirations are her actual dreams, asking "what if" often, and imagining scenarios about victims of her "people watching". *If only they knew their alternate realities!*

CONNECT WITH RACHEL:

Facebook | www.facebook.com/authorrachelmartin

Instagram | www.instagram.com/authorrachelmartin

Website | www.rachelmartinbooks.com

*To my Mom – For enthusiastically voicing your belief
in me in all things, celebrating each small victory,
and showing me what unconditional love is. I feel you with
me on this journey, cheering me on . . .*

BEGINNING IN BLOOD

Squee! The first sound I remember. Pigs, as I slay them—or rather, *watched and learned.*

Left at the doorstep of a slaughterhouse, my teenage host birthed me amongst the tree frogs and slugs before disappearing across the low country fog, more nimbly than a ground lemur. I was never to know or see her again, but clearly, she had instincts about where I belonged.

Despite the electricity of locusts chatter that dawn, a hard-working man named Vernon heard my cries and took me in.

Years later, Darlene, the local malt shop marm who hadn't the good sense to hide from me what Vernon had tried to keep secret, revealed that the teen who'd left me for gator bait was a high school dropout and was known to frequent the prison on the edge of town for "conjugal visits". Except, he and my teenage host were never married. She didn't say who the prisoner was, and I never asked, *anyone*—but Darlene did tell me he was up for murder one, and in her words, that he was "bat shit crazy".

Vernon figured teaching his newborn son the only way of life he'd known was better for me than the alternative . . . being left alone to be raised by his wife, Polly. She'd avoided looking me in the eyes at all costs. The few glimpses I'd stolen revealed a lifeless, angry soul. Likely scorched by excessive whiskey and cigarettes, her womb was dry, and I got to hear about it during her drunken rants for years to come.

Child labor is an ugly designation. I'd heard of camps of kids in other countries working without education, fresh water, or enough to eat. I'd seen them in documentaries with ribs as their most prominent body features. That wasn't me, but tell any red-blooded American about my mornings, after school hours, and summers, and you may as well have called Child Protective Services.

Up to my little thighs, later my knees, and eventually my ankles, in ventrals and blood—this, was my way of life. Rank odors, visual debauchery, grisly screams, and the handling of bowels were *later* to become my drive. All are assaults to normal senses. My senses have never been *normal*. I knew I didn't want Vernon's life, but the buffet of sensory indulgence taught me much about who I am today.

Looking back on those days, *if I could feel,* it would be feelings of gratitude and love. Yes, the slaughterhouse would've been my first girlfriend.

My only other attempt at one was with a cutter named Vicky. Gossip had it, her much older parents gave up on becoming pregnant years prior. She'd been born a miracle child. Their simultaneous passing was a mystery—a mystery because no one in town talked about it. She had been the only witness to what had actually happened. After that, Vicky moved to our small South Carolina town, and lived with her only other relatives—an uncle, by blood, and his wife.

She was thirteen at the end of that school year, and I seventeen, when we locked glances in the lunchroom. The space between us sucked into a vacuum—I still can't recall the physical steps between eyes meeting eyes and standing too close. Awkwardly making our teenage attempt at conversation, we mostly looked down and shuffled our feet. I do remember from that first exchange, that she made me aware of her weekly visit to the town psychologist. I was pretty sure she was testing to see if I'd shun her, but instead I found her intriguing. She became even darker and cooler in my mind.

Those late summer afternoons—when I got off early from the slaughterhouse, we'd slip away to the local bakery and order Puff Pastry Cream Horns. She loved the sound of the cream squirting into their tunnels; *queak, queak, queak*—until the flaky shell was full. I hated the taste of them, but it made her giggle, and I got to see her braces when she laughed, so I'd order one too. I studied the saliva traveling in slow motion down the rubber bands in her mouth and wondered what other fluids inside her might be as lovely. After logging enough hours together, she gave me the chance to find out.

I promised if she'd let me watch, I wouldn't tell a soul. She agreed, swearing me to secrecy. Said it was sacred— made her feel alive . . . feel, *something.* And don't worry because she'd learned how deep and where she could cut so it wouldn't kill her. *That explained her wardrobe of long shorts and shirts sleeves down to her elbows.* I was attracted to what would come out when she opened her skin with a blade—not the act itself.

Our teen tryst was over when I became uncontrollably turned on by an oozing cut she allowed me to witness, for the third time. Could she *not* see the hard-on in my jeans? *I suppose sex wasn't the reason she sliced at her arms and inner thighs.* Probably better it ended. I would soon be an adult with a minor in the world's eyes.

Though I'd saved every dime, I realized the pittance I was paid at the slaughterhouse would never add up to the cost of a college education. A scholarship was to be my only solution. I had no desire *or time* for sports, and fitting in with the jocks would've presented a definite challenge. So instead, I took every possible advanced class, as well as studying beyond the scope of what our small-town school had to offer. A bonus was that it kept me out of Polly's sight.

She'd reminded me repetitively that I was lucky to be there, *and* that she would've kicked me out if not for the memory of Vernon, who hadn't lived long enough to see me escape *his* hell hole. I was not only accepted into top schools, but also sought after, and at no expense to me. Thanks to Vernon's insistence that I work alongside him, I'd absorbed excellent Biology lessons along the way.

My humble yet gruesome roots, by most measures, provided both a hiding place and a launching pad. Since leaving the small South Carolina town, one might say I've "recreated" myself.

I've gotten rid of the glasses hiding my gunmetal blue eyes, through the miracle of corrective eye surgery. My dark-wavy hair has been cut into a clean style, and the uniform of baggy t-shirts have long since been replaced by a wardrobe that doesn't conceal my six-foot-three chiseled physique . . . earned by physical labor, and *not* the gym. I've even taken up sports of the individual variety, mostly mountain biking and rock climbing.

I needn't have grown up playing with "Johnny or Sue". What they may have discovered could've left an indelible mark on their soft fortitudes. I required, and *still* require, anonymity—but to be sure those days are dead and buried, I've changed my name.

ABEL

"Abel . . . Abel!"

Oh, how I loathe that woman . . . "Yes Celeste, *what?*"

"Just a minute . . . never mind, I got it myself."

I knew, I knew the day I married my yoga addict of a wife, what I had gotten myself into. The constant *droll* should come as no surprise now. She regards herself *so* interesting, if not mysterious. She could never pull off "interesting". Painfully predictable is more apropos.

How do I endure such aggravation? I've learned to settle for the sensory satisfaction I derive from Celeste's full menu of insecurities.

My favorite is her absolute radiating jealousy toward any woman whom she deems more beautiful—or better yet, more beautiful *and* more talented than she. A three-course meal plays out so simply. To start things off, I place a compliment upon said target, in Celeste's presence, of course—sit back, and take in the display.

Appetizer . . . the green-eyed monster inside her dilates her pupils, while accelerating her heart rate, and spurting tiny wells of scent from her soft armpits—*the derivative of psyche-induced pinpricks.*

Entrée . . . with erect posture, her B cup chest visibly rises and falls in quick motions, as she quietly grapples to breathe, until a tiny laugh, *the pitch of swallowing helium produces*, escapes her pink lips—*this a retort delivered by her subconscious, no doubt.*

Dessert . . . nervously smoothing her blonde hair, she agrees with said compliment by repeating it—then tries to recover by showering her new enemy with syrupy praise. *I hate dessert.* Still, there is no better gift she can bestow upon me—well, *almost* none.

I'd far rather drink in this visceral display, than the torture of having "conventional" sex with her—an unavoidable task as of late with the baby clock she keeps referring to.

The pinnacle of her jealousy trifecta—my new assistant, Bella Livonia.

At twenty-four, five foot nine, bouncy voluminous breasts, and an ass that makes even straight women drool a little—what are her best attributes? Doing as I say, and keeping her opinions to herself. Rounding out this perfection, she is *not* a gossip.

As an expert on the brain's inner workings, along with hacking into her search history during a few primping trips to the ladies' room, I've deduced Bella too self-absorbed to concern herself with a forty-year-old Doctor's personal business.

Her searches and 'favorites' have revealed shopping habits, in addition to her worship of models and movie stars. Upon further observation, she *has* styled herself after a few of the more glamorous ones, evolving as they do. I certainly hope she hasn't marred that porcelain skin with "tattoo art".

Perhaps her most useful of traits is the distraction she creates for my meddling staff, occasionally fishing for information as to my whereabouts.

Her desk sits center-stage, with a tiger wood surround that hides its contents, until visitors have fully approached its raised countertop. Her chair and the desk rest on a platform behind, allowing her to lord over those who enter through the glass double doors directly in front of her. *Conveniently, the platform also allows a nice view of her from the waist up.* The polished concrete floors announce every visitor for eleven paces before reaching her throne. This gives her time to study their gate, be it with intention or meek.

A camera has been installed at the top of wooden wall behind her desk, which blocks the view of the hall to my office door. When the visitor interests me, I turn up the sound.

I've witnessed her disassemble the bolder of inquiries as to when I'll be back, after she tells them I am not in. Wide-eyed, she leans forward, pressing her breasts together while biting her lower lip—then gives pause as her victim begins to stutter. If they don't promptly leave, she'll stand to smooth her clothing, turning to show off her assets, and allowing her gaze to wander to said target's crotch. The sighting of a *trouser tent* is assured dismissal.

Her best show for me to date—the complete befuddlement of my dear Celeste when Celeste came to my office with a lunch invitation, and the eye-to-eye saga with her soon-to-be nemesis played out.

Introduced for the first time, Bella ended the exchange with "Nice to meet you, *Ma'am*". *Ah* . . . the surname blighted, making Celeste feel like an older woman, by a thirteen-year age gap, and coming from this . . . *bombshell.*

Celeste's tongue rendered itself frozen, allowing me the opportunity to deliver the final blow. Dear, Bella is by far, the most competent assistant I've had the pleasure to work alongside. Her talents *really are* beyond her job's description.

No nervous laughter, no pontificating agreement, just pure internal rage. Celeste's neck veins pulsed, pinching her optic nerves and creating a red-eyed response—as rushing adrenaline muffled her hearing. Still, she stared straight ahead, eyes locked on the body fallen off a mudflap, as "it" stood to shake her hand. Finally, I was forced to utter the word *darling* to snap her out of it.

With eyelids a flutter, and through pursed lips, Celeste finally spoke. "So nice to meet you. I think I'll excuse myself—I have some, *um*, errands to take care of. Abel, dear, I will see *you* at home." Even Celeste had forgotten why she was there!

It was pure magic—insecurities on parade! Unfortunately, I hadn't hit record on my camera before entering the lobby. At least I got *some* entertainment out of it later, at dinner.

As I crossed the threshold of the back door that evening, Celeste's insecurities filled my olfactory, in the form of Beef Wellington rare, and Bitter Chocolate Cheesecake—the one dessert I enjoy—to be served later with a cup of French Roast. She topped it off with real whipped cream in the shape of a heart. She knows I don't eat dairy. The heart was her passive-aggressive way of keeping a disapproving comment out of our mealtime vernacular, while exercising *some* control. I had to bite my tongue . . . *but I'd rather have bitten hers.*

"To what do I owe the pleasure of this delectable meal, my dear?" Knowing that this king's ransom meal was an insecure, yet manipulative gesture—I decided to start my entertainment after polishing off my feast in sweet silence.

"No reason, really. I just thought you deserve to be spoiled occasionally. After all your hard work—providing a wonderful home and lifestyle—it's the least a wife can do for her husband."

"Well, thank you." I left it hanging there. Nothing else needed to be said. I'd enjoy her squirming a bit.

"Not to change the subject, but your assistant, what a lovely girl. Is she married?"

"No, I don't believe she is." *Bingo!*

"Huh, well, I was married at twenty-four, but of course you know that."

I saw no need to respond, as this was a mere statement of fact. *Get to it, woman—my after-dinner entertainment awaits.*

"You were four years older than me, in your residency, genius that you are, and ahead of your colleagues." A little smile popped across her mouth, hoping she'd softened me up with an obvious fact, dressed up in compliment's clothing. "Remember, we had just moved here to Denver, with your new position as head of the Neuroscience Lab and practicing brain surgeon? Of course, I was happy to give up my nursing studies to ensure our home was run with care and grace."

"Three years older than you to be exact, Celeste. Is there a question in there that I missed?" *I despise trolling for compliments.* She'd left nursing school of her own accord and attended in the first place to earn her M.R.S. with a D.R.

"Well, who's counting. Anyway, I was just thinking, there must be *so* many candidates suited as an assistant who would be more . . . *appropriate.*"

"Appropriate? How so?"

"Well, someone who presents her *or* himself in a fashion that is a bit more,' demure', perhaps?"

"Oh? More demure, in what way?"

"Abel, I think you know what I am referring to! Do I have to spell it out for you? Are you really *that* oblivious to her . . . charm? I guess I should be happy about that, but trust me, it is doing your office a disservice to have such a— a wanton siren of a girl plopped right down, front and center! I didn't set out to deliver it to you in this way, but it seems I have no choice."

"So it's her appearance?" *Yes . . . finally getting to the root of it, ole' girl. Dig in now and don't disappoint.* "Maybe I should just talk to her, tell her to wear a longer skirt, or button another button. *Hmm . . .* though it might gape and potentially pop off. I'm sure she would understand. Although . . . she *could* cry sexual harassment and bring a suit against the practice. I know, dear, since you've brought it to my attention, *and* you're not an employee, maybe *you* should tell her how to present herself?" *I had to get more out of this than a good meal and a measly argument.*

"Abel—Dorian—Rhodes . . . I will *not* tell that redheaded *vamp* how 'to or not to' dress. I cannot believe you're defending that obvious, *hussy!*"

"Celeste? Are you actually *jealous* . . . of Bella? Why, she's a baby—however, extremely good at her job. What do you have to be jealous about anyway?"

"Of course I'm not jealous! Look at her and look at me! First of all, I have *never* thought redheads were attractive, poor things . . . I thank the good Lord he didn't give me red hair. I would have to color it for sure."

"I'm pretty sure that Bella isn't a natural redhead, Celeste." That would get her going. Now she'd wonder how I knew the drapes don't match the carpet when, in fact, I'd seen her online hair color purchase 'cherry cola'.

"So she *chose* red hair? *Huh*, how do you know that? There's only one way to know that for sure . . . *Abel?*"

She gripped her steak knife, *hard . . .* almost there.

14

"I suppose when I lean over her from behind, to view the reports she's working on—I've noticed that she smells like lavender and her roots are blonde."

That would do it. Leaning over her provided a great cleavage shot. Smelling her was an intimate offense, and noticing her roots—well that was more than I ever notice about Celeste. Yep, blood trickling out—making a lovely little pool of red on the white linen. *Arousal achieved!*

"How—how dare you!"

Great. Crying . . . always a turn off. When would she learn what turns me on . . . *and off?* Without our game, I'd have little use for her. Emotional blubbering followed by snot—*out of the question.*

"Celeste, why are you so upset? Look what you've done to yourself." I rushed over and uncurled the grip she'd clutched the knife with. Blood was spurting from a vein in her finger. *Oh!* I felt my pupils dilate along with other 'growth' taking hold . . . but my desire wouldn't play well under these circumstances, so instead, I wrapped the cut with a napkin.

"Let's go clean this up." I led her to the kitchen sink and treated the cut. Down the drain . . . all that wasted blood, along with my arousal.

"Oh Able, you're right. I don't know what I was thinking. Why would you be interested in a girl who looks so . . . *ill-bred*?"

Ill-bred. Celeste's go-to. An insult she casts with a wide net—making her feel less inferior. Coming from money, but growing up without the source of it around, her father Myles, who'd moved out when she was three, left Celeste to be raised alone by her pretentious mother Phyllis. Showered with gifts instead of emotional support, Celeste had learned little from her upbringing, aside from an entitled attitude, *which she's still afflicted with.*

"I think I'll turn in early, dear. All this talk about your *assistant,* has spoiled my mood. We need to get up early to catch our flight anyway."

The sniffling and tears, along with the wasted blood, had spoiled *my* mood. At least I didn't have to be concerned about 'us' getting pregnant anymore, thanks to my insistence on checking her fertility a few months prior.

With the help of a fifty-three-year-old woman's test results in the throes of menopause, as well as my self-performed vasectomy—a pleasure compared to what she'd already put me through—she's stopped scheduling "baby sex". No more staring into my eyes during the missionary position . . . *sheer torture.*

Perhaps I'll get on with my real calling, once we're back from India.

HAPPY WIFE . . .

"Oh, sweetheart! Come sit—my poor baby. You must be exhausted after being on your feet for fourteen hours. Everyone *so* admires all the hard work you've put in! Would you like a foot rub, dear?"

A foot rub will hardly make up for you volunteering my services for two weeks of surgery. "Not now Celeste—just let me sleep after I eat this *goop* . . . prepared in who knows what kind of unsanitary conditions. Hopefully, it's been boiled enough to kill any contaminants we're not accustomed to. I'm glad to get the hell out of here after tomorrow!"

"I know it's been rough dear, but you and all the other doctors on this trip are saving lives. No one is ever going to forget that.

Abel, hun, you know how I've tried to introduce you to some of the village children who, no doubt, are without adult supervision? God only knows, if they are *completely* without parents . . ."

"You mean the dirty-faced urchins running amok around here? Celeste, please stop telling people you want to take one of them home. You have no idea what sort of disease they might have or what kind of havoc one of them could wreak on our home. Besides, it doesn't work like that. You can't just steal a kid away from this country."

"*Uh*, I *understand* it doesn't work like that—I'm not an idiot!"

"Oh come on, Celeste! Enough with the water works. You've been on some weird fantasy vacation—weird for you anyhow, agreeing to live in a tent, and use public shower facilities, when you normally wouldn't consider anything less than a four-star resort. Ironically, I'm the one paying the price for this insane little trip you've drummed up. So do *not* expect consoling from me."

"Ok! Enough 'feelings' then! However, you *should* know that I've emailed a letter to update the church on the conditions here and made them well aware that we've encountered an *obvious* orphan problem . . . and well, my plea was read from the pulpit. Thanks to *my* work and *my* ability to appeal to the good souls of the more fortunate back home, a few members of the church have agreed to open their hearts and homes—to a few *choice* children here."

"You mean, by adoption?"

"Yes Abel, I have contacted an agency, so that select, *lucky* children, are being legitimately adopted. Now, the church *and* the foundation expect us, of *all* people, who can't have children to adopt at least one poor child?"

"What do you mean by 'us of all people', Celeste?"

"Well . . . I know you prefer I don't share our personal lives with others, but what'd you expect me to do when I got that news? A few of the ladies from church were praying for us to get pregnant, *so* . . . when it hadn't—I mean it *couldn't* happen—I felt I should let them know that it wasn't possible. They know it's me and not you Abel. Please, don't worry about that."

"Celeste, *we* aren't even religious! We show up at that church on holidays because it makes *you* feel good, or maybe because you can't leave even one social circle in your path unturned—I, well, I don't know . . . or care. But you are *not* to share our personal business with any of them! Do you understand? Let me hear it from your lips!"

"Ok, I get it! And I promise *not* to 'share' again, but this one is out of the bag, and you are not going to distract me by yelling at me, for something I have *no* control over! Now, this is the thing . . . if you can't find it in your heart to adopt just one—not two or three—but *one* underprivileged little girl, when we have *so* much, then you, Abel Rhodes, are not the man I married!"

I *know* her appetite for wealth and living well. *I'm going to call her bluff on this tantrum.* "So what are you saying, Celeste? You would throw away *our marriage*, because you have a little egg on your face? Are you really so prideful, that you would give up every luxury I've given you over a *child* . . . one that isn't even your own?"

"All I'm saying, is that I don't know *how* I'll ever be able to look at you the same if you can't open your heart enough to afford me this one non self-serving thing! And, at the same time do your part to make the life of a child *so* much better than it would be if we leave her here. Over time, of course—I don't know how much time, that kind of thing I fear, will surely affect my love for you. In this scenario, how *could* I remain married to someone I may not love?"

Hmm . . . a trump card I hadn't predicted from the debutante princess. Because I can't afford the amount of time it would take to build a cover with a new decoy wife— *argh, I can't believe what I am about to agree to!*

"I guess I hadn't realized how important this is to you . . . so, with reservation, I'll agree to it—but only with the knowledge that you'll do the lion's share of the parenting. Discipline if needed, should be expected, and will come from me. I won't have a menace living under my roof. However, *do not* expect stories to be read, goodnight kisses, or any other insincere acts of emotion from me."

"Oh Abel, you're the best husband a woman could ever ask for!"

"One more condition—no babies. Only six or older and English-speaking."

"That will work just fine—I think I know just the lucky little girl to pick!"

*****

Celeste's wishes were easily granted. The adoption agency found a seven-year-old who met my conditions and Celeste's physical requirements. We brought back a polite child, with black glossy hair and large almond-shaped eyes.

The only thing I wouldn't allow was for Celeste to change her name, which is Priya. Big surprise, "Priya". I told her it was bad enough her last name was now going to be Rhodes. Celeste thought "Sophie" would have been better, until I pointed out she could've chosen a puppy instead of getting a child—and then made it clear I would never allow a dog in the house.

Though Celeste had become quite house-proud, after nesting into our current home and decorating it to her exact desires—another condition, which I had informed her of on the way back from India—was that we would need a much larger house than the three-thousand-square-foot residence we currently lived in. This was far too *cozy* for me with another person living there. Once I gave her a cart blanche budget, she got over her 'nesting' issue.

A few months later, Priya is proving to be a precocious child, with an intellect I respect. Not that I get all mushy over her, but she seems to be far less of an annoyance than I had expected—plus, the distraction she's creating between Celeste and myself is much appreciated. Celeste's attempts to dominate most of my free time before, are now spent obsessively attempting to win Priya's approval, through any means possible, including expensive gifting.

Celeste has chosen the most elite private school, *of course*, who insisted on testing Priya's aptitude for entry. Though her lack of formal education should've had the *opposite* effect, her scores instead have put her two grades ahead of her classmates. Pure-natural intelligence can't be refuted. Of course, Celeste insisted she only move ahead by one grade. I'm sure with her independent nature, she figures Priya will be out of the house and off to college too soon for her liking.

Celeste's dreams of mother-daughter 'spa days' are also quickly fading, as well as those of having a child to

23

dress up like her personal doll—since, when not dressed in her school uniform, Priya will have nothing to do with clothing outside of her jeans and t-shirts.

We have instead adopted a small human with cerebral needs that Celeste cannot begin to satisfy, *one who obviously needs a parent able to challenge her*. She will do fine on her own.

House shopping in the estate world has helped Celeste lick her emotional wounds. After I nixed the French Country mansion, her first choice—she's finally landed on an eleven-thousand-square-foot Post Modern two-story. The neighborhood estates require too much land for a city setting, so instead it sits off the beaten path closer to mountains. With a nod to Nordic architecture, our home is crafted from natural building materials that fit into the landscape, which is ideal against the surrounding woods. A separate twelve-hundred-square-foot casita resides in the back, next to the lake. I plan to make it *my* getaway.

Meanwhile, no one questions the boss, especially when the boss's work is *so* far beyond their own comprehension. With the lab relying heavily upon the assistants I've hired and groomed, to which I still provide occasional direction—I've scaled back surgeries to only the most difficult cases, leaving the others to less talented surgeons. Add in the nice little distraction named "Priya", and I've had ample time to work on my sanctuary.

ARTIST WITHIN

Colleagues and family, who presume themselves inside my sphere, see an expert surgeon, husband and father. I suppose we all play roles in this world, however it's the artist within that's been left to starve—crouching, in a cold dark corner, as though insidious . . . *something to be ashamed of.* Unbeknownst to others, what is at my core and what's driven me to cultivate said 'personas', also embodies a fervor greater than the likes of all of them combined. *Crouch no more true self!*

Between case studies, surgeries, and Celeste's demands for attention, my Creative has had limited time to flourish. Thus, my dreams as of late, which have been filled with moments of sacrosanct and visions of transformative beauty, are also blighted by looming perils of scarlet lust.

In searing streams of light, voluminous silky petals wave and dance in a silent breeze, beckoning their victims, with whispers of treasure . . . promises of glory. *Entrapment of the entitled . . . child's play!*

Once hypnotized, victims are cuddled within their petal's embraces—where luring promises are transformed into a montage of past lies, and repeated back in their own voices—as if their captor had been watching and listening—aware of their prisoners' lies at each telling.

With every mocking whisper and prisoners in tow, colossal petals dance in unison—joining together as if in solidarity. Some captors struggle to free themselves, while others cry out for forgiveness.

As maestro, conducting the symphony of lies—I cue in the percussion, building to a crescendo of staccatos—cracking decibels produced by the righteous florets, breaking the bones of their convicts until . . . *silence!*

The flowering is complete. I stand outside the boisterous bloom in glorious streams of light—receiving pools of scarlet splendor at my feet. Upon waking, I am fully erect.

*****

The mystique *and* containment of my aphrodisiacal cravings had begun to unravel during medical school. At an age when a young man's carnal desires are in full flourish, a particular incident was to change my course.

During an open-heart surgical viewing, I was spied out by a fellow student, who glared at my crotch, and later asked, "What the hell was that about?" I told him I had taken performance enhancing drugs that morning to pleasure my nymphomaniac girlfriend, and it hadn't worn off. As such, with one wrong move, I had "escaped" my jock strap.

After the incident, I knew a change of discipline would be necessary. Crafting my world of being 'many men' could not be possible for consumption by mere mortals, if this jig were up.

After deep consideration, and a lower red-blood-supply than to other organs, I chose the brain as my field of study. To be frank, I have found it far more interesting a subject than the heart.

Fast forward to years of planning and discipline, my Creative has transformed from dream to life . . . fantasy to reality. The real quandary is, with so much to choose from, what pleases me to root out first? Will it simply fall at my feet? *Unlikely.* Ideally, I will quench my carnal urges along the way.

Possibly an organically-arrived-at reward? Celeste's words, *ugh!* I must deprogram her chatter from my psyche. *Nothing* is organic. She would have me raising money for cures to diseases that plague the suffering . . . not my concern. I too, suffer from an inability to *feel*, which I consider a strength. As such, I cannot get behind these efforts when I simply do not care.

Perhaps I should praise her efforts in this arena. Sanctimonious hypocrisy *is* after all, her calling. As a bonus, it would further keep her out of my affairs. *Hmm*, sanctimonious hypocrisy, hand-in-hand with unjust entitlement . . . *both irritants.*

Spying through Bella's searches *has* opened my eyes to a very real epidemic. Preaching the message—you deserve because you are—shrouded inside espoused knowledge of whatever field their viewers are most willing to follow, lurk endless prophetics who profiteer by way of their glassy-eyed followers. I prefer to think of these followers as lambs who will pay for advice in lieu of making something of their own lives.

Skeptical as to the scores of credentialed so-called "experts" among thousands, I've repeatedly used a background check to find most were without education or real experience behind said claimed knowledge.

After fast-tracking my undergraduate studies with a double-major in Neuroscience to only five years, med-school for four, and five years of fellowship—I was thirty-two before taking on my current roll and eventually leading

29

my field as a surgeon. Three more years passed before the Abel Rhodes Neurology Science Lab was added to our campus. Today, twenty-two years later, and fourteen in training is an accomplishment at warp speed. The nerve of these fraudulent claimers of knowledge—a slap across the face to those of us who have *earned* respect in our fields!

An obvious pattern emerging, is that nearly all hail from a generation receiving trophies for merely showing up. Perhaps their doting parents *are* largely responsible for this runaway phenomenon.

Moreover, it is the herds of human sheep 'following' their con artists that are the real danger. Though pathetic, if gone unchecked, as with ripening fruit, this epidemic of rotting minds and unsuspecting vulnerability runs rampant in society. As generations before them begin to age, they lay us all splayed open to vipers, watching and waiting for the opportunity to devour our ignorance—a society of soft, delicious underbellies we're becoming!

While carving out the fraudulent, one by one, does sound like a good time, their numbers are far too great. And realistically, the holes left behind each rooting out, would surely be filled by the lust for fame from newcomers. *Ugh . . . t*his social terrorism is no longer a trend. . . it is the new way of our society!

30

Only our enemies value the anonymity it takes to protect a covert plan, as we lay ours open for aim. Thus, I must use said "influencers" to my advantage.

With meticulous planning, I shall destroy this . . . debacle. The implosion will be public, of course—*not* public for me. I will be as the rudder is to the sail—guiding its vessel quietly, undercover and with definite purpose.

First, I will choose a Captain for my mission. I don't expect said "Captain" to be excited for his or her role. I must make a thoughtful choice—one who is a shepherd to many sheep. The greater the numbers, the more impactful the revolution.

Once employed, and captive within said vessel, my Captain's first lesson will be learning what it is to make tough decisions . . . the core of real leadership.

COVERT AUDITIONS

"Good morning, Bella. What a lovely dress you're wearing. New purchase?"

As if I didn't know. She purchased it less than a week ago—couldn't wait to wear it. Pastel pink, so fitted the main attraction is the obvious lace of her bra. *Another special surprise will make its appearance when I turn up the air conditioning.* There really is no fat under that nectarine butt either, remarkable. I have no problem with it. It would only be more of a bonus if Celeste were to drop by today.

"No, Dr. Rhodes."

Liar. Why does she bother?

"If you don't mind, my cousin, Sam, is having a baby shower at three today that I would like to attend."

"Sure, not a problem at all."

Another lie. She is going to happy hour with her friends tonight, which starts at four, so she probably wants to go home and freshen up first. Not sure why *that's* necessary—

she'll wash off the fantastic odor she'll have built up throughout the day. Poor thing hasn't been told by any of her boyfriends what a turn on that scent is. Oh, and her cousin's baby shower is tomorrow, so a worthy fabrication on her part. I do respect her brain.

"Thank you, Dr. Rhodes. You are so great to work for."

I know, and you are great to sniff and spy on.

I actually prefer Bella leaves early today. I need her computer for finding my targets, the highest of offenders. She's addicted to the same video crap so many others are. I'll search her history, which she never bothers to erase, given *no one* could ever possibly know or figure out her password. Once inside her head, it didn't take much deciphering to get there.

I happened to notice that she changes her nail polish each week. I've taken the opportunity to go through her purse while she visits the ladies' room every Monday. She keeps the polish handy for touch-ups. I simply put the polish color into the search bar engine, ending it with "24", and just like that, I'm in.

Last week, she was without polish. After several failed attempts, I typed in "nude 24" and got in. Have I said I respect how her mind works?

Come to think of it, I'm not sure *why* she feels the need to change her password weekly. I use a private search and am careful to erase only my activity after each time I've looked through hers. I'm sure it's just a fun thing for her to do.

Scrolling through her favorites, which has been torturous, I've found a myriad of hosts. Why does anyone care about most of the crap they go on and on about?

To be fair, there are *some* legitimate experts online that I've come across, who are actually offering value for their fees.

Impressed by one meditation expert, I tried a free sample of his sessions. I wound up falling asleep about five minutes in. That's where my brain got the real clarity it needed—a catnap. I suppose there's not much harm in his small fees. If the name "Napster" weren't taken, it would be an ideal title for his business.

Perhaps male viewers are too embarrassed to admit they follow. It's clear by the sheer number of comments below the videos, that the greater number of viewers are female. Upon further perusing, there seem to be more female "experts" also—unless Bella simply watches females exclusively. I suppose they know their audiences. Thus, my Captain shall, too, be female.

Though I prefer a more in-depth subject to tackle in this make-believe world, my research is revealing far greater masses following the most asinine of topics—"how to groom your lady parts"; "how to best apply your eyebrows"; "how to build your butt", and worse, just blogging their daily lives, taking us on their *journeys*. I'd rather watch paint dry. Really . . . it is painful.

If not for the endless stream of comments left below their videos, I would assume the number of followers a ruse.

Wrapping up each one, the hosts of said series thank their followers, telling them how special and perfect they are. *Why are they watching if already perfect?*

After the three hours I want back, I've still found no worthy Captain.

Though Celeste thinks I'm working over the weekend, *and* she hardly notices when I'm late, I'd rather keep the questioning at bay. I will resume my search tomorrow.

RED WINE IT IS

Today is Bella's cousin's baby shower. Of course, Bella doesn't work on the weekends, so her computer is fair game.

I wonder, how does a bombshell of a woman like her goes over in a room full of mothers, fighting to lose their baby weight? In walks Bella, with that freak-of-nature body. A room full of pin pricks to the pits, insecurities on parade.

Poor Bella. It must suck at times to be near perfect.

Ding! And here we go again, panning through the drill-of-the-droll. There has to be a standout in this group of "experts". I'd veered off course *so* many times last night, from Bella's favorites to others, all popping up on the right of the screen.

Hmm, I'm noticing one particular woman showing up repetitively. Could she be hocking . . . wine? None so far have. I decide to click on Merlot.

"Hi, dames and gents . . . Merlot coming to you today!"

Dames and gents? She speaks with a light English-sounding accent . . . *probably fake.*

"Thank you so much for tuning in again. As your life coach, spiritual go-to, and health and beauty expert . . ."

Really, an expert at all of that? What credibility is embodied by a "go-to"?

"I'm here today to talk about a slightly off topic-topic, which are the funnest kind!"

Funnest? *Ugh,* instant headache. I'm preparing for a real hustle.

"The 'off-topic-topic', ladies, is kegels! So, much, fun! Guys, if you are squeamish about us keeping our lady parts firm, you may want to hit mute—but don't go away, there's something coming up for you."

Without any diffidence, or apprehension, Merlot covers the bases of kegeling, by presenting a prosthetic vagina to show her followers what it should look and feel like. She suggests they use their compact mirrors to examine their "little boxes" to make sure they're doing it correctly. *I do find her fascinating.* So far . . . the perfect Captain, with the highest following I've seen as a bonus.

I watch video after video, listen to a couple of podcasts, and read pages of comments and advice Merlot has to dish out. She appears to be selling products here and there, no doubt getting paid for it. She also has a book on how to be

37

your "Best Self". Upon researching, she hasn't a degree, that I can find.

She looks like a mixture of African American and something else. Her caramel-colored skin doesn't quite give away her ethnicity. Her hair is curly with a smooth texture, and her large doe-like eyes, in some videos, are gold, where in others, they are light green. She doesn't reveal her shape completely, but I can tell she is curvy and of average height.

Completely confident, she's exotically interesting, and acts as if she has lived everything her five hundred and twenty-nine videos cover. It's no wonder so many sheep follow her. I wouldn't say that her advice is *all* bad, but it's nowhere close to revolutionary.

On one hand, I respect her tireless work ethic, yet I have no respect for its content, or *lack thereof.* Are her sheep following their passions? No—they are following a cult leader. Yet somehow, I cannot seem to hate her for capitalizing on their weakness, no matter the depravity. *Ugh!* Even *I'm* getting sucked into her web—she is good.

Four hours pass, and my eyelids have grown heavy. I'm ready to call it quits. Erasing my day's history, I stop when a video title sparking my interest pops up: "Had I known, I would have saved his life". Despite my longing to end it, I'm compelled to click on this video.

Little Jason Nelson, an eight-year-old with a life-threatening bone disease, needs a blood and marrow donor, from someone who shares his rare blood type. A tear-jerking tale, for anyone with a propensity toward that kind of thing.

Merlot, who *says* she has a rare blood type, wearily pontificates about how she would have gladly saved this young boy, *had she known.* Claiming to have powerful outreach, she lambastes traditional marketing for those in need, shaming the medical community, while glorifying herself—*narcissist.*

How will this help the child now? And what of the gut-wrenching loss his parents have suffered, not to mention how mournful all the people working to save him must "feel"? Mournful, is foreign to my own experience, but I watch my staff go through it often enough to know they're physically affected, instead of at their peak performance when I need them to be.

I shall put Merlot and her rare blood type to the test. She did say "had she known". There are banks of people waiting . . . waiting for rare blood type donations. I will make sure it is clean of disease, of course—but if so, she will make a wonderful martyr. After her public salt-of-the-earth proactivist display, her number of followers will skyrocket—all the more "fun", or "funnest" to bleed her out, little by little! She'll be the saint of the internet, *while I enjoy occasional samples.*

And how dare she call herself Merlot . . . who does that? *That* was her first mistake. *She's beckoning my Creative to come out to play.* Ah, yes Merlot, you just keep it up, you very bad girl. You draw in as many followers as the sticky lies you dish out can attract . . . *flies to honey.*

They *deserve* what's coming to you. If they love you enough, maybe your punishment will cut out their shallow little hearts! It's only a shame *I* won't be there to reap my satisfaction of each their angsts.

HELLO, CAPTAIN

I've reached out to Merlot through her website, introducing myself as a doctor who'd seen her 'rare-blood' video. I told her that I had a proposition to help those in need, as well as a lucrative venture for her, and surprise—she called me!

Promptly accepting my invitation to meet a few weeks later, Merlot and "Dr. Sykes", my alias, are getting together today to go over the details of my proposal.

I've chosen a coffee shop in the business district for our sit-down, after the morning rush. It isn't the trendy spot popping up all over town with lines of caffeine addicts at all hours. No, this place looks more like a French Bistro, with high ceilings clad in impressioned tin designs, little marble top tables, herringbone wood floors, and an old-fashioned pie-bar—housing pastries that even a restrained diabetic would have a hard time resisting. Le Meilleur Café, a mouthful to proclaim "the best coffee". *I will see about that.*

It's a gray, drizzling morning outside for late summer, and for the first time this year, the unseasonably cool temperatures are inviting people to pull out their fine wool suits, sweaters, and jeans. Not Merlot—if she's the young woman crossing the street toward me.

In a pair of nude pumps, that add five inches to her height, *painful looking*—she still has a bounce in her gate. Her breasts and hair follow suit with each step. The heavy wood and glass door jingles, as she uses both hands to pull it open with force. It challenges her heel tips against the pavement, and I stand so she'll approach my table.

"Merlot? I'm Dr. Sykes." I offer my hand, however she has another greeting in mind.

"Darling . . . smoosh, smoosh!" *How original.* She takes my hand as if to offer it for a kiss, and then air kisses each of my cheeks, silly words . . . I'm sure she thinks it's adorable.

"Cheers to meeting you."

She's wearing a red curve-hugging skirt, topped by a thin yellow jacket, which reveals she is without a bra— professionalism—an etiquette acumen missed on her.

"I adore this spot you've picked for our meeting, Dr. Sykes!"

"I thought it would do. Can I get you a cup of coffee?"

"Certainly! With whipped cream, and one of those Almond Financiers to go with please."

42

Interesting . . . she's either studied french patisserie for our meeting to impress me, or has a sweet tooth spanning across cultures. This one, baked in the form of a gold bar . . . *perhaps she is sending a message?*

While waiting for the sales clerk to gather the order, I notice Merlot shifting uncomfortably in her chair, and looking around with a less than confident expression, than the one she's been wearing for me thus far. I make eye contact as I walk toward her, hoping to put her at ease.

"Thank you, Dr. Sykes. I haven't had one of these since I was a little girl."

"Please call me Doc, Merlot. We don't need the formality of the whole title." *I'd rather not make up a first name, or answer to a fake one.*

She polishes off the Almond cakette quickly and gets right to our discussion.

"So, Dr. Sykes, I understand you want to learn how to effectively use social media to attract more rare blood donors?"

And to get your rare blood out, in general.

"Yes—unless you have another suggestion? I was thinking of either a seminar type setting, in order to train both me and my colleagues, or a video series with our financial support, starring you of course. I think you'll find our association has deep pockets, and we could use an expert of your caliber, as well as a spokesperson that the public responds favorably to." After giving her an obvious choice, by which to gain agreement, a pensive expression in her eyes, as well as a tensed mouth, tells me she's treading lightly into my web.

"*Well . . .* though either of those sounds smashing—if you want my Petunias to donate, and there are hundreds of thousands of them you know"—*she's waiting for me to behave in an impressed manner*—"they will need to hear it from their Merlot, so I would much prefer to do a series of video programs. Seminars are a bit . . . stiff—not really my style."

"By 'Petunias', you mean your followers?" Suddenly her body language is transformed into that of a teenage girl.

"Why, of course. Don't tell me, you're a social media virgin—you *are*, aren't you?"

"Well, I, I mean I know what it is . . . for the most part. I just don't indulge."

"Ooo . . . I like how you put that—indulge! Yes, it makes me feel like a dessert. And I *am* sweet."

Overt flirtation—*teenage girl turned vixen . . .* I'll bet her blood is like bitter chocolate—my favorite kind.

"Not to change the subject, Merlot, but do you have a filming crew and set?"

"Oh no, nothing that fancy, Doc. I record in different rooms of my apartment for different topics." I sense an explanation of everything I've seen in scores of videos coming . . . *painful*—I focus on her pouty mouth and cleavage to stay somewhat engaged. "My bathroom is for beauty. I shoot footage for more intimate topics in my bedroom, and my office is for life coaching. For what I call 'me time', which is about balance and unwinding, I sit in my living room with coffee or wine. Film crews, sets . . . who needs them? The talent steals the limelight anyhow!"

"That would be you?"

"Of course, silly! You see, I don't think my Petunias would respond to a fancy setting. They feel safe and at home in my apartment."

"So no other talent or team . . . If you don't mind me saying, I think any other personalities would look drab next to yours anyway."

I've got to bring her defenses down for what I'm going to request next.

"Oh, Doc! Such sweet words coming from *such* an intelligent man. A compliment's worth so much more from a smart one, it is."

"There's just one thing . . . how shall I put this—while I appreciate your abode being a comfy place for your 'Petunias', we have something with a more clinical vibe in

45

mind. Of course, we could still add some finishing touches to make it more fitting for your followers."

She can't wait for me to finish . . .

"Sure, sure, I get it. We'll be doing a more medical sort of show, so I understand how it needs to look a *tinge* sterile. I would like to give it my 'brand' like you say, put *my* 'touch' on it, so I could go for that. When should we get started!"

Not so fast eager one.

"First, tell me your favorite colors, and I'll make sure our design team searches for items that you'll want to surround yourself with." A huge smile takes over her face at this suggestion.

"*Ooo* . . . I do so appreciate everyone catering to my needs!"

At this, I'm subjected to a rendition of a clapping little girl who's nearly jumping up and down in her seat.

"Well, I despise orange. Greens and browns are just dumpy colors. I look best in magenta, aqua, some yellows— yes, splashes of these colors will liven it up a bit against a clinical-canvas."

She seems primed for "the ask".

"One more thing, Merlot, and it *is* rather important." She's batting her eyelashes at me in anticipation.

"Go on then, never hurts to ask, now does it?"

"I want to prepare our set-shoppers. I wouldn't normally impose in this way, but since your Petunias are so comfortable with *your* place, I don't want to veer too far from your rooms—so would it be acceptable for me to drop by and take a few photos?" She's narrowing her eyes slightly as she considers my request.

"Well, typically I *would* say no. I don't let anyone know where I live, given my high profile you see, but you bein' a doctor, *and* helping *me* help who knows how many people— I suppose I will trust someone such as yourself . . . just this once."

Yes! "Thank you, Merlot. I don't take your trust lightly."

I pull out my chair as if to end our meeting, when it hits me what a media hound she is, and I pause. "Oh, and until we're ready to get started, the foundation doesn't want any press coverage, not even on social media." An obvious drop in her facial muscles, accompanied by bulging eyes, prepare me for her objection.

"But . . . I don't understand? *Why* wouldn't they want to build up the viewer numbers in advance?"

Her heartbeat has picked up, and her posture is tense. *I'm preparing for a verbal sparring.* Thinking fast, I come up with something she'll have no rebuttal for. I lower my voice and lean in, as if to be discussing a top secret with her—

47

exclusively. She follows my body language . . . and now the delivery.

"You see, Merlot, there are laws we adhere to of the strictest nature, medically speaking—which our legal department is still working through, *and* we don't want our competitors jumping on the bandwagon—you know, stealing our thunder before it gets *really* big. We're afraid they would use *another* 'Merlot' to bump us. And, even though contribution is always better when more people get involved—ultimately, we're still a corporation, and profits peak when our nonprofits explode."

She sits back and crosses her arms and legs—not happy, but it's evident that I've taken the fight out of her.

"*Ah* . . . I see. Not that there *is* another Merlot, but mum's the word—I will keep it on the low."

Ego play—*check!* At this, we agree to the day of our appointment at her apartment. I pause waiting for her to end our meeting first this time.

After she's up, I scoot out my chair and stand. Her gaze follows the path up my body, starting from my feet, until she's locked eyes with me.

"*Ooo* . . . Doc, you are a tall one, aren't you?"

As I break her stare and look away, she giggles and gives my lapel a soft, playful swipe.

48

I look down at her again . . . nice cleavage. "Yes, Merlot"—*an awkward exchange.* I'm unsure how to end the obvious statement she's posed in a question, so I go around her to hold the door, and leave it at that.

Now that I have my Captain, it's time I pay a final visit to the vessel of my labor . . . my sanctuary.

SANCTUM

A few years ago, while cycling through the mountains outside of town, I happened across a trail, barely visible as such. It spoke to me, *Abel . . . come hither, see what I have to offer.*

Fairly flat, the trail would appear inviting to a novice cyclist were it not so grown over with tall weeds. In part, it runs adjacent to a narrow strip of grass, siding a steep drop off. After a good rain, the creek bed, forty feet below rushes with deep waters.

On the other side of the reservoir are towering Douglas Firs, hiding an ebony mountain—all unfriendly territory. I had to explore it.

During that expedition, once beyond the ancient soldiers, I stood in awe of their majestic castle. I'd earned the right to climb her—a mountain of mostly shale— stitched together similar to an old quilt, only by black foot daisies.

Not far into my climb, her stone skin began to break away in sheets under my foot's pressure—as if to be a self-defense mechanism, devised to keep me from whatever mystery lay at her crown.

I made it just over halfway to the top, but ill prepared for its treachery, I decided respectfully, to leave this side of the stream to Mother Nature's children, and thus made my descent.

Something far more interesting lay on the other side of the creek, not far off the road. Bike hoisted atop my shoulder, I walked down the gently winding path, where to my right, rose a hill the height of a tall building. Fortressed by roots and boulders, a crown of lush foliage—mostly pines—topped its peak.

On my first trek, I noticed something unusual hiding beneath a thick web of growth in its hillside. Had someone else been here . . . done *this*?

With my knife, I freed the jigsaw of stubborn vines to reveal . . . a decaying door? Gamuts of weather events, no doubt, had glued the heavy relic against a boulder formation under its old bones. The door creaked and moaned as I pried it away . . . *you've done your job well, old friend.*

Entering through the large hole behind it, flashlight in hand, a cave unlike any other I'd seen, unfurled before me. After all, what cave boasts . . . a foyer?

51

I scooted my feet, clearing layers of dirt to reveal flat rocks—intentionally laid with tiny gravel binding them tightly. Countless hours were spent toiling away on this. *Hmm . . .* was this an elaborate bomb shelter? Or had it *actually* been . . . someone's home?

Moving beyond the foyer, I found a soaring ceiling—an arena-like space, where from it resided six arched openings. The mighty arched walls were painstakingly made of stone and crude mortar. Construction of this scale . . . fascinating—a natural curiosity to a surgical architect. Beyond each arch lay rooms that, though open, were possessing of a dank atmosphere in the still of their blackness.

After exploring each one, I studied the middle arena once more. As my vision began further adjusting, piercing obscurity high overhead—load points secured by bundles of rebar came into focus. My assumption was that these were installed to keep its structure from caving in—which meant the cave had to have been excavated beyond Mother Nature's intent.

I thought I knew of all the caves and mountains for fifty miles. How had I never discovered this one before? Perhaps because the trail outside dissipates quickly into the forest—it hadn't been trod on enough to create an obvious path?

Not one to believe "fate" is a controlling force in one's destiny—even I had to admit to myself that there must be a cosmic force at play here. Yes, this giant gemstone was waiting for me—and it was to become something special by my hand!

Every spare moment since that glorious day, I've devoted to finishing its inside. Celeste thinks I've been cycling excessively to prepare for competitive races. Many long hours and how-to videos later, I've transformed it into my pristine sanctuary.

At the early stages of my labor, I'd discovered a curious dampness outside the entrance of the cave—moist, even in drier weather. Setting out to find its source, I discovered a spring, near the top of the hill—treasure!

On my next trip, I came prepared with parts for a pulley system, a harness, and pole climbing cleats. At an ideal spot, I dug out as much earth as the terrain would safely allow, and installed a large basin. Much of it hangs past the hill's shear. Using metal stakes and tree branches, I've created a platform to accommodate the overhanging container. For camouflage, I've wrapped it with foliage, which has grown in quite nicely.

A filter keeps debris out of the line, which is buried behind vines and runs down the hill. Given its steepness, no one will tread on it.

The flow is teed off at the cave. When not in use, I allow the spring to take its natural course—only diverting when necessary for bathing and drinking. Stopping the flow to build up for a few hours creates a thunderous pressure into the tub. When Merlot arrives, I will close off the tee.

Since its installation, after hours of filthy work, I've tested it out—so that bike sweat is the only evidence I've arrived home with.

After nearly two years of stealing every hour possible for its completion, my sanctuary is now Merlot-ready.

However, to assure its perfection for the "Queen of the Petunias", I'm going to try it out on a more . . . *expendable* subject—one without potential transformation. Perhaps someone who brings me personal pain or discomfort? After all, why wait when the world needs my silent judicature.

Conveniently, Celeste has a half-sister from a different mother she's become close to. Libby lives in the next state by a half day's drive. Now that we have the estate home, she, the husband, and her eight-year-old son, from an estranged dad, have come for three vacations in less than a year. *I see a troublesome habit forming.* I wouldn't hurt her sister, who's a mousy sort of woman, or the kid.

In fact, I've good reason to think the boy either is, or *has been,* abused in some way by an adult—most likely a male figure. The child's behavior smacks of it, and the abuser *deserves* his sentencing.

On their last visit, I observed said husband, Derick, take Libby by the wrist, and jerk her like a rag doll into the garden while checking his surroundings to ensure that they were alone. *He failed to look up to see me in an upstairs window watching.* Apparently, not private enough, he grabbed her by the back of her neck and forced her deeper into the trees, off to the side of the lake.

I couldn't see what happened next, however, with my sense of physiological reactions—I knew for a fact later that she had been crying. Her cheeks hinted of salt, and her irises were murky.

I'm not one to judge a marital scuffle, but I'm pretty sure after manhandling her, he'd bruised her in places where the evidence was hidden. Whatever, she's an adult. She should have known what she was getting herself into— not to mention that her kid would be exposed to that idiot's temperament.

They're arriving tomorrow for another visit. I was going to have a talk with Celeste about them being in my space so often, but I've rethunk it. Undoubtedly, Libby wants to escape the violence as often as she can, and I'm sure he is isolating her from everyone in her family.

Assuredly, he allows these trips for the free vacation time away from the shoe box they live in.

After lifting weights for hours in my gym, shaven head and body on display in his man-kini trunks—Derick lays by the pool for hours. The eagle tattoo across his back and his edgy man jewelry smack of narcissism. He does appear to be quite strong, but that kind of bulk *could* slow a man down.

I rarely speak to the neanderthal, and he seems to appreciate it. I'm going to watch him around Felix this visit. If I have enough reason to believe he's guilty of what I think he is, I'll free both Libby and Felix from what torments them—*while testing the intricacies of my secret domicile.*

FAMILY VACATION

"A...be...l!"

"What, Celeste!"

"Oh! There you are . . . you startled me."

"Just getting a glass of juice . . ."

"I thought you were in the foyer. Anyhow, remember, Libby, Derick, and Felix are coming for a four-day visit, starting today. I want all of us to go to dinner tonight."

"Okay . . ."

"It'll be interesting to see if Felix comes out of his shell around Priya. Have you noticed how shy he is?"

I'm sure there's good reason for that.

"I haven't paid attention, Celeste, but now that you mention it, I don't think I've *ever* heard him speak."

"Well, I've tried to engage him several times, and he stares at the ground every time."

"Perhaps it has something to do with Derick."

"He does seem a *little* strict, but Libby says Derick is a great dad."

"Your sister's picked a few real losers. Tell me you haven't been uncomfortable with his nonchalance—nothing but a shred of fabric between us and his 'Johnson', running around back and forth from the pool."

"Yes! That 'swimsuit' is embarrassing—for me! And *he* should be the embarrassed one. It's like he's so proud of his bodybuilding, he's got to show off his physique. Still Abel, that doesn't make him a bad husband, just . . . different, I guess."

"The guy's a classic narcissist. They're almost always cheaters in a relationship. It's a matter of time if he isn't already doing it." *That doesn't explain why his wife and child all but salute him while in his presence.*

"Really? Poor Libby. Don't say that to her, I don't want to give her a complex. I think she feels lucky to have him."

"When's the last time you saw me converse with Libby? And also, what could possibly make her think she's lucky to be married to that dead beat? I'm sure her Trust Fund is the thing that most attracted him to her—and by the looks of how they live now, he's probably gambled or wasted most of it away anyway."

"I do think she funded that vitamin business he started. She dances around a straight answer when I ask how it's

58

going, so you may have a point—*oh,* she's texting me. They're coming up the drive. Their ears must be burning . . . *shh*! Get the door Abel, and let's not say another word about this."

"Well hello, Abe! We don't usually get greeted by you. I'd be less surprised to see a butler!"

"Funny, Derick. Butlers are peculiar. I wouldn't have one lurking about in my home. Let me help you with your things, even though I'm *not* the butler."

"Celeste told Libby we'd be going to a steak place downtown. It's nice of you to treat us."

More like her favorite French restaurant. All he needs to know is steak is on the menu and—once again, obviously *not* expecting to pitch in on the bill.

"Is it couples only, or are we bringing the rugrats?"

"Yes, Derick, the rugrats are coming. Once you're settled, we need to get going. We have early reservations."

"Well, la-tee-dah. We wouldn't want to be late for 'reservations'. Just bull-shittin', man. Loosen up! We'll shake a tail feather—I'm starving."

A "starving" Derick seems to be a chatterbox. The sooner he's full of charred flesh, the better for me.

*****

"Bonjour, Celeste! So lovely to see you and your guests. We have your favorite spot waiting."

"Merci, Raphael! So wonderful to be back, darling!"

Ah, Celeste in her glory . . . air kissing with Raphael, receiving her accolades like a Queen. *Someone* doesn't seem impressed. There he goes, charging off to get a seat at the table of *his* choosing. It'll take the rest us twenty seconds to catch up . . . though Raphael is on his heels, still managing to display the decorum of a Maître' D.

"What's the thickest steak ya' got? Bone in' of course."

"I'm sorry, sir. We don't serve 'bone in'.'"

"What! Alright then, I'll take the biggest, juiciest one ya' got, I mean hangin' over the plate big . . . after I get a mug of beer, Jack D on the rocks, and one of them little skillets of rolls. Do you all *serve* that?"

"I will alert your wait person as to your 'desires', *sir*."

"Well, ain't he got a stick up his ass!"

"Hun! Inside voice please. He probably heard you."

"Libby, what've I told you about sassin' me? I don't give a shit what that twat heard! I should take the 'French' right out of his mouth. Do we need to talk about this later?"

"No, Derick. I'm sorry dear. Let's just enjoy the evening."

"Yeah, yeah. Hey man, sorry 'bout that, Abe. Guess I just need some food and drink. I've been a little stressed. Sittin' in a car with these two for nearly half a day don't help none either."

Keep digging your hole, Derick. I'm looking forward to never spending another evening out with you.

Two giant mugs of ale and five whiskey shots later, he's lit, belching and loud. Celeste's expression is giving away her regret in choosing this restaurant. Her cover is blown among those who've assumed her upbringing to be that of a dignified socialite.

Even Priya, who normally seems sickened at Celeste's displays of pretention, appears to be embarrassed with each guttural belch—shifting in her seat and looking away—her only possible move of disassociation. She hasn't tried once to engage Felix. To her credit, she is completely comfortable with what others might deem 'uncomfortable silence', but then again, he is a child, and Priya is an adult locked in a child's body.

On cue, Derick disappears with the arrival of the check. He's taken Felix with him to the men's room. I let them know we'd be close behind, getting the car. He'll think I've gone on to the valet station with the ladies.

The men's room appears to be empty. All of the louvered stall doors are open, except one.

"Go ahead little man, pull it out . . . Daddy won't bite."

"But Dad, I really don't need to go."

61

I'm not allowing this. I bang the door shut next to their stall to get his attention.

"You finish up here, Felix. Dad's gonna wait outside the door for you." Derick slithers out to find me standing at one of the sinks. The cologne attendant's chair is empty, so he was safely alone—or *so he thought.*

"Abe!" He slaps me on my back. "You're one of those quiet sons of bitches . . . kinda creepy, man."

I don't flinch. He's far too ignorant to see the resolve in my expression . . . *my sanctuary awaits!*

THE SEDUCTION

How do I get two hundred and fifty pounds of muscle, even *with* a pea-sized brain, to willingly follow me into the web awaiting him? I could drug him. I am strong, but I could only manage to carry him down the path from the road to inside, at best. Traffic is quite sparse on this road, but still not a chance I am willing to take. No, I will need for him to follow me. But how—without *some* suspicion?

I decide to tell Celeste at breakfast, in front of the others, that I've been asked to fill in teaching a group at a seminar, in the place of a colleague from an affiliate hospital. I'll say he's come down with something at the last minute and explain that I need to go over for the weekend in order to prepare for Monday and Tuesday's classes. This will give me three days to exact Felix's revenge.

With guests to entertain, she won't ask to tag along in hopes of a shopping trip—her usual mode of operandi.

Celeste seems to have forgotten the embarrassment from dinner. She's laid out an impressive spread of croissants, jams, scrambled eggs, bacon and fruit, along with coffee, teas, and juices—over a white linen cloth on the patio table. The sun is holding on to the last few days of late summer, offering heat that has forced us to pull out our shorts. Celeste let everyone sleep in until ten before ringing the breakfast bell.

Priya has been up for who knows how long. I saw her coming out of the casita to breakfast from my bedroom balcony—probably avoiding Felix. She acts awkward around him, or is it she has nothing to say, as he has nothing worthy of her intellect to converse with him on. I've languished, avoiding our guests. Something Priya and I have in common.

Derick is particularly quiet during breakfast this morning. He's nursing a hangover, I strongly suspect. I've caught him stealing glances at me over the table. *Still wondering what I heard in the men's restroom stall last night?*

After explaining to Celeste that I'm helping out a fellow Dr. in need—at said "imaginary conference"—and gain approval from her as to its worthy reason for abandoning more family time, I deliver my next excuse—a ploy to leave the table.

Derick perks up as I speak, ticking his head slightly to the side with the raise of one eyebrow. *Hmm . . .* he smells a rat in my explanation—perfect. I've laid the cheese, now I need to get my mouse into his trap. His headache could've played *against* my ploy to get his attention with this excuse, but somehow, it seems to be helping him cut through the more languid of the hosts residing within his thick skull. I won't underestimate that quieter sleeping giant.

Felix excuses himself to skip rocks across the lake—getting an eyeroll from Priya, before she takes her plate to the kitchen sink and disappears upstairs.

The ladies are engrossed in a conversation about a show I haven't seen, as I excuse myself to make my call to let my "affiliate colleague" know I will fill in for him. Until this, Derick's thoughts are elsewhere. Suddenly, he snaps to attention. *I've laid the trail of crumbs.*

Walking down the hallway, slower than normal to my study, I leave the door cracked a few inches.

As I move behind my desk, I hear the wood floor make an ever so slight popping sound—no doubt under the strain of the meathead—so faintly that I determine he is in his sock feet. I put my phone to my ear and begin having my "phantom" conversation in a hushed tone, in order to draw him close outside the door.

"Hey, baby. Yeah, bring your friends, we'll make a freaky party of it. Uh huh, the new place in the woods, super private, you'll love it. The Mrs. thinks I'm going to a seminar for three days. She's got relatives in town so no way she'll be checking in on me. I'll bring the good stuff, yeah, the ecstasy. You are sooo hot baby! What do the other girls look like? Oh, the ones who posed in that nude magazine—great! They are unbelievable, and they're into it . . . right? Okay, sweet! You betcha, I want to do all of that stuff. I'm getting excited just thinking about it. Yep, headed out in less than an hour—see you soon."

My secretive tone and the neanderthal's headache have worked in my favor. Otherwise, he would have busted in at this moment, demanding an invite to the party—*or else.*

I hang up and walk around my desk, then act like I'm writing something on a piece of paper . . . I am. It's going to make its way into Libby's suitcase pocket.

I need to give the cretin ample time to get back down the hall. He's either going to approach me with a blackmailing proposal *if* I deny him entry, or follow me and deliver the threat closer to the cave. Either way, he's going to have to come up with an excuse for why he's leaving. I've got one for him. *He just doesn't know it.*

PARTY TIME

To cover my tracks, I take a cab to the airport, suitcase with supplies in tow—leaving no phone record of the second cab, I hail *it* at the airport. This trip takes me to a storage space on the edge of town, where old hospital furniture leftovers have conveniently found their temporary resting place. I keep an extra bicycle here as well.

I'd committed to donating the items from an overhaul of the hospital's interior renovation a few years prior—a job no one wanted.

Every thirty days, I give Accounting a receipt of donations taken away for that month. Little by little, it has freed up space for my sanctuary's renovation materials.

Once my driver drops me at the storage shed, I transfer my suitcase of supplies into a large backpack for the bike ride. *I wonder if the blockhead is still following.* He was conspicuously close behind in his own cab, until we got separated by a red light. Must have left the family car for

Libby. I wonder what he told her. He obviously believes he's spending all three days with me, the "Jerk Doctor", and a few hot babes—having sex and doing drugs.

I ride eleven miles to the trail, which leads to the cave. With a towering tree line overhead nearly closing in on it— I'm not sure how I ever found the place to begin with.

As I come to the path's opening, I hop off. *Did I lose him?* I wait a few minutes and a yellow bumblebee-colored cab appears in the distance. It's slowing now . . . too much. He'll reveal my spot to the cab driver, *dimwit*! Jumping on my bike again, I cycle for half a mile, before dismounting again—this time the cab is slowing closer behind me. Derick sticks his head out the window.

"Hey asshole, need a ride to our party?"

I'm relieved to be concealed behind a bike helmet and large windshield style sunglasses. I move up close to the lunk head, who's grinning in anticipation and whisper, "Hey shithead, it's a secret spot. Get your dumb ass out—we're within walking distance."

He pops out of the cab like a kid running for their spoils on Christmas morning, with only a full plastic grocery bag in his hand. After he pays the cab driver, we're on our way back to the trail.

"So, Derick, you obviously heard my phone conversation this morning. What tipped you off that I wasn't going to a seminar—enough to follow me down the hall to my office?"

"Hey Bro—"

I'm "Bro" now that he thinks he's getting a hot piece of ass.

"I know a good excuse to chase some tail when I hear it. Pretty masterful—wish I could use that one."

"Yeah, well it's been used, so it's doubtful Libby will buy it now." *Building rapport with a mental mouse is painful.*

"True that! You'll have to let me know if you think of any others I could steal. You're definitely smoother than I am."

I've got to get a clear shot at his neck. The syringe is burning a hole in my pocket! *Just a little further.* I lay my bike next to a large stone, hiding it in the bushes as we arrive at the trailhead.

"Where in BFE are we going? I don't see any houses?"

Perfect, this is my opportunity . . . *turn your head, Derick!*

"It's hidden around the bend of this path, built into a hill. You won't believe how cool it is!"

He takes off walking faster ahead of me, so swiftly I'm fumbling in my pocket—then pulling the rubber tip off the needle behind my back. He's spotted the door, which I'd purposely left cracked open yesterday. I've replaced the heavy old relic with a lightweight metal patinaed one, shaped to blend into the hillside.

"Oh cool, I see it—wow! Are the ladies here?"

"They may be. They know there's no parking, so they're getting dropped off."

Just a few steps away . . . I've caught up with him now. He's bending over to get the handle and duck inside. His neck is exposed—*yes!*

I jab it into his exposed skin, and shortly, a potent level of GHB, liquid ecstasy, will be coursing through his bloodstream, a date rape drug rarely detected with certainty given its rapid elimination—eight hours in the blood and twelve in urine. It stays in hair up to four weeks, but thanks to the "vanity machine", who shaves his head and body, I'm in good shape—in case he were ever to be found. He reaches up to slap at his neck, but I've already ejected the needle.

"Ouch! Holy shit! What was that?"

I think fast, realizing his muscles stretched taut probably increased the sting from my needle.

"Oh, wow—I just saw a wasp fly away. Did you get stung?"

"I hope to hell I didn't! I'm allergic to those little bastards!"

"Don't panic, Derick. I carry an antivenom for these occasions. We doctors come prepared. Sit and I'll take care of it."

I pull out a second syringe, same dosage of the first one. He must be on steroids; this isn't making him sleepy yet. I also may have miscalculated the dosage ratio for his body mass, but this next one should take him down.

He looks away as I stab him with a hefty dose in the thigh between his quad muscles, which he has so generously developed—unwittingly for this occasion. He pretends to be tough, but flinches and catches his breath.

That was fun.

He changes the subject in hopes I don't notice the tear he's wiping from the corner of his eye. "Hey, are the girls here? I wanna see what they look like."

"Not yet, Derick. Let's head inside and wait. They'll be here soon."

He yawns. "Oh wow, that antivenom must be making me sleepy."

I love it when patients self-diagnose.

"Hey cool—is that gear for S&M play? I've never done it, but I saw it in a movie once—looked hot."

"Yes, that's what it's for. So you've never done S&M?"

A small corner room to the right of the foyer, designed especially for torture and clean up all in one—*genius.*

"No. Why?"

"Well, one of our girls, the sexiest one, is a Dominant. That means she needs a Submissive, *and* she rewards handsomely for good behavior. It doesn't hurt anyway, just a bit of acting submissive, and saying 'Yes Mistress' a lot. If you play your cards right, she should be impressed with you right away. She'd make it worth a little role play on your part."

"What—what should I do? Ya' know, to get in 'submissive mode'? I want her to pick me and get right to it! *Damn!* I'm getting pumped just thinking about it!"

"Sure, let's get you ready for her."

This is far too easy. I open the thick plexiglass door with air holes and tell Derick to disrobe down to his underwear, which of course, are the man-kini trunks—black no less. I then pull out a black blindfold, and tie it around his eyes. Next, I instruct him to put his hands overhead, as I secure his wrists with handcuffs hanging from a steel beam. Last, I have him spread his feet to secure his ankles with shackles bolted into the stone floor.

"You're ready for her now!"

"Oh dude, this is sick—in a cool way! Can't wait to meet this crazy-sexy bitch . . . only, could you take off the blindfold 'til then so I can get a look at her first?"

"Sure, Derick."

I roll the mask up onto his forehead. And now, he's yawning, eyelids fighting to stay open. His head begins to bob, until finally his chin rests on his chest, and he's breathing a sleep-induced cadence.

One last detail before I get to work. Using clear surgical tape, I secure his eyelids open, along with his slumbering jowls, cooperating in their relaxed state as I pull them upward. He appears to be awake—and smiling a ridiculous smile. I carefully tilt his head up, resting it slightly to one side against his massive bicep, to balance it from falling forward. Stepping back, I take a few photos—*these will be useful.*

He's admitted to cheating on Libby, and I'm sure he's abusing both she and Felix. Add to this list, inappropriate behavior caught in an incriminating photo—which will make it to Libby's phone by "accident" from Derick's number in a few days, addressed to his *Dominant Mistress.* It should nicely support the letter she'll find from him, which I stuffed deep inside a pocket of her suitcase on my way out, before catching a ride to the airport.

Better for Libby and Felix to hate him than to know the truth of his demise. Not to mention, the police won't look for a cheater who's left his wife. Hell, he never even adopted Felix, so it's doubtful she'll even *try* and find him for any kind of support.

I've got several hours, as he slumbers, to contemplate his demise. An eye for an eye? His crimes cannot be exacted by his victims, and I'm not engaging in that sick behavior, so, maybe not. *Hmm,* I do have zip ties. I imagine no better way to humble the narcissist than to take away his manhood—a game I'll call "Truth or Lies". A fitting justice, one notch at a time.

In his haste to be slapped lightly with leather straps from his imaginary Dominant Mistress, Derick has failed to notice he's standing on a grate, lodged in the floor over a deep hole, with rocks at its base. It's designed for cleanup, in order to dissipate the odor of decaying blood. I've stocked a natural cleaning solution, as I wouldn't want to harm the environment surrounding my sanctuary in the cleansing process. I intend to keep this place private and thus, it must remain lush.

Though its plumbing was the most arduous of jobs, each facet of construction held new challenges. The accomplishment is now my reward—*well, one of my rewards.*

Derick's current stay is in the clean room, also known as Merlot's patio—doubling as a torture chamber when necessary. Excluding a suite for Merlot's stay, I've outfitted a hidden viewing room—my private nest within the sanctuary, which contains all of the electronic equipment.

There's also a supply room storing living necessities, including a refrigerator, and a room which mimics Merlot's current living room in her apartment.

They encompass the larger middle space, which I've dubbed "the arena". Strategically, it's been left free of furnishings, enabling one to see into every other room all at the same time. I didn't need to change the floor plan. The stone walls where arched openings once faced the arena, are now closed off in front by thick plexiglass with ventilation holes.

I've made living wall screens, covered with air-moisture fed plants, which lower to cover the plexi-walls. Because the cave's excavated ceiling is high over the arena, they easily raise straight up using a pulley system.

A patina-finished false ceiling made of tin, and faceted to look like a rock formation, hovers just below the cave's real ceiling. It gives the illusion of a shorter cave, atop the living walls when lowered by its pulley, along with handily concealing the rebar structure holding the cave together.

I removed the well-laid rocks from the original floors—which was back-breaking but muscle-building work, exposing the cave's black shale that I had discovered. For the most part, it is an even surface, and more practical in the event of blood cleanup—which will sink into nature's trough.

The brain receives information mostly through the retina, but to answer the quandary of our second most suspicious of senses, I've recorded nature's songs from outside the cave. Blending the forest's sounds could come in handy in the future. They are ready at the touch of a button from my mechanical viewing room.

Though the living walls have a natural woodsy smell, most caves put off a bit of a musty aroma, largely due to dampness. Now that I have eliminated small leaks from the outside spring threatening the integrity of this side of the sanctuary—to emulate this natural effect, I've concocted a musky freshener in my lab.

Were my sanctum to be discovered at any point, the look, sounds, and smells, would all be that of a natural cave—better an *obscure* find.

As I wait for the sleeping giant to get the last of his final slumber, I decide to try out Merlot's mattress for the evening.

I'm sure I will have sweet dreams of this ethereal place. This wonder . . . my sacrament—has been planned with the closest definition of love and passion I'll ever know. It renders me . . . "whole".

ASHES TO CARBON

"Ahhh . . . !" The beast is stirring. I've been up for an hour. Letting him wake naturally is the least I could do on this, his last day. I greet him in front of his room.

"Good morning, Derick, how was your night's sleep?"

I've lowered the walls and the ceiling, so he will assume he's in a cave.

"Where the hell am I? You . . . *freak!*"

"Tsk, tsk, who are you to be casting shame? It appears *you* are the one in Freak's clothing for the time being."

"Clothes—where are mine? And where are my underwear? I always knew there was something *gay* about you!"

"Now Derick, let's not stereotype others just because they do not share *your* sexual preferences, which are far more disparaging than mine. As for your "panties", I cut them off last night, in case you decided to urinate into the grate you're standing over. Obviously, I couldn't get them over your feet."

"What are you talking about, my sexual preferences? I dig women."

"And little boys? That's right, Derick, I heard you in the bathroom."

"I was just helping him get his little ding-a-ling out. Felix gets anxiety in public restrooms."

"That's pretty quick for a brain of your capacity. Save the lies for my later enjoyment, *please.* I know the tell-tale signs of sexual abuse. Felix is the poster child for it, just as Libby has the classic signs of an abused wife."

"I would never touch Libby!"

"Once again, I am asking you, politely, save your lies— at least for a while. Besides, I couldn't care less if you hit Libby. She's an adult who should have gotten out *and* taken Felix out with her by now. There's no excusing her for that. Besides, it *is* other women you prefer to 'touch', as we both know."

"Then why isn't she here—and who are you to talk? You were the one to set this up with those babes. Hey, they never showed up, huh?"

"Your mental prowess is astounding, Derick. Standing *there* on a grate over a deep hole, bound by chains for hours on end, and you're just now beginning to question *why* they haven't shown up?"

"You think because you're a brain surgeon you know *so* much, but look at you. You're a pathetic freak, who has to tie strong men like me up in steel, so we can't kick your ass— probably makes you feel like a big man, huh? Just staring at me completely naked. I bet you want some of this! Tell you what, you *fag*, let me go and I'll give you all you can take!"

"Oh, I've warned you about insulting others, Derick. I'm going to assume that because you've probably got an ecstasy hangover and haven't had your coffee, you're coming across in a way you'll later regret. Speaking of your nads though, they are particularly small . . . steroids?"

"My body is all natural. I've never taken the stuff!"

"I'll stop questioning your 'shrinkage'. For now, save the lies. I'm asking nicely . . ."

"I don't know what you're getting at, but really man, let's just move past this. Gag's over. You win. Just unlock these metal things and let's get out of here and go get some breakfast."

"Derick, do you know how bulls are castrated . . . *no*? I'll tell you then. A band, made of rubber, is placed around the top of the scrotum, and eventually the lost blood supply causes their 'Rocky Mountain Oysters' to just . . . fall off. Though dishes containing them are revered in certain cultures, with claims of making men who eat them quite virile, it kills the bull's desire to impregnate the cattle, or run the other bulls off. Instead, they become . . . docile."

"Hey man—I don't like where you're headed, but if you think for one second you're putting a rubber band around my nutsack, you've got another thing coming!"

"Oh Derick, you *are* amusing, even in your position. The steroids really have done a number on your sense of reality. Tell you what, I'm *not* going to use a rubber band. I have a little game I'm calling, 'Zip Tie, Truth or Lie', and you're going to play."

With Derick's ankles bolted to the ground in a spread-eagle position, wearing rubber gloves—with a pre-readied zip tie loop in hand, I use fast and steady aim to lasso his scrotum. Tightening to a slightly uncomfortable pressure, I assure him that the teeth of the plastic edges will only dig deeper with each writhing movement. This suggestion steadies him. After the zip tie is firmly in place, I stand back in front of him. He's finally quiet—his eyes larger than his balls.

"Here are the rules, Derick. With each lie, I tighten one more notch. Since you seem incapable of telling the truth, I suspect you'll be a eunuch in no time. Once you've answered each question truthfully, the game ends."

"First question—do you hit your wife?"

"Only if she makes me!"

"Lie!" *Click . . .* I tighten it a notch.

"She doesn't do as I ask, that's how she makes me. She knows what sets me off!"

Click. I tighten another notch.

"Hey! You said one notch! You didn't like my answer, but it's not the same as a lie."

"Half-truths in your world, Derick, are lies in the real world. Second question, and this one is good for two notches, just to warn you. Do you abuse Felix in any way?"

"No! I love the little punk."

Two notches, *click . . . click.*

"Ahh! Why are you doing this! What have I ever done to you? Okay, I probably say things to him that ain't so good for his confidence. Sometimes, it's hard to resist. He's such a little mama's boy."

"Insults flung at Felix are *not* what I was referring to. You *know* what I meant. I will ask again, and let me caution you, your 'boys' are turning from a shade of red to slightly purple. You'll want to answer carefully. Do you abuse Felix, in *more* than an emotional way?"

"Okay, okay, I've hit him a few times! I know I shouldn't, but he does things like drink the last of the milk, or eat my leftover steak. Any guy would lose it!"

Click.

"*Argh!* I was telling the truth! Come on, man!"

"You weren't telling the whole truth. You know what I was referring to. All I am asking for is the whole truth, so you are essentially neutering yourself with each lie. Again, answer the question!"

"Yes! I have done some things—touched some things—I shouldn't. I don't know why, okay! I guess I'm a sick son of a bitch. Please, please! Take that thing off my balls before they drop off. You can't imagine how much it hurts!"

"Okay, Derick, thank you. Thank you for telling the truth. In all honesty, I didn't think we'd get here this quickly. You've . . . perplexed me, as to what I'll do next. I was planning on a quick end to this part. But now, you've made it more, well, interesting."

"Oh man, come on! I'm standing here with a zip tie squeezing my nuts nearly off, and I've done what you asked. You gotta keep up your end of the deal, let me go—please!"

"Silence! Your pleading is gauche on my ears . . . there is nothing more repugnant! I've said nothing about letting you go, only ending the game. And, you are correct—breakfast is long overdue. I'm stepping out for a bit."

"Look man . . . Abe! I don't know what you're planning, but I'm telling you—you do *not* want to do this! If I go missing, there's gonna be trouble. I swear, you'll regret it!"

Ignoring his pleas and empty threats, I step outside and have my hikers-meal of dried fruit, jerky, and water—while I figure this out. He's merely attempting to save his manhood, which he would use to destroy another kid, if not Felix. I don't believe child molesters *are* curable, and with the added element of his narcissism, he's certain to continue.

Hmm . . . Celeste *is* always going on about how Libby never got a diamond engagement ring. There must be a sizable amount of carbon in a man Derick's weight. Under extreme heat, and enough pressure, his remains *would* make quite the rock. Most companies performing this service would surely require a form of consent and a death certificate.

My lab, however, has an incinerator for biohazardous materials. I'll send his remains off to a Swiss company who transforms by far the greatest number of human remains— once I've turned him into ash. I'll make it appear official. I doubt they'll bother to check the false name or death certificate. Worst case scenario, they won't know *who* sent it. Libby will get him for a belated birthday or Christmas present from Celeste—a pendant on a necklace, perhaps?

My trophy, which I will only get to enjoy when Libby is around, may make family visits more . . . bearable.

83

Because I do not have the time or tolerance for starvation—and I don't care to mar my sanctuary with the likes of *his* blood—I set out with my hazmat suit and a five-gallon bucket and shovel. It shouldn't take long to find yellow jacket's this time of year in the woods. Their nests are at their peak sizes in August, and though it's the end of mating season in early September—I should be able to find one on the other side of the stream, where the flowering bushes are plentiful at the base of the mountain. The enclosed room will be the perfect space to free the aggressive creatures.

An hour later, buzzing bucket in hand—I tape the air holes in the plexi-glass, and introduce the full-grown nest to one very panic-stricken man. A hyperventilating Derick will quickly use up the air—if the venom doesn't take him down first.

Upon their release, Derick's screams take me back to the slaughterhouse sounds—similar to live red fox meeting their ends, trapped and brought in by hunters. It was unpleasant work, with which that I was never charged.

The theatrics are taking longer than I had expected. It gives me more time to savor this momentous occasion. In order to properly delight in the reward of my countless hours of blood, sweat and well, no tears—I've put on the soundtrack for Vivaldi's concerti, "The Four Seasons". I turn up the volume, but not so much as to drown out Derick's accompaniment. The acoustics in the cave are stupendous! I can't help myself—the milestone of this most joyous ceremony deserves my full accolades—as I "air-conduct" like my life's work depends on it!

First "Spring", a playful classic, has me bouncing and beaming. Next, during the violin-heavy number, "Summer"—a schizophrenic piece ranging from delicate to frantic, I'm possessed through my core with wild fervent motion. The chipper notes of "Autumn"—has me skipping as my imaginary baton dots "I's" in the air. Finally, with "Winter", showcasing its acoustical joy in my cave—the full regalia of my performance wraps up all parts into one.

And while it's true, Derick's "song" is raw—and *not the accompaniment with which Vivaldi would have approved*— his unbridled screams are worthy of absolute dramatic critical acclaim. Brava, Derick . . . Brava!

HAPPY BIRTHDAY LIBBY

Three days after leaving, I arrive back from my "seminar". Libby's car, which should've been gone with her and Felix in it, is still parked outside.

Upon entering the foyer, I hear whimpering and the sound of sucking snot coming from the kitchen—*yuck!* Though I dread the display, I know I must appear to care.

They're both seated at the snack bar—Libby's an ugly crier, and she's covered in disgusting liquids. Celeste looks more helpless than I've seen her in a while.

"Hello, Celeste . . . I'm home."

"I heard you, Abel, and anyway, can't you see Libby is quite upset?"

"Oh?"

"Really, Abel. She doesn't want to talk about it."

"It's okay, Celeste, everyone will find out anyway. You can't keep anything quiet these days, what with social media and all."

"I beg to differ, Libby. I have not joined any of those services, and rather enjoy my privacy as a result. No need to tell me why you're upset. It's none of my business."

"Abel, can't you tell she *wants* to confide in you now? Please, give her your handkerchief."

I'm one of the few men left who carries one, and now this one will be ruined.

"Libby, honey, feel free to cry on Abel's shoulder if you need to. He has a way of comforting a girl when she's upset."

Who the hell is she talking about?

"Derick . . . uh, sent me this photo of himself, naked— with his arms and legs shackled . . . spread out—in some strange room!"

Glad that went through.

"That's just . . . weird. Why would he do that?"

"He accidentally sent it to me. He meant to send it to his 'Dominant Mistress', Dahlia! He told her he was ready and willing to obey her every desire—*ahh!* I, I just can't believe this! It has to be some kind of joke he's playing on me. It's going too far though!"

Celeste shoots a knowing look my way as if to say, "She's in denial".

"Libby, sweetie, look at your sis. I don't want you to hurt like this but, why do you think this is a hoax? I mean,

Derick did *leave* almost three days ago, and you haven't heard from him. Why, he left right after Abel did."

"He did? Where did he go? Did he say?"

This should be interesting.

"He said he had been asked to judge a bodybuilding contest, which he's done a few times. Since it was a last-minute request, the flight was too expensive, so he said he was taking a cab to the bus station, but he should have been back by yesterday—*and* I haven't heard from him! Well, not until *this* came, but it wasn't even meant for me!"

"As your sister, Libby, I hate to say this, but isn't it obvious he's cheating on you?"

Or dead?

"Even if he is cheating, he hasn't divorced me! I deserve an explanation . . ."

"Ahem, well, did he take luggage with him, to um, indicate how long he'd planned on being gone? Or did he leave any clothes here?"

"Those are odd questions, Abel. What are you getting at?"

"Well, if he didn't leave any clothes, he's probably not planning on coming back." *They're stuffed into the lower part of a toolbox in my sports garage.* I'll be sure to get rid of them later.

Libby's dialing Derick's phone number obsessively. Good thing I have it on mute.

"You know, Abe has a valid point. Why don't we check your luggage to see if Derick's left anything? You've been too worried to even think of anything like that."

I play the concerned brother-in-law and follow them upstairs. I may have to subtly guide them to the letter I'd planted on my way out before heading to the "conference". After tearing through the suitcase, Libby has found nothing of Derick's, so I prompt her.

"Did you check all of the pockets? I pack my underwear in those side pockets, so if he does too and he's left any in them, he's probably coming back, right?"

Weak excuse, but I'm grasping at straws.

Libby unzips all of the pockets . . . nothing, until the last one.

"Look! Here's a pair of his underwear!" She has hope in her eyes.

"Hey, what's that sticking out where the underwear was?"

Celeste reaches in and pulls out the envelope.

"It's addressed to you, Libby. Do you want to read it or should I?"

"You go ahead—I don't know if I can bring myself to."

Celeste takes the note out of the envelope and hesitates after reading a few lines. She looks at me, and I nod as if to say, "go ahead, you have no choice now."

"*Ahem* . . . Dear Libby, I'm off to 'get off', for the first time in a long time, Hah! Do you like how cool that came out, almost poetic. Anyway, I hate to break it to you this way babe, but you just don't do it for me anymore. I have needs you can't satisfy with your 'limits'. I want more than one partner, and at the same time, often. I'm into kinky shit you won't agree to. Sorry, but you knew who I was when you married me, and you've kept me from being that person by refusing these requests. Oh and P.S. There's a reason I never adopted the kid. I didn't want to be responsible, financially speaking, in case this didn't work for me. So I guess what I'm saying is have a nice life, and peace out!"

Celeste drops the note and looks at her sister, whose face has turned to a burgundy shade of purple.

"That . . . Bastard!!"

Yes, quickly moving out of denial, and into anger. The second stage of grieving, *thanks to one very descriptive letter.*

"I can't believe what an asshole he's become! I wonder if he's on steroids and it's making him crazy?"

"Well, Libby, speaking as a doctor and brain specialist, there is *no* evidence that steroids cause these effects.

90

Violence maybe—but usually the person on the drug is *more* possessive of their partner, so I don't think any steroids are responsible for this behavior."

Have to keep her out of denial.

"Abel, shh! This is not the time for your doctor's analysis. But Libby, Abe is right—you shouldn't write off his behavior because of steroids. First, you get that disgusting text, and now the note? It sounds like he's chosen to be with very unsavory women, and I'm just gonna say it, he doesn't deserve you anyway. You can do much better. Besides, Felix needs a *real* dad—one who *wants* to adopt him."

"Poor Felix! He's losing his dad, all because I'm not open-minded enough in the bedroom department. He's gonna be so upset..."

Something tells me she's wrong about Felix. I can't let her slip backwards.

"Libby, there is no logical way to take the blame for his brutish ways. This is not your doing, and Celeste is right in what she says." *Ugh! My mouth feels dirty for saying, "Celeste is right."*

"I just don't know what to do now, I feel so . . . *lost*. I don't want to face anyone we know. I'm too embarrassed to bring myself to talk about this with any of our, well, *my* friends. It is so humiliating!"

"Tell you what, sis, you just stay here with us, for as long as you'd like. You and Felix are always welcome in our home. It's so huge anyway."

Geez . . . I didn't think through this wrinkle.

"Not to be insensitive, ladies, but I have some case studies to go through before I'm back in surgery tomorrow, so I need to excuse myself."

That went exactly as planned . . . except for the longer stay part.

ONE FINE DAY

I wake . . . refreshed. Is this what *excitement* feels like? Stretching high overhead as I rise, after exhaling a bounteous lungful of air, a broad smile makes its involuntary way across my face. Careful not to wake Celeste, I ease out of bed and walk out to the edge of my balcony, overlooking the lake. The sun sparkles off the water's ripples, as American Goldfinch nested on the edge of our woods, sing their melodious morning chatter—no doubt in jubilation of my victorious coup. Silently, I revel in the satisfaction of my spoils, so richly earned—my farewell, to summers 'day after' glow.

Though lamenting the last few days of Derick's demise *are* memories to savor, there is one query left undone, which could take years to realize its resolution. Will the damage Felix has experienced result in assured emulation? Such is the case with many victims of abuse. If so, I will be forced to deal with him as well.

Ah ... inspiration!

Playing the role of said "reaction" to the cloning of their abusers. I shall stamp out the diseased inherent at the first sign of replication. Surely, this is an original quest *and* it supplies an abundant repertoire of targets. Naturally, the *creator* of its underling shall be the first to go . . . and the chain of familial abuse ends. My Creative thrives once more!

After several minutes of lounging in the warmth of a perfect morning, the surge of satisfaction I felt upon waking is beginning to fade. Thoughts of my trophy hanging from Libby's neck, as well as newfound inspiration, are things to look forward to—yet something washes over me, rendering me ... unsettled.

Determined to enjoy my triumph a bit longer, I draw in another deep breath, slowly exhaling as I close my eyes. This meditation gives way to glorious fields of red flowers, waving in a silent breeze. One by one they melt into a sea of silk-like sanguine . . . blood? *Merlot's blood . . .* she's in my psyche.

The appointment to see her apartment, in order to reproduce a "set", for the sake of her rare blood and organ donation promotion, is scheduled for this morning.

Suddenly, I'm back to reality. Birds' song has been replaced by sweat trickling down my back. Time for a shower and coffee.

"Good morning, Celeste. Rise and shine! I'm hungry for breakfast."

"Seriously, Abel? *Shh!* Have you forgotten Libby and Felix are here? Grab some fruit, and let them sleep in. Libby's devastated. She needs to rest as long as she can."

I did forget, in my newfound purpose, that we have house guests. I haven't that much time to get to Merlot's apartment, so I decide to heed Celeste's advice. Taking a pre-packaged cup of fruit Celeste keeps on hand for Priya to snack on, I hit the drive-thru for an espresso on my way.

Merlot's complex is on the other side of town, in the middle of a much less affluent area, with most of its architecture dating at least fifty years. Pulling up to the building, I park on the street in front of the four-story Colonial that, if not for the brick, would look far more run-down.

I enter behind a resident with a swipe card, *newer security.* The lobby consists of a corridor only large enough to hold small, locked mailboxes, and a tiny lounge space where two uncomfortably small chairs, and an accent table holding a lamp, reside. The numbers on the mailboxes appear to match the apartments—old school *lack* of security. I take the stairs up to Merlot's apartment, careful to avoid possible eye contact or conversation that occurs in elevators.

On the third floor outside her door, I hear an old—yet familiar—smooth song playing. I pause before knocking.

I hadn't planned on her working my imagination.

"Why hello, handsome Doctor, right on time you are. Come in, please."

You never invite a vampire into your home.

"Thank you, Merlot. This is . . . cozy." *I get right to our meeting's purpose.* "Would you like to be *in* the photos? Perhaps sitting where you normally do while shooting?"

"Of course! But first, come in, Doc, relax. Can I get you a mimosa or some chardonnay?"

Two offers without anything "red" in them from Merlot.

"No, thanks. I've had my coffee, so I'm fine. I don't mean to be hasty, but I've got meetings in an hour or so, so . . ."

"I get it, Doc. Just being civil. To answer your question—of course I'm going to be in the photos! Please let me have a say on which ones you use though. I wouldn't want any of my bad side *ever* published. Where shall we start?"

"How about here, in the living room? You do shoot in here, do you not?" *I know she does.*

"Yes silly, I usually sit on the sofa's edge like so, this shoulder rolled slightly behind, arch my back a wee bit, with this side of my face tilted toward the camera. I look more 'knowing' this way. The Petunias trust my advice when I look more *knowing*. Now that I'm perfectly set, I don't want to move. Could you reach around this side of me and pull the drapes slightly? It casts a glow on my face and highlights my bone structure."

She's intentionally sticking her lady parts out and batting her eyelids at me.

"Sure, I guess." I carefully bend around her, so as not to ruin her perfect pose. She smells lightly of pheromones mixed with jasmine. *Oh yeah, she digs the Doctor.*

"Perfect. Now hold that pose and smile."

She raises one eyebrow, and the opposite corner of her mouth, after wetting her parted lips. She's giving me a salacious look that says—*"you want to bend me over, don't you?"* Such a bad girl. I'm going to have more fun with her than she could ever anticipate. I snap the shot. "Perfect—see what you think." I show her the photo.

Looking down, she catches a glimpse of the bulge in my loose trousers. *Uh oh . . . too soon.*

"Why yes, a good photog you are. You'll have to text it to me."

"Where to next, Merlot? How about your kitchen? You don't regularly film in there, correct?"

"I see you've been watching! I rarely do anything in the kitchen, so you must have checked out my thread *rather thoroughly*? I suppose we could get a photo in there."

97

I'd like to give her a thorough checking . . . control yourself, Abel!

"On second thought, that probably isn't a good idea. It's a bit too . . . 'home-makerish' for my brand."

"Okay, how about your office? You said you conduct life coaching there." It's barely more than an alcove—enough to fit her small pink desk, fuzzy chair, and a floor lamp.

"If you don't mind me sayin', Doc, you look like you could use the bedroom?"

So brazen. Swallowing the lump in my throat, I meet her "dare" as cool-headed as possible. "Merlot, you're an attractive woman, however I'm afraid anything you might be referring to would cross the lines of professionalism."

Whew! Good save.

"We don't have to take our clothes off, Doc. I could just undress one *very,* desperate, member there, and take care of him?"

So tempting. I really just want to go for it—all of it. It's been a long time since a woman's allure alone has made me erect. What am I thinking! She's my target, not my temptress. *Pull it together, Abel!* There's work to be done here.

"Merlot, I didn't come over to seduce you, really. It would be so far out of line for me to engage in anything of that nature with you, not to mention it could hurt the foundation's cause." *I'm going to have to get control of myself.* "Is it alright if I use your facilities?"

"Sure, Doc. Use whatever you like."

Ugh, she's twirling her hair while she bites her bottom lip with that wide-eyed stare . . . not giving up easily.

Careful not to meet her eyes, I smell her panties warming up as I slide past her. *Hurry, Abe!* In her bathroom, I turn on the fan and the water on full blast, as I proceed to do something I haven't done since college. It takes less than a minute. *Ahh,* at least now my focus won't be a problem.

"Everything coming out all right in there?"

She's giggling. I mustn't succumb to her obvious flirtation. She probably gets a kick out of having this kind of control over men. *Naughty.* I will not go easy on her. I will remember this. No one puts me in a position of weakness . . . *no one.*

When I come out, she meets me with a lower lip pout, sticking out enough so I want to bite it until it bleeds in my mouth. *I wonder how she'd like that?* I'd better stop this train of thought before it's showing in my trousers again.

"If you don't mind, I'll just shoot the rooms, quickly, and be on my way."

"Whatevers!" She turns away as she flings her hand in the air, as if defeated—then whirls back around to face me. "I hope I haven't done anything to offend you, Doc?"

"Quite the contrary. I will finish up here, and be in touch soon, once the sets are complete, and we're good to go with the website. It shouldn't be more than two or three weeks before we start filming."

I'm going to lock this side of her personality away deep. Even though it makes me feel so . . . *normal*, I will not let it take control of my plans. "Normal" *is* the problem I have with it.

One side of me would like to pleasure her until she's writhing and screaming for mercy. Once she's at the height of her begging and I hear her heart coursing with that *rare blood,* my other side imagines plunging in and holding it, while it beats in the palm of my hand. *Ah, there's the real me, back in no time.*

SETTING THE STAGE

Though we doctors are not IT experts, I've spent countless hours in the last year, hacking into medical records which, aren't all that foolproof. Given *my* credentials, no one would suspect anything if I were to be caught nosing around in their files.

I've become quite adept at collecting details online, in order to unlock keys to assimilating passwords. My fellow colleagues have provided all the practice I've needed to hone these skills. Not one for small talk, I know very little about their personal lives. However, thanks to social media sites, and their posts, I have a window into their home lives—names of their family members, pets, where they went to school, associations they belong to, and anything else they've so generously "shared". The world they've built for themselves says much about *who* they are.

Facial expressions, along with body language in their photos, tell a subconscious story about them as well. Simply put, the brain automatically tells the body and face what to do, so much so, that even *faux* poses can be counteracted by facial expressions. A smile may say, *I'm happy to be standing next to the person on my right*, but the eyes and facial lines created by any underlying stress of this social interaction, tell me if the opposite is actually true. An involuntary response . . . *my favorite kind.*

Passwords *can be* quite individualized, but once I've combined the silent cues, along with the obvious information in posts, I've been rewarded with a plethora of them.

I'm not snooping to find out information about their personal lives, per se. What I am looking for, are the lists of potential donees waiting for organs. I could simply ask, but that would raise too many questions . . . no, this has to be a carefully orchestrated mission, as my gifts will not come from any "donor lists".

Though it seems a long shot to find healthy enough organs in the hosts of Merlot's choosing, I will make good on this promise, whenever possible. I had not anticipated it, but she has become a muse to my Creative—*I've always wanted one.*

My little bird won't be enthused to see her new abode, *at first.* Its rooms are dressed as closely as possible to the décor of her apartment. In her bedroom, vibrant purple silk bedding, *identical to that which I nearly took her on.* A little pink desk with four drawers, and a sparkly framed mirror attached, accompanied by a sheepskin-covered desk chair, sit on one side of the room. Both are anchored by a generously sized, lush leopard print rug. *Nothing but the best for Merlot.*

She had a poster of her favorite rock star, which I have nixed from the room's design. *I suppose it rubbed me the wrong way.* There were a few other items which I had deemed *too* dangerous, in case she does not appreciate my efforts more than anticipated. Thus, I've omitted them too.

In her bathroom, opposite the desk wall made of mortar and stone, and divided by plexiglass—rests a sink, toilet, and clawfoot tub where she will take cool baths. *This should force physiological responses for my viewing pleasure.*

As for hygiene, I will provide only enough hair and skin product for her to not make a mess with, just in case she decides to get sassy. I will let her know that the sample size products will be provided every seven to ten days. Her natural response will be to use them sparingly. I also don't want her washing off her natural scent so often, as to not have the chance of enjoying it.

The living room is positioned at the end of the arena— on the other side of her bathroom. Its couch, and all interiors, match her apartment's to the detail—except for a faux backlit sky scene over the sofa.

The brain can be tricked into serotonin production induced by sunlight. As such, no privacy has been provided between the bedroom, bathroom, and living room, so that the sky scene will force *some* subconscious normalcy—even if she doesn't choose to "feel" normal.

I noticed her apartment's patio had not appeared in any of her videos, thus could not be recognized as a new one online. I've afforded her the luxury of a small one to be controlled at my discretion, which doubles as the clean *and* torture room with a floor drain. It sits next to her bedroom opposite the bathroom. In its ceiling a cover, camouflaged by grass matching the hillside, can be moved from the outside to expose sunlight. Under the grass covering is a soundproof plexiglass ceiling. In the event a hiker happens by, there will be no suspicious sounds coming from the cave.

When she is on her best behavior, I will reward her with time on the patio, to bask in the natural light. I alone hold the key to its door, of course.

Across from her boudoir, and on the opposite side of the arena, is the white room with splashes of color she has requested for our new show.

Between the white room and her living room sits a small viewing room where I'm able to watch all rooms by camera, should she not volunteer to share her private time with me. Its plexi-wall dividing it from the arena is covered on the outside with a living plant wall, as are all of the others, so she will not be aware of its existence.

Last, when entering on the left side of the foyer, adjacent with the white room, is my supply closet. It houses a generator, refrigerator, sink, washer/dryer and a composting toilet—so I need not share hers.

Finding this place, I knew that I had stumbled onto something that I alone could bring to its full potential. Now, all that is left is its permanent occupant. With careful calculation, it's time to introduce Merlot to her forever home!

EARNING TRUST

Photographing Merlot's residence had proven fruitful. I'd discovered a naughty side of her to be cautious of, gotten all of the information needed for her new rooms, and her financial account numbers—which I had not anticipated finding so easily.

Merlot isn't as "neat as a pin". Her checkbook lay open on her desk, so of course I was able to blow up the photo I had taken of it, retrieving an account number for banking references. I will inject cash for all of her bills, which I'm sure she pays online, mostly because the check on top is #0012.

Someone as computer reliant as she wouldn't write checks and actually *mail* them. After retrieving her mailbox key, I'll check her box under cover of night, just to get rid of flyers and advertisements, occasionally.

Residents in her building seem to keep to themselves. Sitting in one of two chairs, reading a newspaper, which I unfolded across my face, I had spied out their interactions from the corner of the tiny excuse of a lobby, during the two weeks before my first meeting with Merlot at different times of the day and evening.

They're mostly younger adults who moved about, fixated on their devices, rarely speaking or making eye contact with one another. I doubt any of them have ever picked up a newspaper.

Strangely, Merlot hadn't emerged. I would wonder if she were an agoraphobic, had she not agreed to meet me at the coffee bar. Though most humans reveal their patterns, if not daily routines—as far as I can see, she was not regimented at all.

Luckily, upon seeing her place, she had no pets to contend with, and definitely no love interest—unless online or long distance. I had done a background check, but nothing turned up. Even her checkbook read only "Merlot" in the top left corner. *Who is she really?*

Upon today's introduction to her new home, I've decided if she needs a sedative, it would be a mild one, something natural and not harsh like Derick's. After all, I *deserve* to enjoy the fruits of my labor—I *deserve* to appreciate the wonderment when she takes in her new home. I will blindfold her so I am able to drink in her surprise upon its unveiling.

She's expecting me today for the first shoot of our show, but she won't know why I'm in dressed in formal attire. Every woman seems to appreciate a man in a suit—and with respect for all that I've worked toward, I'm paying proper tribute toward the occasion.

As I raise my hand to knock on her door, I feel my blood course and my breathing become shallow. Surely, *this,* is "excitement"? The aroma of diffused Ylang Ylang, an essential oil commonly used as an aphrodisiac, wafts under the threshold of her door . . . *she is up to something.*

"Hello, Doc! Mr. 'on time', I see—*ooh*, and so dapper!"

Wearing a short silk robe, she's unabashedly staring into my eyes and twisting her long dark curls. *I'm going to play the part of the bashful brainiac she takes me for.*

"*Um* . . . do I need to wait in the lobby while you get dressed?"

She's determined to seduce me. Guessing she doesn't get told no much, and I doubt her ego can take another rejection.

"No, silly! Come in. I have coffee, or if you prefer, a glass of champagne?"

She's biting her lip now, still twisting her hair, and leaning on the counter so that her robe reveals cleavage—just shy of showing me her nipple. *Bad girl.*

"Champagne is for celebrating. Are we celebrating, Merlot?"

"Why, of course we're celebrating . . . the first day of my new show! And we're celebrating for the people who will benefit from rare blood donations."

"Well, in that case, I guess one glass of champagne wouldn't hurt."

She's tiptoeing as she poses sideways to pull out a glass. With her stretch, the robe opens slightly in the middle, showing me the front of her panties, and a toned stomach with a bit of roundness below the belly button.

Glass in hand, she slowly bends over to retrieve the bottle from the refrigerator, revealing that the panties between her legs are a thong.

"Getting a nice view there, Doc?"

As she straightens up, she pulls her robe together, as if she didn't mean to give me the "slow-motion-show" and pours my glass close to the brim. *I think she's looking for affirmation that I find her attractive.* She locks eyes with me again, while handing me the flute of champagne.

I take a nice long sip, holding her gaze captive—showing her I can compete in the stare-off she'd started. *This won't be an empty compliment just to anger Celeste.*

"I don't know what to say—should I apologize for looking? I couldn't seem to help myself."

109

The first to break rank in our visual game, she moves her attention to the growth in my pants. My cock was already hard, but now that she's eyeing it like a greedy bird—a new rush of blood joins the ranks down below!

Steady yourself, Abe . . . let her do the seducing.

"What we have here is a *very* lonely boy. I think *he* needs some socialization, don't you Doc?"

Not waiting for a response this time, she goes right for it, cupping my entire package with both hands using just enough force to let me know she could give me heaven, or hurt me with one false move. *Not going to let me finish myself off this time.* It's *so* difficult not to take control—to be controlled—but I must *earn* her trust if I'm to lock her away soon.

"Do you plan to see that *he's* socialized?"

"*Uh huh . . .*"

Instantly on her knees, and unzipping me, Merlot takes her time. She treats me like an artist molding a masterpiece with her mouth. I'm transported to a place that isn't her apartment. All I see are vibrant colors, floating, then waving . . . *now whipping in circles!* Just when she senses my knees may buckle, she stands and yanks me back to my senses by the tie around my neck.

"*Uh-uh*, Doc. Not yet."

She pulls me toward the bedroom by my necktie—needing control—and I am at her command.

"Now kick off those shoes and lose the clothes. You can keep the tie on."

That sounded like a command, so I do as she says. After sauntering over to a camera on a tripod, she pushes a button and I see a green light appear. *I must remember to retrieve that.*

"You're shooting this?" *I don't care, I'll keep it for my viewing pleasure later.*

She doesn't say anything. Instead, she opens a nightstand drawer, pulls out braided ropes made of silk with buckles on them and instructs me to lie down. One by one, she uses the ropes to connect each wrist and ankle to the bed frame. I let out a gasp, involuntarily.

"Nothing to fear, Doc. I'm happy to see you're still *excited*. Watching yourself on camera can go a long way on a lonely night."

Hmm . . . she must have lonely nights.

"How could I be anything *but* . . . excited?"

Merlot makes a real show of slowly letting the silk robe slide over each of her shoulders, until it lands in a plume around her feet. Next the thong—a neatly trimmed package makes its appearance, as do erect nipples. Her body is imperfectly beautiful, not tall or model thin, but curvy and real. Merlot's skin is like nothing I've ever seen—creamy, slightly darker than tan, and without marks or tattoos. I'm just sure she will sit on my cock . . . *begging for her to is more like it.* I can't contain my "excitement" much longer. *Somehow she can tell . . .*

"That's good, I want you to explode."

She stands over me writhing while she manipulates her clitoris with one hand and wraps the other around her body, stroking every inch of her skin she can reach—and then running it through her hair. Her moans are *so* real. She *truly* loves herself—and having control.

"You heard me, Doc! Explode! *Ahh . . . oh!*"

It hits me that she's not going to ride me at all! But watching her on the verge of her own ecstasy is more than I'm able to contain—so I do as she says, and fully uncork!

"Very good, Doc. I hope you enjoyed it as much as I did." She jumps off the bed as if nothing happened, sticking her landing, wearing stilettos I hadn't even noticed.

"Now you can honestly say we've *not* had sex, if asked."

She's got a snarky tone as I lay vulnerable, spread eagle and messy. I've earned her trust *and* she feels in control—confident, as though I am her nerdy puppet. *Perfect.*

She cleans me up tenderly, then unbuckles the ropes. This should be the awkward part, but knowing what's coming next, I am at ease. Now that she is completely trusting, it's my turn to be in control.

TAKE ONE

I've told Merlot we're filming a sunset shot to use at the end of each show. The natural setting has a babbling brook in the background, so I'm driving us to a perfect spot for the footage—*my secret trail.* She's brought her camera, as well as a few changes of clothing for the shoot. I've collected her laptop to review each take. I've also switched out the drive—*and apprehended the scandalous one.* I'll snag her security card so that there will be record of her comings and goings, when I visit to collect her mail, as well as her keys from her purse.

I had helped myself to her medicine cabinet, on a last-minute trip to her bathroom, where I found Melatonin, an even milder sleeping aid than the little pill ready-to-go in my pocket.

As we approach the trail, I look over at her in the passenger's seat, and she looks as though she'll nod off at any moment. "Okay, Merlot, we're here."

"That was a long ride, Doc. *Ahh!* I'm actually a bit sleepy." *She's slapping her cheeks and talking to herself to snap out of it.* "Wake up—the camera loves energy!"

Once we've gathered our gear, we walk further down the path to a spot not far from the faux rock door in front of my cave. After setting up the camera, I position myself behind it. She clears her throat, widens her eyes, and springs as toothy a smile as I've seen her use in other videos.

"Okay ready now, Merlot! Wow the camera with that bubbly personality you're famous for!"

Giving me a quick nod—*a real pro's gesture*—she tugs at her clinging white dress, so that it's perfectly smoothed over every curve. Though it's apparent she's braless in the cool temperatures, she looks mother-nature-esque, with the forest as her backdrop—somehow seeming less salacious.

"Ladies, Gents, Petunias—that wraps the first of our new segment! Remember to give us a thumbs up to 'like' our show, and please check out the link below with instructions on how to offer your beautiful blood donations. If you aren't able to donate, your monetary help is lovely too!"

She raises a glass of what appears to be *red wine?*

"As always, cheers to me, cheers to you. Keep it real, my flowers!"

115

Ugh, so corny. At the risk of denying myself her *real* reaction, I'd emptied a capsule of Melatonin into her glass. She made me hold it while she went behind a bush to pee, and I couldn't help myself. Just a tiny bit of natural sedative.

"Merlot, that was amazing! Now, I have a surprise for you, but I'll need to blindfold you first—and carry you, of course. Those shoes are barely safe on a flat surface."

"Well now, Doc! I hadn't taken you for the 'surprising' kind?"

Giving me a half-crooked smile—she loves surprises, even though control makes her feel secure. *Classic Cinderella complex.*

"Doc, should we check first to make sure that camera take worked . . . you know, before all sunlight is gone?"

"No need to mess with perfection, Merlot. Now, close your eyes madame."

"*Ooh!* Since you insist, kind sir!" She's wriggling like a little girl as she squints her eyes closed, hoping for something special. Though she's doing her best to hide it, I sense anticipation in her perky stance and uplifted chin.

Not sure *what* she's relying on "the Doc" to give her— the same thrill, if not a greater one than she gave me? *Oh, she's right to anticipate.*

I drape her eyes gently with a scarf that opens into a lovely envelope shape, an expensive designer-patterned silk

I knew she'd recognize. By the curve upward on one side of her mouth, she had peeked and I was right. A spritz of rose infused into it, from Celeste's collection of parfums, didn't hurt either.

I scoop her into my arms, and a silly smile spreads across her face, a relaxed version of my earlier video-vixen. Vulnerable and trusting . . . I *should* feel sorry for her, being completely out of control, but it's my turn now, so . . . no.

Her heartbeat hastens with each of my steps, coursing that "rare blood" through every cell of her body—the same body that writhed over me only a few hours ago. *I suppose I'm anticipating this too.*

As with the days of old, a bride-and-groom's destined end of chastity, so our journey halts at the cave's door. I contemplate whether to throw her over my shoulder, but the half-smile still on one side of those full lips and the churning intensity I sense in her core, tells me instead to simply savor this moment.

117

WELCOME HOME

Three steps into the foyer—I gently set Merlot upright onto the cool stone floor. First, I take a remote from my pocket and click on a sultry song—I think she'll recognize it. She audibly exhales . . . I was right.

Carefully untying the blindfold so that no hairs on the nape of neck are pulled, I press my nose into the skin just below her ear, and inhale deeply. Chill-bumps appear on the backs of her legs. *Nice!*

Positioning myself in front of her as I peel the scarf away from her face, and she blinks a few times, as if what she's seeing isn't real—then spins, slowly, smoothly, as if on a turntable. She's processing with her eyes, yet, for once, I'm unsure of what's behind them . . . *say something.*

After a few full circles, Merlot plants her feet and looks upward in a slow, methodical gaze, then back down, finally resting on the white room. It's splashed with accents of turquoise, fuchsia, and a sunny shade of yellow, *as promised.*

Resting in the middle of the room is a surgeon's table, *which I plan to make full use of.* For now, it's covered with a comfy pad and accompanied by a down-filled pillow, as well as colorful throw pillows.

A painting centered on the back wall, behind the table, is a vibrant abstract of a woman's face—whose bone structure resembles Merlot's. Below that is a slick white credenza, where my surgical tools are stored, topped by five small cacao and musk infused candles, "sexual chocolate". Flanking the abstract of the "Merlot" painting are tall, narrow mirrors framed in gold. A modern chandelier, I knew she would approve of, dripping with oblong smoke-colored crystals, hangs centered above the middle of the room.

Two shallow side walls are camouflaged in greenery with little white lights sprinkled inside them. High overhead, I've draped ethereal streams of white tulle, which glow in contrast to the rugged faux cave ceiling.

"Well? What do you think?" I decide to break the silence, hoping for an honest response.

"I . . . I'm not sure where or *what* this place is. It's like a *fantasy*, romantic . . . yet ominous. What is it for?"

Oh no, not ominous—not what I wanted her to say!

"It's your studio. I promised you a room of white with accents in the colors that you requested. Is it not to your liking?"

"No—I mean yes, it is quite beautiful, but this is not what the Petunias will be comfortable with . . . as we also discussed."

I want to show her the rest, but I'm not sure she's ready for it yet.

"Merlot, this is only the setting for the part of the show where you interview medical experts. A professional setting—yet stylish, is it not?"

"Yes, yes, it is stylish. However, I *am* surprised such professionals are making the trek to be interviewed all the way . . ." She's relaxing in her stance and her eyelids appear to be getting heavy.

"*Ahh!* I'm not sure what's come over me. I'm getting *so* tired. I guess what I mean is, *ahh*—sorry to keep yawning Doc. I'm certainly not bored . . . really. Oh yes, I meant to say, we will need some "Merlot" atmosphere that the Petunias are accustomed to—a cozier setting in addition to this space, perhaps? Also, why is it located in the woods? Is this a cave?"

"This 'cave' was a discovered resource, and since we want the environmentally-conscious minds of today to see donating blood is as natural a thing as nature itself, it just

120

fit." *A weak story made up on the fly.* I don't appreciate having to lie *or* that she isn't in awe of all I've done for her.

"Look, Merlot, resources and time were put in here to make this setting special. If you do not approve, I suppose that we can scrap the whole idea, but we won't be shooting in your apartment."

"Oh no Doc, it's just all so new to me. It *is* beautiful. You just moved my cheese a little, that's all. I'm not sure though, why there isn't a more interview-like setting inside the white room? Why this, table?"

"Oh that—well, it moves, so we could put a few lounge chairs and a coffee table in its place for interviews. This is just to show how easy and comfortable it can be to give blood. Come over here. Hop up."

She seems tentative about this, for someone who doesn't know of my fetish.

"Here I'll help you." I lift her from her sides and pop her up onto the table. "See? Comfy, right?"

She's running her hands over my upper arms. It appears my muscles have distracted her. A foot, which has freed itself of the high heel, is making its way up to my crotch.

"Doc, this table may have other uses."

She's not going to tie me to it, if that's what she's thinking. I want her blood—I'm not letting her take control this time, but I may have one final loose end to finish, so that she trusts me completely. I want the next room's introduction to be a smooth transition.

"I was going to save the next surprise a little longer, but since you've gone and played with my 'friend' again, let's put your blindfold back on."

I place the blindfold around her eyes, changing the track of music to one I'd spotted from her collection in a basket next to her desk. A wide grin uncontrollably makes its way across her face.

The distraction allows me to raise the plant-covered screen that was concealing the plexiglass, dividing her bedroom from the arena. Next, I disengage the floor anchors holding the clear wall in place, and electronically hoist it behind the greenery wall so that it's hidden. I don't want her attempting to retreat like a caged animal, *just yet*.

"Come now, Merlot."

Standing between her dangling legs, I use one hand to scoop her up by her buttocks, while I lift her with the other wrapped around her back. *"Mmm"* escapes her lips. The warmth of her breath cascades my neck and catches involuntarily, as I set her down and slip off the other shoe. The floor is cool and smooth. I know it feels good to sore feet tortured by unforgiving shoes. *She won't need to put herself through that from now on.*

Holding one hand and leading her with the other, we make our way across the arena and into her bedroom. I lean down and whisper in her ear. "I'm going to take off the blindfold. I have another surprise for you—*and* the Petunias."

"Oh! Doc! This is magnificent! It's my bedroom— almost identical. You really didn't move my cheese *too much* after all. My Petunias won't even know the difference!"

"Great, music to my ears!"

Even though she must be feeling heavy-legged, Merlot finds a burst of energy to run and flop onto the bed, but in seconds, she's stretching her arms out, woozy and yawning again. "It's sooo cozy! *Aww . . .* I'm sorry Doc. It must be the wine, plus these sheets feel *so* good."

Don't be, I put just enough Melatonin in that wine to relax you.

"What say, this time I tie *you* up, Merlot?"

She's laid on her stomach already, and with this suggestion, she looks over her shoulder, giving me a side-eye and smirk that says, "I dare you". I meet her challenge eye-to-eye as I run my fingertips along the middle of her butt, then reach up into her short dress, and lift her thong away from its snug position. She's accommodating me with open legs offering up what's between them.

"Oh yes, Doc . . ."

I accept her invitation with a gentle squeeze and strategic kneading. She's responding nicely. Peeling the bottom of her dress over her smooth mounds, I lean in and breathe a hot breath between her legs . . . then inhale to let her know I appreciate her scent.

"*Ahh* . . . Doc!"

Finishing with one slow lingering slide of my fingertips, without exploring her smooth insides, her quivering reaction tells me she's ready.

"Oh please . . . Doc, I'm *begging*! Don't do what I did to you. I withheld on us both!"

In one smooth motion, she pops onto her back and sits up just enough to whip the rest of the dress over her head, tossing it onto the floor. Always the actress, she's squirming on the purple silk like an animal in heat. This may be the last time I get this chance—and she's asking me for it. I wouldn't take her any other way.

"I am just the man to give it to you, Merlot."

I grab her by the ankles and flip her back over onto her stomach—she's not resisting. I pull out my ankle restraints with a bar between them from under the bed—*great planning*—and lock her into them. Her legs are apart just enough.

Next, I put cuffs on her wrists and run a cord through the welded rings on them, tying them around the bed frame.

124

She can move her arms, but she can't get to me or flip over. Next, I take surgical scissors and cut the panties from the thin string of fabric running through the valley of her ass, and the ones on each hip. *Panties destroyed.*

"This is quite a view, Merlot."

"I'm aching, Doc . . . please!"

"There's just one thing, and it *is* necessary if you want me as bad as it looks, sounds, *and* smells like you do?"

"What? Anything!"

I pull out my blood-drawing equipment—also stored under the bed. "I need to put this needle in your arm and give you the privilege of being the first to donate . . . to the cause."

She looks back on the bed and sees I have a bag for her blood, a cannula and a needle, along with a tether for her arm.

"What? You want my blood—*right now*?"

I raise up on my knees so she can get a good look beyond the needle at what else I have for her.

"Oh . . . this *is* hard, and I am not making a play on words. Why my blood? Is this something that gets you off, Doc?"

"*Oh*, more than you can imagine. To watch your blood flow out of you, while I satisfy you at the same time, there's nothing that gets me off more. And trust me, it will be better than any sex you've *ever* experienced. So . . . what do you say? Are you in? I'm not going to force you."

"It sounds freaky, even for me, but you do make it sound thrilling in a good, kinky sort of way at the same time."

"So you're in?"

"Yes, okay, but only on one condition—you can't donate my blood. It's clean, it's just . . . well, I can't explain. Just promise you won't donate it?"

I find this odd from the woman ready to save a child's life, but I promise.

"Don't worry, Merlot. I'll keep it for myself. You won't be needing it again anyway."

She's officially given me permission to "enjoy" it later.

"Okay, Doc . . . just do it—don't make me wait any longer!"

I'm a master at placing the needle, so it isn't going to hurt her arm, even during physical motion. I'm in her vein quickly, and she doesn't flinch at all.

Time turns into nothing more than a concept, as the glittering trail of red running through the cannula hypnotizes me. In seconds, my aching bird relaxes onto the bed, breathing more slowly—turning into a human puddle, as I am transfixed by the most beautiful shade of crimson I've ever witnessed.

I know the safe amount to take. Perhaps starting the second bag, though it isn't full yet, may have been going too far—or was it the natural sleeping aid that caused her to pass out? I decide to put a glucose drip on her and remove her restraints.

Too bad I don't get to finish her off, but I'm far from a necrophiliac—and in this case it would've fallen under the offense of date rape, *a punishable crime.* Once the drip is empty, I tuck her in, and bring down the plexi-wall along with the green living-wall screen. Merlot is safe and secure in her new castle.

In addition to a set of PJs and her silk robe, I'd snuck into a side pocket of her bag, which I've left folded for her in case she wakes feeling cold, are snacks and orange juice— for her to regain her energy in the morning. There's also a journal encompassing all fetishes on her desk, in case she cares to discover her own. Last are bath products and a note.

*****

Dearest Merlot,

I had a wonderful day and evening . . . you as well? I have to be at work tomorrow, but I'll be back late in the afternoon with more of your clothing, the rest of the equipment needed for our show, and extra food of course. The bath has toiletries like the ones you use at home, in smaller sizes, so please use them sparingly as they will need to last a week to ten days. There are also clean towels and washcloths. I've left a few magazines for you to stay up on current events for the sassy remarks I've seen you use with the Petunias. There's no Wi-Fi here, and you won't be needing your phone, so it is safe with me. Get comfy in your new castle—or should I call it what your generation has coined your "Forever Home".

REALITY HANGOVER

Good . . . morning world! I feel *so* rested. I don't even remember going to bed last night. I must have been toast!

Silk sheets, my dearest friend, a tactile pleasure you are. Mmm . . . *tactile.* Merlot, your imagination *is* insatiable. Perhaps a little satisfaction is the right way to kick off this day. PJs be gone! Wait, no knickers? Where did I put you?

It's awfully dark in my room this morning—must be cloudy out. *Ah,* there you are with my robe, just out of reach, and folded *so neatly.* I don't recall doing that? *And* . . . just like that, I'm distracted. Pleasure postponed. Oh well, up you go, Merlot.

Ahh, a good toe-wriggling in the right rug is certainly underrated. It feels more plush than usual . . . *huh?* This *is* my rug? It's leopard print but the pattern seems slightly, off.

Where is my rock star? I didn't take that poster down. *Ouch!* The bend of my arm feels like it's been bitten—*and why is a cotton ball taped in it?* Holy wankers! What have I done!

Come on, Merlot—think. What is the last thing you remember? Oh yeah . . . you committed to giving your blood—first, *before sex*. What were you thinking—oh right, you weren't thinking—you were horny! What else? Put this together . . . you're naked, *and* you remember being with the Doc. Did I—I mean did the Doc and I . . .?

This *isn't* my room. It's that damn studio, or cave, or whatever the Doc made for my next series of videos—*and* I've slept here!

Huh? Are those *glass* walls? They're shiny yet shadowy . . . like a forest outside of a museum—*huh?* They feel like glass. Let's see how they sound when I knock on them. Nope, that doesn't sound right.

A surge of bile is ganging up on my throat—I'll swallow to keep it down. I'm going to pound on the walls to get his attention. "Doc, let me out of here! Come on, I know I was a bad girl yesterday. I crossed a line. But seriously, *ha-ha-ha*, the joke's on me! It's over now—I've learned my lesson! Let me out, *please* . . . I need to pee!"

Adrenaline is rushing to my eardrums—this feels like the beginning of a panic attack. *Calm yourself, Merlot.* Breathe . . . in through your nose and out through your mouth—*and* one more time. *Ah* . . . that's better. My eardrums are clear as a bell again—speaking of which—why *is it* so quiet? I'm starting to wonder if he's here at all.

Scanning my studio bedroom, I spot a crack in the smooth-as-glass wall, on the other side of the bed. Perhaps a door? I'll push on it—yes! It opens easily, but it's pitch black in here.

Stroking the walls next to the opening, I feel no light switches. What *is* in here? I'll search with my foot. Hmm . . . something cool and smooth—a pedestal. It's a sink! I must be in a washroom—only logical for a toilet to be nearby. And, there it is—oh, thank God! I'd rip down my shorts, if I had any on.

Ahh, sweet relief.

My thighs relax as my bladder deflates—the right one is pressing into a cool surface. What's this? A tub next to the toilet? Did Doc actually think I would take the time to bathe in here?

While reaching around to find toilet paper, a faint glow catches my eye. It's lighting up the bathroom and a bit of the bedroom. Is that . . . *a window?* I was sure this was a cave. It appears to be in another room next to this one. Mesmerized by its glow—revealing enough space to walk around the end of the tub—I'm headed for a closer look.

Ouch! My forehead! I've found another clear wall!

Damn it!

I cup my face and press into it for a clearer view. The room resembles my living room, and the glowing window is brightening to a "woodsy scene" as if automated—so, *not a real window.*

Feeling perplexed and now hungry, I sit on the edge of the tub. The thought that I've *possibly* had sex *is* making me feel grimy—like I want a bath. Should I?

The glow has spread through the bathroom completely, and I see tiny bottles of shampoo, conditioner, and body wash—all the same brands as mine at home!

What is the point of this? *The little hairs on the back of my neck are standing at attention.*

"Doc! I know you're watching . . ."

Think, Merlot. There's got to be a way out of here. Maybe, he's trying to find out how resourceful you are. Maybe, *this* is a game or a survival test, to see how you'll do under pressure. But *why* would he do that?

Chills are spreading up my thighs—miniscule informants, heightening my internal alarm. Breathe, Merlot. What if he is watching. *This paranoia is making me feel like a mental patient!*

I head back to the bedroom for more space to roam, which is now lit from the glow of the bath. "Doc, seriously! You've thought of everything. Now please, let me out! I'll starve before passing your test!"

132

Wait, what is that? Covered by a white napkin on the desk next to the bed, it appears there's a tray of something—*food?* I bounce onto the bed, sliding across the sheets. It's a replica of *my* desk and chair! Of course it is. I'm too hungry to care. Under the napkin, I discover a carton of juice, jerky, and a small package of granola. I don't want to eat it, *out of spite*, but I can't help myself. I scarf down the feast—meant for a Barbie Doll.

My bed-bouncing activity has loosened the tape in the bend of my arm, which is hanging from one side now. No need to keep this. *Huh?* There's no bruise or even the smallest of holes on my skin. If not for the spot of blood on the cotton, I would question if this is part of the game, except, I regretfully recall letting him draw my blood. *I'd better flush that.*

I'm not sure he's watching or if I'm alone, but leaning toward the "Doc is not here". With the realization that I'm on my own, at least until he comes back, I'm feeling braver. I need to have a closer look around.

Scooting out from the desk, the chair's feet screech on the stone floor. Its cry ends in a jingle. *What the*—a chain bolted from the leg of the chair into the floor? Gripping the edge of the desk, I give it a good tug. Nothing. It's bolted into the rock, too!

133

I'm *not* going to cry—*I'm* in control of my destiny. This is merely a bump in the road that no one *ever* need know about. *Be calm, Merlot. Be very, very calm.*

An elaborate hoax, the whole thing. Your bedroom, your products. Why *would* someone go to all of this trouble if your show weren't real? On the other hand, you were left—no, *trapped*—in a cave overnight! You're locked in, and you've no way of getting home. Hell, you don't even know which way home is!

I feel a part of myself from within, whom I haven't needed for a very long time, paying me a visit . . . my alter ego. I traded her in for Merlot years ago, but she comes in handy when Merlot can't get a grip. *"There's nothing you can do at this moment. Do, not, panic. You've survived worse than, whatever 'this' is . . ."* Anj is right.

The stress of my panic is wearing me out. Overwhelmed, and accepting that for now I'm trapped, I let go of the anxiety hunching my shoulders—as if to have been wearing them for earrings. I allow my gaze to relax, and the sheets invite me to take comfort in them.

Giving in to their call, I lie down. They *are* cool against my skin. *Ahh . . .* the pillow feels plush as I dig my face into it. More deep breathing exercises help the strain in my neck, one vertebra at a time. That's right, Merlot—calm your "fear thoughts".

Still fighting the mind-minions prodding me to cry, I roll on my side, while gripping beneath the pillow. *What's this* . . . an envelope? On the front is written, "Now that you've found this".

I read it over and over again to confirm—*he, is, certifiable!* I doubt there's a show at all, or ever has been. I'm destined to be forgotten to all of my followers . . . all of my work thus far, wasted. *No-no-no-no*—I refuse to live life a prisoner! I must escape . . . I *will* escape!

Up and splatting the cool floor at a militant pace with my bare feet, I replay every event since yesterday as if trying to find something I've lost—in this case, my freedom. I don't know why, but it's the only strategy I think of.

One minute, I'm begging for sex and then . . . then, he sticks a needle in my arm, stealing my blood—why? *Ugh!*

Did he take advantage of me in my sleep? I don't think so—I would definitely be sore. He probably thinks I'm promiscuous, but I've had very few partners. It's no wonder I'm horny all the time.

One thing I do know is, I *must* outwit him. He's much stronger—and obviously more cunning. I mean . . . just look at this place, and the plan it took to create it—and no one knows about it except for me . . . now!

He'll definitely take me for a mouse in a cage. *Yes, let him believe he has the upper hand.*

What I need is to find *his* weakness.

A question keeps nagging at me. Why would a handsome doctor, with the world at his feet, go to such elaborate measures for the likes of me . . . well, who he *thinks* I am?

I know one thing he doesn't—what I've survived!

MAESTRO

I'm almost ready to leave when Celeste pings me. "Darling, dinner with the Trudans at eight—don't forget." *Ugh!* I despise it when she commits my time to social engagements. This one, however, is a rather important task. Now that she's finished decorating our monstrosity of a home with her high-profile interior designer—which I insisted on her using so she didn't turn our modern masterpiece into a French Chalet—I've gotten her involved with the Children's Hospital Fundraising Committee. When she gets bored of Priya, or the other way around, it will keep her busy.

After six hours of a particularly challenging tumor removal this morning, all I wanted was to focus on getting to Merlot's apartment. I still had rounds to complete on the Neurology wing, as well as swinging by the lab, and signing off on the studies my technicians require before proceeding to the next stage of our current project. My schedule is down to a science, so it took only ninety minutes in total.

I park a block short of the apartment to keep my car from becoming a regular visitor out front, and head in with a duffle bag of tools in hand, as well as two empties for her extra clothing. Wearing my navigator shades, bike gear, and a winter cap, the age gap between myself and most of the younger residents is nearly bridged. Not one of them looks up from their devices as I pass them—*good.* I'll not check her mail in the light of day. She may have a secret admirer who has memorized her box number.

After taking the stairs, I slip inside her apartment and lock the door before turning the lights on. I close her blinds, just in case she's got any peepers in the building across the way.

Since constructing the cave, I've become mechanically adept. Recently, I'd converted its pulley systems to an electronic one. I'll be changing out her switches and thermostat to be operated by an app, which I'm conveniently putting on *her* phone as of today. This will allow the lights and temperature to be operated on a normal schedule as if someone lives here.

I turn the sinks on full blast and flush her toilet while I work, providing water usage for her monthly bill. To make sure nothing spoils in her refrigerator, I've brought paper bags for cleaning it out. I'm surprised to see very little inside. Her diet seems to consist of frozen dinners, bread, peanut butter, mac and cheese, and an array of canned goods. Of course, various bottles of cheap wine and a bottle of champagne are members of the guilty cast of shit she subjects her body to. It's unbelievable how nice her skin is, eating like this. I take out the items that will spoil and leave the ones with a "forever" shelf life. I'll need to shop for her new-improved diet.

In the bathroom, I find tampons. I forgot about this— *menstruation*. I pull one out and examine the little blood-sucking machine. *Mastery and a criminal waste all at the same time.* Oh well, I guess I'll let her use them, for a while anyway. Another item I've forgotten—a razor to shave with. I don't think she'll like being hairy. On the other hand, if anyone is to use this . . . it should be me. I might actually nick her by accident . . . *stop daydreaming Abel, there's work to be done!* I won't have her using it on herself, or on me. I'll have to give this bit of grooming some thought.

I've collected the rest of her filming equipment, and stuffed an extra duffle with my favorite items for her to wear—which are mostly articles showing as much skin possible, and just a few comfy items. I'll not wash the comfortable ones as often, so she doesn't opt for them all of the time.

139

After a quick run to the grocery, away from my usual route, I'm on my way. I didn't have time to park at the warehouse and ride my bike today, so I'll have to pull in behind the sparse stretch of trees. *Risky.*

Anchored by two duffels of clothing and a grocery bag as I walk toward the door of the cave, I'm experiencing trepidation—which is an instinct, *not an emotion.* What if someone has found her—sprung her free? What then! *Stop it Abel!* Fear is an imaginary weakness.

I enter to find Merlot at her desk. She's not acknowledging me—probably angry and obviously pouting.

"Merlot, I'm back! How was your day? You had a good rest, I hope."

She doesn't look up—just flips through a magazine, *definitely pissed.*

"I know you're probably wondering *why* I have you locked in. I know this is not what our agreement was, but you will see, after some time, that it's the right thing. You don't go out much anyway, so now you have the same environment with just a little more . . . supervision."

"What do you want from me, Doc! How *the hell,* do you think I'll ever, *ever,* agree that *this* is the right thing!" I'm up and pounding my fists on the clear wall in Doc's face. For good measure, I let out a tear—a frustration cry.

"I guess it's fair that you see it that way, for now, since I haven't filled you in on our real plans. By the way, you'll find the plexiglass you're pounding on to be unbreakable. Now please, sit on your bed, and I will fill you in."

"No! I will not sit on this bed, or be 'amicable' just to appease you, *sir*!"

"Merlot . . . such big fancy words, not your typical mode of speech." *Hmm, is there more to her than I'd realized—has she hidden her true self from me?*

He's up to my face with only this clear wall between us, looking wild-eyed, almost hissing, and . . . excited? *Damn it, Merlot! You've already given too much of yourself away without realizing it.* Time to turn the focus back on him. "Answer me this, Doc . . . did you rape me?"

"What? I am *not* a rapist . . . though you *did* beg me for sex."

"I knew it! You did rape me—it's rape when one party isn't awake!"

"I said you begged me for it—you fell asleep too quickly, maybe from the bit of sedative in your wine. I wouldn't have sex with you while you're asleep. That's the epitome of a date rape or a necrophiliac in the making, not that I judge the latter—to each his own, but a limp body holds no excitement for me."

"So *that's* why I was sleepy? You put something in my wine? That's probably why I begged for it too. My defenses were down!"

"Now Merlot, you and I both know *that* is not why you begged, and besides it was only Melatonin. You have some of your own fetishes. You just haven't come to owning them yet, as have I. Those silk braided ropes with buckles on their ends—the ones that you used on me—I'm sure they have come in handy long before we met, no?" She's turned away from me. *I've touched on something here.* "Anyway, I only wanted a little blood—though I will admit starting another bag may have been going too far. I was going to get it one way or the other. You only made it more pleasant to retrieve."

"Is that what all this is about, your fetishes . . . finding *my* fetishes? We can do that in a normal setting, like my apartment. You didn't need to lock me up to play. Can't you just let me out, Doc? We can do all the playing your heart desires." *I know this won't work, but I've got to play the dumb girl, and get him off my trail.*

"Tsk, tsk, Merlot. You're sounding ungrateful for all that I've done to make this magical world for you. Not to mention, we both know you don't plan to go back to 'us playing' at your apartment, after I've confined you." *I don't think she's ready to hear any of my plans yet.*

142

"Such a civil way of putting it, Doc—confined, huh!" I wave my hand in the air and walk away from him for effect, and then thoughtfully turn around, as though the next thought is just now hitting me—*Good acting is key.* "Doc? When you mentioned 'real plans' . . . what exactly were you referring to?"

"We can discuss it later." *It's hard to say if she's being genuine—I don't think I've broken her in quite enough.* "First, I'll show you the rest of the place, so you know how absolutely secure it is. Oh, and I also brought you some comforts from home." I show her each outfit, one at a time. "I've also brought you extra food and feminine protection as well. According to my sense of smell, you should be needing these anytime now."

"But how did you know . . .?"

"Merlot, darling, I have *very* keen senses. I could smell you the first time I was at your apartment, leaning over you. I knew then approximately where you were in the month as far as your 'cycle'. Oh, you probably thought I was interested in your cleavage—it was nice, too. You see, I'm coming clean about *my* fetishes . . . however, that is *not* what this is all about. Before I say anymore, I will take you on a tour."

"There's a purpose for each room in your forever home. You've already discovered your bath, I'm sure.

143

Opposite your bathroom, on the other side of the bedroom wall, is a treat. I will show it to you if you promise to be good—but first your patio."

"Of course, Doc . . . don't treat me like a child." *I'm going to knee him in the crotch and make a run for it.*

"Come with me, Merlot. You're going to like this." I open the door, reach in, and take her by the wrist.

"Easy on my wrist, Doc." I step out quietly and then, in one swift hard blow to the crotch with my knee, I think I've done my damage—but he doesn't let go. Instead, he coughs twice, and tightens his grip.

"Oh, Merlot. So predictable. I think you may have broken the skin around my cup's edge. I will forgive you, but next time it won't be so pleasant. You're feeling high-spirited today, so for safe measure, I'm going to bind your hands behind your back." I tie them uncomfortably tight, sure to enjoy the red marks when I take them off. *My thrills may be sparse for a while.*

"This is your patio, for when you've been good for a few days. At the top, I've installed a luxury feature hidden in the hillside—a skylight to let natural light in. It's soundproof, should you decide to scream for help."

"Well Doc, you've outdone yourself. Once again, I *am* impressed."

"Sarcasm does not become you, Merlot." I lift another wall of foliage, disengage the plexi-glass pins in the floor, and lift it with the touch of a button. "There is no access to your living room from the bathroom. As with your patio, it is to be enjoyed only when you've displayed good behavior and is to be operated by me alone."

"If you don't fill me in on our plans, how will I know what good behavior will earn me time in these rooms?"

"Given the fact you tried to incapacitate me only five minutes ago, we're not going to review 'plans' today, but nice try. However, I have brought a lovely meat, cheese, and fruit platter, along with some of your favorite wine. You can watch me open it and pour, so you know I'm not drugging you. This is the last time I will provide dairy as it is not healthy—so savor the cheese."

I untie her hands and re-tie one to the coffee table, which is bolted to the floor. She looks despondent. "It won't always be this way, Merlot. You'll just need time to adjust and I'll have to see that you've acclimated to your new way of life."

After fifteen minutes of watching her eat, I think she's had enough—*and* I have a tedious dinner date with Celeste and the Trudans.

"It's getting late, time for me to go. Let's get you back in your room." She's walking slowly ahead of me, with re-tied hands and her head down—dreading the time alone, I think. Something on the back of her silk robe catches my eye . . . a red spot.

"Merlot, you've stained your robe. Guess I was just on time with those tampons."

"*Uh*, thanks for pointing it out." *Ew!* I never wanted to discuss this with a man. But Doc is obviously not a normal man. An idea springs to mind. I turn around giving him a sly smile. "Hey Doc, if you've got some time, I've got some blood."

"Oh, Merlot . . . not to compound your rejection today, but I've got somewhere to be, so I'll pass on your offer."

"You can resist? I'll let you do anything you want with it." *I'll do anything to have a chance to get out of here.*

"I'm sure it's lovely 'menstruation blood', but I could take it or leave it. The least pure, aside from diseased blood. I do not prefer it, so no thank you. Now, would you like to give me your robe for cleaning?" She doesn't know I have facilities for washing here. I purposely left the supply closet and my viewing room out of our tour.

She's sliding it off, giving me a similar show to the last time I was at her apartment. She's naked underneath, and a bit more round bellied. *Must be the period bloat women complain about.* There's a nice patch of red smeared on her

146

inner thighs. Lovely. Luckily, this cup will hide the beginnings of any excitement.

I watch her crawl into bed without cleaning her thighs—she's definitely tired. I lower the foliage screen in front of her room, do a quick wash of her robe, and hang it to dry. The machines in this room are silenced by soundproof insulation, so she's none the wiser that I'm here waiting for another twenty minutes.

As the washer swishes and spins, my mind begins to calculate the day's pros and cons. Its planning and execution was flawless, yet it fell flat with Merlot. Logically, her human emotion would not yet align with my goals. I'll write it off for now, especially with her "hormonal time". Why is it that I do not revel in her negative physiological reactions, as with Celeste's?

Speaking of Celeste . . . time to get to the *insufferable* task of dinner with her and the Trudans.

147

QUARTERLY ITCH

Celeste is waiting for me as I enter the foyer, wearing one of her designer party dresses—black crepe, with a V-neckline and an ombre of metallic beads on the cuffs and hemline. Of course, her classic pearls and diamond stud earrings keep it from going *too far* into the edgy look she consciously avoids. Standing at the bottom of our stairway with crossed arms, and a tense expression—I can hear her mental foot-tapping as she times her verbal vomit, for after I've closed the front door.

"Abel, we are going to be late—*where,* have you been?"

I open my mouth to give her a "working late at the office" reason, but she cuts me off.

"You know what—never mind. I don't have time for excuses. You've got exactly fifteen minutes before we need to leave."

"Not a problem for me." I dart up the glass staircase two steps at a time, for a quick shower and change of clothes.

"This is an important dinner, Abel"—she shouts up the after me. "Put on a nice suit and *please hurry!*"

Celeste is all wound up to impress Lance Trudan, who is head of all of the fundraisers at the Children's Hospital. She's gotten her feet wet with a few tasks, but wants to be the lead on the next big soiree they throw—pretty nervy of her to toss her hat in the ring *this* early. The amount of time, out of my business this could provide, makes it worth my full support, so I will be on my best behavior.

She wanted to order a luxury ride to the restaurant, but I assured her that I wouldn't be drinking, so not to be concerned. *I think she had a more impressive arrival in mind than my hundred-thousand-dollar SUV.*

Arriving at Bon Vivant—Celeste's suggestion—she waits for the valet to escort her out of the passenger's seat as if royalty.

The restaurant is elegant without being *too* romantic—white linen tablecloths, crystal stemware, and high ceilings in a wide-open room. The wait staff is excellent, and the fare is a mix of French and American prepared with a gourmet slant. There are a few beef selections, Le Gigot D'Agneau—

French Roast Leg of Lamb—and a salmon dish—*probably farmed.*

Out of the cuts from the slaughterhouse growing up, the delicacy which I was never treated to, is the Chateaubriand Filet—the most expensive part from the cow. It is on the menu, and I am *sure*, prepared in a more savory way than Polly could have ever pulled off. It will be the best part of my evening.

Two glasses of Chardonnay in, and Celeste is becoming too chatty. At least she's taking up my slack. As I had expected, dinner conversation with the Trudans is grueling. On *its* menu, I suffer through a long montage of talk about kids needing lifesaving procedures—*blah, blah, blah.* There's a bit of conversation about the lack of rare blood in the donor bank as well. *I do need to check Merlot's sample of blood I've collected a slide of . . .*

"Isn't that right, Abel? . . . Abe?"

"What . . . Celeste?" I had drifted off, thinking about my caseload tomorrow. *A forgivable reason for not being engaged.*

"I was just mentioning to Lance and Deidre how you were the one to suggest I get involved with fundraising and party planning for the Children's Hospital."

Time to interact. "Oh, yes, it's Celeste's specialty, really. There is no 'socialite opportunity' or event that she misses.

She knows all the right people who'll want to be in the Party Pages of the 'who's who' for charitable events."

"Thanks, Abel . . . *I think*."

"Anyway, the point is Celeste is an asset to any organization who wants to throw successful fundraisers *and* she's pro bono, so what else could you ask for?" Now that I've done my "duty" for the evening, it's time to zone out again—that is until Lance starts talking about where most of their organ donations come from, as well as the process of shipping them.

My ears perk up. This topic interests me, given I'd told Merlot, albeit in luring her, that our show would help garner organs to those who are having a difficult time finding a donor. Though it is *unlikely* one of my candidates, less deserving of their parts than those who are in need, will have contributable organs—I'm a man of my word whenever possible. The timing and details would be delicate—details I will study.

The conversation moves back onto family, things "we" like to do—Celeste goes into details about the India trip, *and* . . . I'm out again—until *finally*, Deidre says it's time to relieve their babysitter. Thank you, Deidre!

All the way home, and up to the bedroom, Celeste babbles excitedly about the dinner. She's had far too much wine, and now that we're ready to change out of our dinner attire, she's swishing around the bedroom, batting her eyes at me like a peacock in heat—as if *this* is going to lure me sexually.

"Abel . . . it's been a while now. Have you forgotten how to do it?"

"And by 'it' . . . use your words, Celeste." *Don't make me suffer through "it" please.*

"You know what I'm talking about. I've been so wrapped up with Priya and now the Children's Hospital. I feel like I've put *us* on the back burner. I'm sorry for that, but I do have needs. Don't you?"

Ah, taking half the blame for our piss poor sex life now—diplomatic manipulation. If only that creamy white skin would pop a blood vessel . . . *anywhere.* I could at least fake it more convincingly with her. One session could last her a good three months, with our track record. Plus, I don't need to have her following me around out of insecurity, like a puppy beaten with the newspaper for peeing on the rug. *I'll have to give "it" to her.*

"Of course I have *needs*, Celeste. I think all humans do. I've been busy with work too, so don't beat yourself up over it. You're doing a generous thing working for the kids at the hospital."

I hate this sweet crap! Like a good soldier, I move behind her to remove her pearls, and unzip her dress. *Let's get this over with.*

"Oh, Abel . . . that's nice. It's my turn now."

She loosens my tie, slides it off, and then gets on her knees to unzip my pants. The zipper sticks, and she moves in close to see if it's caught on my shirt's tail.

"Let me help, Celeste." I yank it in an upward motion, just in time to catch her bottom lip in it.

"*Ow!* I'm—I'm bleeding! My lip, it's bleeding all over your pants!"

"*Shh!* Let me help." In one swift motion, I rip the zipper down freeing her lip skin . . . *that had to smart.*

"*Ow,* Abel! That's twice now!"

"You were stuck, Celeste. Only one way to fix it. Here, let me see." I pick her up and examine the lip. Beautiful bloody lip, swollen and gushing down her chin. "It's only a surface wound, Celeste, no stitches necessary. The lips are just sensitive—they bleed easily."

"I'll go wash it. It wasn't your fault, Abe. I was trying to be sexy and, well, it wasn't."

"Au contraire Celeste, it *is* sexy. You stay right here and let me take care of it for you." *If I'm going to do this, she's not going to waste blood again.* I engulf her bottom lip in my mouth, and bite down just enough to make her lip spurt a little. She whimpers slightly until I slide my hand between her legs.

"*Oh*, Abel!"

I strip her clothes off like a savage, while focused on the bloody mouth and chin. *She's never been so beautiful.* Her look is that of a lost lamb . . . until I throw her onto the bed and give her a good hard screwing, missionary style— her favorite position. This view is a handy aphrodisiac for me, *for once*. I tell her to lie still when I'm finished.

"Here, Celeste, hold a cold towel on your mouth and open your legs. I'm going to take care of everything."

After cleaning her up, I try to convince her to roll over and sleep. She's still slightly drunk, and obviously loves the attention, so it takes some time for her to doze off. More conversation . . . *great.*

"Oh, Abel, I don't know what came over you tonight."

She's blushing . . . *really?* Aside from the blood, the most boring sex ever. At least I've checked my three-month duty off the list.

"I don't think I've *ever* felt so . . . alive!"

Uh oh. I hope my blood-induced passion didn't backfire. I decide to change the topic. "You know, Celeste, the thing Lance was talking about tonight—the lack of rare blood donations? It might be a good cause for you next, as far as an awareness event. It's not that you *need* a job, but if you prove your abilities, you never know what it could lead to in the future."

"I had never thought of it that way. It does sound kind of interesting, but I wouldn't want our family to suffer with my time being taken away for work."

I've got to shove her in a different direction other than focusing on "us". Two ships passing in the night, that's a comfortable arrangement for me.

"Don't worry about where any of this *does* or *doesn't* lead. Just take all the time you want. And above all else, enjoy yourself."

LANDMINES OF GOLD

Ah, planning. A task of patience and diligence.

I've caged my bird. Soon I'll begin plucking her, but first I need some *instant* gratification, and therein lies "part B" of my plans.

Where to find my future organ cadaver. I had told Merlot in the beginning, merely as a ploy that our "organization" was looking for rare blood and organ donors, however, a promise is a promise, so if it's possible, *and* I have the logistics safely worked out, then I will see it through.

Watching the news at my work computer, as Bella has left early and my work tasks are completed—I find a few robberies, nothing serious. I divert to the Internet's "unsolved crimes"—this should be easy pickings, thanks to the lack of anonymity they've earned for themselves. On second thought . . . *that* could pose a problem.

Though not the primary driver, if I find a few subjects who fit into the organ donation puzzle rather neatly, I will keep it in mind.

A close enough geographic location is also preferable, so that my calendar isn't changed *too much* by luring and capturing the prey. Unexplained holes in my schedule *could be* risky if a savvy agent were sniffing too closely on a missing persons investigation.

I'll begin my search with subjects high on the spectrum of psychopathic or sociopathic behaviors. *This*, I understand. Though we share a similar limbic system, I have much more control than these offenders, sadly, will ever learn to exercise.

Some waste their talents haphazardly killing on "whims", while others practice by method, typically involving exacting the same pain they've received—to a greater extreme, of course. They're a menace to we who master the control it takes to *equitably* inflict our justice.

First, I'll begin in the most-wanted list found on the Internet. Gentry Harrisen, who likes to burn things. She's on the FBI's list for burning her family—a brother and parents—alive in their home on Christmas Eve five years ago. No teeth were left behind. *Trophies perhaps?* She's not been tried because she hasn't been found. *Hmm* . . . this one is high profile. I'll move on.

I decide to take a different tack. Tapping into the national registry of suspicious deaths through the morgue's files that our hospital uses, I deploy the hacking skills I've acquired as of late. The registry is attached to a national database, so I'm able to view information throughout the country accessing it. None of the perps tied to these victims have been prosecuted or imprisoned, mostly because they're missing and haven't been tried. Once they're found, the files are removed from our system and are strictly in the hands of the police, *or* the FBI for investigation.

Here we go: Miscarriages Caused by Severe Beatings. None of the women died—that is, except one, and her cause of death is listed a car crash. Why then, have they made the registry? Abuse and miscarriages happen multiple times daily.

Ah! Though he isn't mentioned as more than a boyfriend at the time, a deep dive of research reveals that they were all dating the same man—Lonnie Baker. Only one woman called the police for domestic abuse, but refused to file a report when the police arrived. Unfortunately, I won't be able to speak with her. She's the one who died in the crash, after paramedics found her hanging on by a thread; *however*, the baby was saved.

This file is listed as a low priority, which makes it slightly more interesting.

Perusing the landmines of possible death-by-domestic-abuse from obvious random kills is getting old. I'm looking for repeat offenders, if possible.

I come across a string of couples, all elderly, who've died in what looks like suicide pacts.

One couple, maybe two, wanting to die together? Understandable. But eleven in less than a year's time? Now that's a pattern. They've all kicked it on a few different iterations of painkillers—so they didn't feel much. *Generous of the bastard who took them out.* It's clean—respectable, even.

It doesn't appear there's an investigation tied to these. The morticians seem to believe it's merely a trend that's caught on within the older couples of their communities. Reporters speculated that perhaps they wanted to go out while their quality of life hadn't degraded to the point of great suffering—however, only one of them actually had a terminal illness, according to the reports. There's no suicide note and no record of assisted euthanasia—which would be legal only in certain states, for those who are terminally ill and suffering. How then, were they convinced, to take their own lives? *This* is not legal and *not* euthanasia.

The death pacts have occurred in a spread-out fashion. For it to be deemed a "trend", it would need to be taking place in a tighter area—*well thought out.* I respect this criminal mind master for their prowess, control, and ability to remain invisible.

Most want their prizes to be revealed for the guts and glory, like roadkill. This one seems an interesting challenge—however, I may need to hone my skills before taking it on. Nonetheless, I'll put it into the *maybe* pile.

One more worthy candidate, and then I'll leave it to Merlot to choose. It will be my gift of sharing, *and* she needs to learn real leadership for our future project.

"O Negative Corpses Presenting Nearly Bloodless"— *Fascinating!*

O negative presents in only five to seven percent of Americans, but can be used for most other blood rare types for transfusion. *I am immediately intrigued.* I think this will be *my* pick. I only hope it is Merlot's.

So far, reports of ten corpses have shown up, different nationalities, who carry O negative. There are no clues as to *who* is draining them. They show up in separate databases with varieties of reasons for death. Their *varieties* must be skewing attention. *Smart.*

More than one appears to have drowned. Two died in car accidents, one was a subway tracks victim, and four jumped out of a window. All are labeled accidental or suicide. They range from eighteen years of age all the way to fifty-seven—both male and female. The only constants are their drained blood and the blood type. No mention of homicides. The file is simply marked "unusual coincidences".

There are no coincidences here. This purveyor of O negative is either on a mission to save other lives, or a psychotic hemophiliac with a perversion toward O negative, for some reason.

The time frame of these deaths are all within the last five years, at two a year—the only pattern this offender observes. I could enjoy the hunt, along with the kill, on this one. He or she is an insult to those in *my* fetish community.

After clearing my search history, articles in hand, I set out to visit my rare bird.

MANIFEST INITIATIVE

No longer in need of building material space in the storage bunker, I park my SUV where they once resided. I've convinced Accounting and Administration that the lease on the building was too costly, so we've purchased it and are holding it for ongoing storage needs—which I have agreed to continue managing.

I'm thankful, in this moment, that my afternoon's caseload was light. It's unusually warm today—seventy degrees. The leaves are beginning to turn to golds, reds, and oranges, illuminated by streams of sunlight breaking through the branches overhead. A cool breeze evaporates the sweat on my brow as I ride toward the cave.

My backpack is equipped with the files that I plan to entrust Merlot the task—*and honor of*—choosing our first worthy victim. Hopefully, she will see that any of them are appropriate candidates. I will get more insight into who she *really* is and what drives her, by her choice. Though she appears a bit shallow from the outside, I do suspect there may be more to her than my first blush impression unveiled.

Upon hiding my bike in the thicket of brush on the trail to the cave, anticipation mixed with the glorious weather, has put a pep in my step today.

After lifting the remote wall of foliage, and turning on the lights, I see Merlot up and ready for my greeting.

"Good afternoon, Merlot! How are 'things' today?"

Chit-chat . . . I suck at it.

"Is that what you're going to ask me—really? I'll tell you how *I am*—completely bored out of my mind, lonely, angry, and just in total disbelief of . . . *all* of this!" *I've got to play the role of the typical victim—your time is coming, Merlot. Stay cool.*

"No worries! I have the solution to your boredom—boy do I! I have an intriguing homework assignment just for you." I remove the comfy pad and pillows exposing the cold steel table and lay out the articles of the three perps I'm giving her to choose from.

"*Eww* . . . what's with the gory photos? These are all, dead people?"

"Yes, and you get to take your pick of—"

"My pick of what! Are you bringing me a dead roommate, or are you asking me . . .?"

"No, I am not asking you to choose *your* method of death, Merlot. Nothing of the sort. Why would I go to all of this trouble just to turn around and kill you? And of course, I wouldn't leave a corpse in here to stink the place up. That would be unsanitary."

"Then what's with the articles Doc? And why tell me I get to take my pick?"

"Please calm down. Now, the victims of these hideous acts whose evidence I lay before you, have not been vindicated—mostly because our justice system is constipated with lackadaisical bureaucracy, *and* the murderers have outsmarted them. They've either gone AWOL, or made their crimes look 'circumstantial'. But I ask you, do these photos look circumstantial?"

"Where did you even find this information? I thought you weren't tech savvy . . . and how do you *know* these were homicides?"

I decide to skip her questioning, as all of it is quite dismissible. "Oh Merlot, see beyond the page and the print. Look into the stories, how they relate, and stop feeling sorry for the victims long enough to think logically."

"Sorry for them? I'm completely revolted! I don't understand *why* you want me to read *any* of this garbage?"

Hmm, interesting that her sense of empathy isn't the first emotion to kick in. *I'm learning more about her already.*

"Those responsible for these crimes may have escaped the justice system, but they will not escape justice itself, and *you* have the honor of choosing the order of who I will exact it upon first!"

"You mean, you're going to *kill* the 'supposed' guilty person of these crimes? And you expect *me* to choose who gets it?"

"That is precisely correct. As I said, read what they've done, and choose who goes first."

"So you're going to kill *all of them?* I don't want to choose—no, I *refuse* to choose! I'm not having anyone's blood on my conscience. I will *not* play your sick game!"

She's spoiling my good mood. Opening her bedroom door, I throw her onto the bed and pin her down by the wrists over her head. "Oh, you're playing! In case you've not figured this out, *you* are the one under lock and key, and *you* will do as I ask! Once you've actually read what these . . . *animals* have done—you'll see that they deserve what's coming to them!"

"What makes *you* any different than them! High and mighty talking about justice, yet you're planning to—"

"To do what? What the law should be doing? That's what *I'm* doing! And what makes *me* different Merlot, is that I exercise control in my urges. I believe in stopping the criminal *before* he commits more crimes! *And luckily,* there are enough of them to go around for me to exercise my controlled urges for as long as I enjoy doing so!"

"So that's it? Is that why you've kidnapped me? To be a party to your crimes?"

"Such an ugly word, kidnap. *Do not* use it again."

I dismount and release her wrists.

Wearing a short dress has afforded me a visual trail up her leg, all the way to her panties, except . . . she's not bothered to put them on today. I run my finger along the top of her leg—until she jerks her foot away.

"That's only part of the reason you're here, Merlot."

"What's the rest? I'm *dying* to know."

Sitting on her bed is too intimately close for this part, *especially with no payoff*, so I stand away from her to explain something she's not going to appreciate. *Time to let her know what I really think of her "business".*

"I did find you on social media. I confess I've watched dozens of your videos. Don't get the wrong idea, I'm *not* obsessed with you. I actually deplored most of it."

"Well, that's a fine thank you! So you outright lied when you said you were impressed with my work?"

She's sullen, wrapping her arms around her legs, beginning to rock on the bed. *Spoiled baby*.

"I never said I was impressed, Merlot. You assumed it, perhaps because you are so consumed with the image of who you believe yourself to be. You suffer from a huge amount of self-importance, as so much of your generation does, without having earned it, *or* actually acquiring a real skill through hard work, much less education."

"I beg your pardon! I earned over two hundred thousand followers! They didn't just pop up one day and say, *Oh, Merlot, let me watch you faithfully, please*? It took *knowing* them, what *they* want to hear and see, and fine-tuning it as rapidly as possible."

Sitting on the bed as I lord over her, apparently left her feeling too out of control. She's animating with arm gestures, then crosses them as she plops onto her desk chair.

"First of all, thank you for admitting you're merely manipulating them to get your numbers. And second, what education do you have in psychiatry for the life coaching you give? What business degree for your business advice . . . *hmm*? Have you ever actually worked back-breaking hours in the beauty industry or *paid for* and *attended* the classes professional stylists do to keep up with the latest trends—which, you espouse as your own? Moreover, how much actual *real-world* work, and how many hours, have you put into doing any of these things that you claim to be an expert of?"

She jumps out of her chair at this . . . *more arm gestures*—definitely on the defensive now.

"Well, I . . . I am watched for being fabulous! I don't *need* to do all of that to be who I am—and I don't know *how* I know what the best advice is, or what trend is going to be the 'next big thing'. I'm a sponge when I'm not even trying to be—so I learn things that most people can't remember, even when they're taught. I'm doing a real service! And besides, I've only *earned* enough to pay my bills anyway until . . . well, until *you* tricked me into believing I was going to finally enjoy the fruits of my labor."

I meet her threatening tone, only in a quiet controlled voice, moving into her personal space, and looking down into her eyes . . .

"Oh, you thought you were going to make it big, huh? Don't worry, Merlot, you're not done shooting footage for your Petunias. It won't be live, and *I* will be in control of its content as well as its editing, but together *we* will teach your generation they aren't deserving just because they exist. We're going to have them looking at all of their participation trophies and feeling like pathetic failures for accepting them."

Merlot looks as if she's ready to cry. To show her tears of manipulation will have no effect, I give her more space and stand in the doorway.

168

"The good ones will rise from the ashes and actually do something with their lives, and you'll have led the charge. Oh, and if I haven't said it . . . I *am* impressed with your number of followers. Congratulations! That's the main reason why you've won *this* prize! *You* are the Captain of this change to come! Now, read the articles I've laid out for you. You've got twenty-four hours to pick who goes first. Once you're done with that task, think about what you're going to wear for your next video *and* what little 'truth', that is *actually* true, about yourself—something unflattering but real, not meant to impress your Petunias, that you're going to confess. This ugly truth will be the theme of your next video. And, if I do not approve of your truth, then I will choose one for you. In fact, I think we'll name a series of videos—Truths About Merlot, You Didn't Know."

She's standing completely in awe, mouth dropped, dumbfounded expression, and ready to melt into the floor. I was right to let her in on our plans—it was time.

After locking her in safe and sound, I cycle back to the storage shed. I'm refreshed and actually smiling—a rare occurrence. *I'd better stop before my face gets sore.* My hard work has just begun to pay off!

INDIFFERENT WORLD

As I pull into the garage, the skyline's last plea at daylight streams neon orange across the horizon. It's as clear a night sky, as the day's had been. Twinkling stars litter the deepest indigo in the earth's spectrum overhead. They cast a glow down below, so that temporary clouds visibly waft from my mouth—announcing that I am alive and well in the crisp night's air.

I enter through the front door, greeted by the constant green dot of light atop the smoke detector, and a warm haze in the hallway, illuminating from the kitchen appliances around the corner. Their hum is the only sound in an otherwise silent foyer.

It seems the house is empty—until I walk upstairs and down the long corridor to the master bedroom, passing Priya's room on the way there. Her door is ajar. Wearing earphones and lying across her bed, she's surrounded by journals, an opened computer, a neat stack of notecards at her ready, and a pencil in hand.

She enjoys her studies in the casita. I think because it affords her privacy away from Celeste . . . and lately, Celeste doesn't seem to mind that she frequently stays out there until all hours of the night.

I had planned for that to be *my* getaway, but since she's taken it over, I'm resolved to using my office downstairs. It *is* practically on its own wing of the house, near my gym, which no one else uses—*now that I've transformed the meathead into a more perfect state.* I decide to knock before opening her door any further.

"Hey there, busy?"

"Yes, kind of."

Typical short answer from her. I push it open anyway.

"It looks like you're multitasking. Studying for a test?"

She looks over her shoulder, tipping her head slightly in my direction. "I'm researching colleges for credentials."

"College? Aren't you jumping ahead a few years?"

"I have to make these decisions in advance, *Dad*. That way I know I'll be taking preparatory courses for the highest possible exam scores and testing out of those that are a waste of my time. The faster I move through Pre-Med, the sooner I'll get to my specialty. You should know *all* about that."

"I see. When did you decide that you want to become a doctor? I'll take it as a compliment if I've had any influence in your decision."

"When I saw what the physicians, who came from America and other more prosperous countries, did for the sick in India—I knew then it was for me."

"You *do remember* that I did that once, right? That's when we found you."

"To be clear, that's when *Celeste* found me. It doesn't take a brain surgeon to deduce you didn't want kids, but you took me in anyway, so I should thank you—seeing how that made it a greater sacrifice. Anyway, if Celeste hadn't pushed to adopt me, I wouldn't have the opportunities and privilege that I do now—and I *do not* plan to squander them."

"*Hmm*, that's an interesting perspective. I'll leave you to your research—carry on."

What a brilliant kid. Her attitude begs the question—do kids who get everything from parents, like Celeste, automatically become a spoiled burden on those around them . . . a *thorn* in society? Priya seems to refute this assumption.

Normally, this time of evening I'd head to my office and prepare for tomorrow's hospital roster, which is sometimes needed—but mostly something to do, since I rarely watch television. I have tomorrow's schedule memorized, and I'd rather lament today's 'unveiling of purpose' to Merlot.

On my ride home from the cave, I'd forced myself to stop grinning like a schoolgirl about the day, but now that I have this rare time alone in my Nordic Castle, with Celeste out, doing who knows what—the bedroom balcony beckons my presence.

A slight blast of cold air hits my face when I pull open the telescoping glass door to the balcony. It's nothing a warm cup of *something* and my Navajo Blanket won't fix— one of my only mementos from childhood.

Celeste had insisted on a small bar in the bedroom, with a juice refrigerator, sink and drawer microwave. With so much space to fill, I had agreed. I don't keep up with what she stocks in the cabinets and fridge, as the aperitifs do not interest me, mostly because mostly they are sweet. She has, however, pushed "special teas" under my nose repetitively—swearing by their health benefits. I've been a hold out as a hard-core coffee drinker, but since the pre-packaged pouches are handy—I decide to try one.

The little tins have names on them, like Matcha, which sounds like chewing on grass. I peruse Vanilla, Raspberry Spice, Ginger Cacao, and finally one called White Shark Chai Tea. It's made with white tea leaves and organic spices. The "shark bite" comes from hints of black pepper, complementing its citrus notes. *Whatever,* I'm tired of reading—I decide on this one.

Wrapped in the stiff old friend of red, black, orange, and twisted wide fringe on its ends, I head out onto my balcony with tea in hand. Snuggling up on the cushioned sofa, the steam from my cup warms the tip of my nose. *Mmm* . . . the "shark bite" is actually tasty.

The stars are bright, and the moon is beginning to peak over the pines at the bend of the lake, straight ahead in my view. An ebbing breeze blows ripples against the water's surface, joining in a distant waltz with old man moon's illumination. They creep closer the higher he goes in the sky.

At times I long to have "feelings", and then ask, is longing a feeling itself? I certainly do not wish to think as other *emotional* humans do, but the satisfaction of achievements as of late—have me asking what the smiles brought on by their epiphanies are about.

Rather than question my internal intent and reactions, I reform to play out the conversations, and results of the day. Merlot needed my honesty and it *is* only fair. After all, I've been demanding the truth from her. I couldn't hold it back any longer—time to move ahead with my glorious plan. She does not seem excited, and of course at this juncture, what else could one expect.

174

After being told that I do not admire her work, her childish display brought me no discomfort. But *huh . . .* replaying it now, her internal reaction was definitely off—how could I have missed it! There was no heart thumping anger, no red eyes or sniffling. I didn't even smell a *hint* of her rant's fervor. Rather than question my own fortitudinous lack of feelings, perhaps I should dial in on Merlots? I do not believe she's afflicted with what I, or other closely related psychologically *different* humans embody. The closest to any of my relatives, could be a mild case of narcissism. Or perhaps, something has happened to her in her past? This seems like the most plausible of explanations.

The chill of the night has gotten frigid, and my tea is long gone. I head inside to put my cup in the sink when I notice the clock on the microwave says ten fifty-eight. Climbing into bed, the house is still silent—nearly three hours have flown by.

Waking from an ethereal sleep, I hear Celeste soft-shoeing it across the bedroom floor. She turns on the spout of her sink to its softest flow, and after ten minutes of washing up, slides under the covers facing opposite my direction. A slow anxious breath expresses from her mouth, as her chest falls from a fully inflated rib cage.

Having an inkling she's been or is being unfaithful. I turn on my back, and quietly fill my olfactory with her

175

plethora of scents. Toothpaste, face wash, and a floral powder, patted between her thighs—all fail to mask the musk of vaginal manipulation.

I roll my head toward her to see that her hair has fallen away from the exposed skin on the back of her neck. Moonlight's refection beams off the lake, generously filling our room with a soft bluish light—spotlighting her strawberry-colored splotches—a giveaway if there were any doubt. She routinely rubs her neck during orgasm.

I'm trying to *feel* some way about this, but after a few minutes, I muster only ambiguity. No anger, no hurt? No. I hope she doesn't think she's fallen in love and decides she wants a divorce. I don't have time to create a new "cover life".

I also *do not* plan to get saddled with part-time fatherhood. Like Priya said, I never wanted a kid to begin with.

If Celeste follows in her mother's footsteps, she'll want to keep up her lifestyle, while playing on the side.

Her dad, Myles, caught Phyllis cheating and actually gave a damn. In reality, if Celeste can balance this with her conscience, it's better for me anyway—another distraction to keep her from meddling in my affairs.

On the other hand, if the asshole she's screwing is wealthy *and* they fall in love . . . great, now I'll have to find out who he is in order to assess my risk.

LITTLE EYES

Doc *so generously* left the folders of these gory photos and cases with me in my bedroom to study. What am I gonna tell him? Kill this guy instead of that one? And what's this string of blood-drained bodies about—all coincidences? I don't even see that anyone is *definitely* guilty here. Plus, I'd prefer to stay away from the topic of blood with him—too bad. I thought we'd have at least *some* sex. Now that I know he's a psycho, that could be dicey.

Looking at all of this gore is making me queasy. Time to get this over with. I pick . . . this good-looking librarian abuser—also known as the baby killer. Looks like he *did* beat one of the girlfriends to death . . . nope she died in a car crash. At least the baby lived. What a hell of a way to start out in the world. Regardless, he caused a lot of miscarriages.

If he *is* guilty, Doc was right to put this one in the pile. I'll bet he's knocked up another one by now, based on the timing of his other assaults. I guess offing this guy might be okay.

What's with the blonde-haired, blue-eyed chicks? I'll ask the Doc if he thinks there's a reason, or if he has even noticed this pattern. Okay, task number one—done!

On to number two. Let's see, what *isn't* flattering about me? How bloated I get during my period? That's a pretty raw thing to talk about. Maybe he'll go for that. How I eat too many french fries and drink too much rosé?

Nah, pretty sure my Petunias are guilty of that too. They'd probably just relate. There are some obvious things, about my past . . . I just can't tell the Doc—and no way I'm telling my followers. I *could* shoot with no makeup? No . . . that's *too* embarrassing, but it might be good enough for Doc. A stripped-down version of Merlot. Yes, I'll try that one out on him.

I'm polishing off a dinner of crackers, hummus, and a pear at my desk. Doc has supplied me with a mini fridge, which he stocks just enough food in to keep me from starving.

I wish he'd brought my rock star poster. I used to get off imagining things he would do to me. What's a girl with a starved love life supposed to do?

Falling back onto my down filled pillow, I feel my eyelids getting heavy. I'm not going to fight the urge to crash early, except . . . *huh?* What's that? I know what *that* is! I freeze—eyes cracked open to mere slits, and pray my eyelashes conceal them sufficiently. I don't want them to give away my discovery of the camera I've *just spotted*!

I know equipment, and *that* is state of the art—the smallest camera available. It's mounted between the two plastic walls, adjoining the bedroom and bathroom, at the top corner. My senses are in overdrive—but I must remain chill.

Still hiding behind my lashes, I roll from one side to the next, acting as natural as possible, while checking the room's perimeter. There's a camera in each corner! *More recon necessary.*

I get up and walk into the bathroom, where a light comes on automatically now. After pulling my thong down to sit on the toilet, as if I have business to attend to—I drop my head so that my hair falls over the sides of my face. Nonchalantly, tilting my head to see through the veil of my curls—*there's another one!*

I carefully scan the rest of the room in the same manner—three cameras . . . *holy overkill!* I don't know if I'm streaming live, or if he turns it on and off. What I *do know* is *now,* I'll need to be extra careful. *Damn him!*

Before climbing back into bed, I peruse the rack of clothing he brought from my apartment. I need to choose

180

something to wear taping my show—a show that the Petunias have been anxiously waiting for. I pick the best color out of the small wardrobe, to compliment my bare skin. He'll be surprised to find me in it tomorrow when he arrives—and more surprised to find me bare-faced.

Feeling eerily exposed, I slide under the covers as naturally as possible.

I'm going to try to have dreams about my rock star.

TRUE LIES

After attending to a day of tasks my "cover life" requires, I drive to the storage space, park, and hop on my bike. Eagerly anticipating Merlot's choice, as well as discovering *what* truth she's going to reveal, I pedal to see her in record time.

After raising the wall of the bedroom's foliage, through the plexi, I see Merlot sitting on the end of her bed, with a look in my direction as if she's playing the role of "cat who swallowed the canary".

"Hello Doc, how are you today?"

"Are you mocking my mood from yesterday, Merlot?" Again, she plants that *knowing* smirk on her face, but something else looks different.

"You decide . . ."

She uncrosses her legs slowly, giving me a glimpse between them, donning a purple suit with a mini skirt riding up to the top of her thighs, as she speaks in a low, calm voice.

"I'm great actually, and ready to film. I've missed it— my Petunias must be Merlot *starved* by now."

Leaning back, she braces herself on each straightened arm, highlighting the fact that she's *not* wearing a shirt under the blazer, and it's secured by only one button at her waist.

"I don't want them finding another *'me'* to worship. I suspect they distract easily. Plus, I need to keep up my endorsements to pay my bills."

She is decidedly cool, calm, and collected. I *suspect* she's practiced this speech.

"That's a nice purple suit you're wearing, Merlot . . . no shirt though? A lot of skin, don't you think?" She doesn't respond, but I think she's on the verge of breaking character.

"*Hmm* . . . what else looks different?" Finally, she can't take my oblivious questioning any longer, and jumps up.

"I'm not wearing makeup! I always wear an on-trend-face, as part of my show! Going completely without is going to shock the Petunias."

Now that she's perked up to the more fiery version of herself . . . I'll play along. "Okay, not bad. I think we'll use that from now on, but I'm gonna need you to put on a shirt. The chest skin is detracting from your natural face."

"From now on?" *Damn!* Detracting from my face was the point. "No, Doc, one thing at a time, please. I'll lose my makeup endorsements."

"Yes, we'll shoot your show with your bare-face from now on. But before we begin your segment, tell me first, who did you choose for me to extinguish?" Her body language changes again—to a happier version of herself.

"It wasn't easy, Doc, but I'm choosing . . . Lonnie Baker! Do you want to hear the thought process I used to make my decision?"

"I appreciate that you recognize there *is* a 'process' in your decision making—so, go ahead."

"I said to myself, *he's supposed to be charming, like a good sociopath should be.*"

Interesting . . . she understands what a sociopath is.

"All of his girlfriends have been blonde-haired and blue-eyed, and each woman is or *was* a librarian—perfect targets—quiet, with a tendency not to socialize too much. They're probably flattered when a good-looking guy comes along acting interested in them. He also appears to be *very* physically fit."

Healthy organs. Good.

"Then I started to actually get mad at this guy. I thought to myself . . . that's it, Lonnie, knock 'em up and beat the shit out of them. And, it looks like they all quit their jobs around six to seven months of pregnancy."

"Many good observations, Merlot. Anything else?"

"Sure, Doc, I'll draw the pic for you." I'm pacing for effect, like an investigator, and the Doc is smiling. "He treats them like they're precious until—and he's waiting for this part—they do one thing he can poke at. Like wearing makeup after he's convinced them months ago to stop, or perhaps they go to the gym to workout, when they know he despises other men looking at them in tight clothing."

Hmm, she sounds awfully *close* to this analysis.

"Then he's in their face, grinding his teeth, red-faced, and spewing as he yells at them, 'You're a *slut* aren't you! Who are you trying to impress? Does he *screw* you and make you scream like I do . . . you, *whore*!'—Yeah, I know this guy's mode of operandi. It's total brain washing."

She's definitely reliving something here.

"Now, confused and shattered, she's ready to leave him . . . *until*, he convinces her he's 'protecting' her from others in the big, bad world who want to take advantage of her 'naivete'. At this, she knows his undercurrent of threat is over, and she yearns to ride the wave of security he's promising instead. Still feeling raw and vulnerable, the

185

scene ends in tearful makeup sex—only she's the one crying, and he is oblivious to her pain. The vicious cycle repeats itself, in varying degrees, until he knocks her up, and now she relies on him completely!"

"That was an exciting tale, Merlot! So why do you think *she* would stand for this cycle of abuse?"

"Don't know. Maybe she's addicted to the feeling that only a guy who's torn her apart can supply—when he puts her back together again that is."

"Long, yet interesting analysis. Have *you* ever been pregnant, Merlot?"

"Me? No! But I'm guessing that's part of what he gets off on."

"You may be right about that, and something that I didn't share with you is that, technically speaking, there is evidence that he knows where to strike during his kills. Strike high on the abdomen with enough force and the blow will take out the baby. Strike low and hard enough, and the hemorrhaging caused can kill the mother—possibly the baby in the process. The last one, Tonya, must have challenged him enough that he decided she needed to die based on the bruises to her lower abdomen. Of course, the cause of death was recorded as a car crash."

"Doc?"

"Yes, Merlot?"

"Now that he's killed a mother, do you think he'll have a taste for it again?"

"That's quite astute of you. The baby's death alone is most likely *not* going to quench his craving now. I'm sure he assumed putting this one behind the wheel of her car, then crashing it into a tree, would get the cops off his scent. He doesn't know that she survived long enough for the baby to be saved. She refused to name the father on her deathbed, so the kid is a loose end he doesn't know about. That was over two years ago."

"So how're you going to find him?"

"Lonnie's quite the traveler. I've mapped out his kills to see if there's a pattern. Geographically speaking, they're random—check out the map. His kills are drawn in red lines, connected in chronological order."

"It looks like . . . like *initials* to me."

"*Huh*? It does look like initials—that aren't completed yet."

"Hey, did you discover any information on his family or his past that could help you find him?"

"Because you seem *authentically* interested, I'll share with you what I've found. His stepmother, who he mostly grew up with *was* a librarian—however, she's brunette with brown eyes. His birth mother was a blonde with blue eyes. She worked as an exotic dancer and died when Lonnie was four, *and* she was never married to Lonnie's father. One night after work, she was beaten severely and taken to emergency, but then hemorrhaged too badly to recover. They never found the culprit, and the account of a shaken four-year-old boy would never have held up in court, especially in those days, so the case fizzled out."

"Oh wow, I almost feel sorry for him, like maybe he should just get help."

"Don't go soft on me now, Merlot. There's no helping him. And, you were right about Lonnie probably being a sociopath. It's absolutely possible that he never felt *anything* after seeing his mother bludgeoned to death, and most likely repeats these acts to try and make himself feel *something*."

"Wow Doc, it's like you're a detective—or a psychologist!"

"It *is* kind of like that, isn't it, Merlot?"

"I suppose you're right about Lonnie. If he isn't stopped, more innocent lives will be taken—brutally too."

I sense she is dragging this out to deflect from talking about the "truth" she's going to reveal.

"Leave the justice part to me. Now, on with your second task . . . something true your Petunias *don't* know about you?"

"Well . . . I usually have an outline and fill in details as I go. This was a tough one to figure out. The bare face was my main reveal."

"The bare face isn't enough. Dig deeper or I will come up with something for you, and I *don't* think you'll enjoy it."

"Okay . . . but I'm a pacer. It helps me think. Can I have more room to walk, out there?"

"Yes, but know that if you attempt to run, it won't be pleasant."

As I set up the camera, Merlot instructs me on how to operate it. "Ready now, Merlot . . . on your mark, and go."

"Hello, Petunias. It's been almost two whole weeks and well, I've just been a bit 'tied up' as of late, so I apologize . . ."

"No!" I stop the camera. "First, you're *never* to use references toward being tied up, caged, or detained in *any* way. Second—and I only want to say this once—*never* apologize! I absolutely loathe apologies, and hearing them. No one ever *really* means it, and it's shallow. I'm going to stop and start as I need to prompt you. Now go."

"Hello, Petunias. Starving for a little Merlot today? Let's do an early afternoon toast then. It's happy hour somewhere! You may notice something a bit . . . different. I'm not wearing a face trend today, or any makeup at all! That's right, stripped down. We're going to do a little series of 'stripped down' where I go without makeup—sorry makeup sponsors."

I stop again. "*I said*, no apologies! Now start from 'stripped down'."

"Okay!" *This is going to be harder than I thought . . .* "Stripped down, where I wear zero makeup, and you learn something new about me each week. Today, I'll come clean about being a bit of a 'control freak'. I like things to look a certain way, in my home as well as at my friends' homes. I've been known to go so far as to rearrange their furniture."

"Merlot, this is boring, and you're still trying to be relevant. If you're going to own being controlling, dig deeper. Expose something *more* revealing."

"Okay! The most controlling thing about me is, well, I don't like to be kissed. It's too . . . intimate."

"Good. And why is it too intimate?"

"It is too intimate because, because, *oh*—I just can't say!"

"Oh but you can, and you will. Now go!"

"I'm used to men watching me, perform—but not touching me—and *never* kissing me."

"Perform? In what way?"

"In the bedroom, I dance—to be sexy."

"Come on, Merlot. You and I both know that you do much more than dance. Now tell your Petunias—damn it!"

190

"I don't just dance . . . I—I masturbate in front of them—so I don't have to be touched and I don't have to kiss them. I haven't actually *had* a real relationship, okay!"

I stop the camera and step back this time for a moment. *Now I'm getting somewhere.*

"How is it that a pretty, vibrant 'internet sensation', such as yourself, hasn't had a *real* relationship—*and* has had to please herself to avoid human contact? What happened to you, Merlot!"

"Stop yelling! I can't take it! This is *too much* honesty! Every teen watching this is going to make fun of me or tune out, and the young adults will think I'm pathetic. Please, don't make me say anymore!"

"This is only the beginning. We're going to show them how to be real *before* they're in the state you're in. Now tell your Petunias what happened—go!"

"I got this way because—because, I have an uncle who used to abuse me, okay! Now I don't trust men, and if I don't let them kiss me, then *I'm* in control!"

"*Ah* . . . now doesn't that feel better—and such drama for the Petunias. You should be proud of yourself for owning those secrets and saying them out loud. You may have even helped a few girls and boys out there."

"You are *so* cruel! How could you make me do that? You aren't really going to post that, are you?"

191

"Actually, I'm going to save that one. I think it's in the middle or toward the end of our 'Truth' series. Maybe the 'climax' even, if you get my meaning. Of course, I will edit it as I see fit, based partly on your numbers. Like you, I will see what the Petunias *do* and *do not* respond to. Only, I'll take the information in the opposite direction until they've all *stopped* watching. We're going to start with the truth about your manipulation of them for numbers on your next show."

"What are you talking about? I'm not a manipulator!"

"You've admitted that you shape your show around what the Petunias respond to and what gains sponsors."

"Well, what's wrong with that? I have to make a living, just like everyone else."

"What's wrong with that?" I grab her face and she flinches. She'd better get used to being touched because I'm going to do it whenever I please. "You're giving advice to people who are taking it—and *you* are not qualified to give 'said' advice, or pretend you're an authority on anything. *You* haven't earned the right. That makes *you* a fraud!"

"Well, I haven't heard of anyone being hurt from my advice. I mean no one's written in on my blog that I've given bad advice. Doc, you're hurting my face. Let go!"

She bats my hand from her face and retreats into her bedroom. "We should get one thing straight, Merlot. Don't mistake your 'giving people advice without being an expert' to mean I care about what happens—to *any* of them. They're lazy and probably deserve bad advice because they're stupid enough to listen to someone who talks because she loves to hear herself talk *and imagine*s she's famous."

"That's some high opinion you have of me, Doc." *I'm starting to tear up, but I'm fighting it.*

"Don't take it personally. There are many more like you, but I could only choose one to change this course. *You* are my 'Captain'. What you *should be* is flattered! We're done here today. Dry it up and think about how absolutely honest you're going to be for our next 'real' show."

Flopping onto her bed, she curls up in a ball, and turns away from me. I stock her fridge with the food I had brought, and secure the walls again.

She's off dairy, and other processed crap, that's given her skin blotches, which I can see now without the makeup. It's also contributed to those extra pounds on her belly.

Over time, I'll transform my caged bird into an unrelatable vixen, and watch as her Petunias fall away.

In the meantime, I have hunting to do . . .

OMINOUS REFLECTION

Merlot's story about abuse *seemed* real, and it's sticking with me. I shouldn't care; however, I do see how another victim getting her revenge could make for a gratifying kill. I'll need to turn her into an angry savage before we get to the uncle she mentioned in her confession. Right now, I need to focus on Lonnie Baker.

I've done my research on his birth mother and flown to St. Louis. My first stop is a bar down the street from where she worked years ago. I'm dropping by to see if anyone happens to remember the incident of her death. It's a local watering hole called Rusty's. My rental car's navigation just announced I'm a mile away.

Celeste thinks I'm going to check out a new laser machine, which could assist in spinal surgery, at a medical trade show. It would never occur to her that *I* would fool around when I'm away. In fact, I sensed she was holding back the excitement at the news of my little departure for a few days. This gives her time with her lover, who I've discovered is a muscular mental-midget she met at the gym. He has no financial wherewithal, so not only *won't* she think of divorcing me—he's probably too roided-out to impregnate her, which is good, since I'm sure after diagnosing her infertile, she's not using any protection. I couldn't ask for a better match.

Pulling into the parking lot, I choose an unmarked spot away from the few small windows in the joint. It's a dusty place . . . to be so humid here. With a light push on the screen door, I'm greeted by a creak—and the jingle of a little bell on a string—*classy*. The screen provides minimal ventilation for the stench that hits me inside, tightly embedded into the green indoor/outdoor carpet—*nice*. I'm guessing its stains could tell stories dating back at least twenty years. Dark paneled walls transport me to Polly and Vernon's dimly lit prefabricated home. *Its squeaking floors and thin walls made privacy an impossible feat.* Neon beer signs and Nascar posters top off the milieu.

In an adjacent room open to the bar area, a few women, wearing thick makeup and dated hairstyles from the days of heavy metal videos, are laying on the flirtation with four guys playing pool, who are eating it up.

A meticulously shined wooden bar looks to be the cleanest part of the place. There's one bartender—a big guy who looks more like a bouncer, with a shaved head—and another, who's an older, wiry-looking female, with lip lines that reveal she's been a smoker for many years. Against my nature, I sit near the middle of the bar as "Madge" approaches.

"What can I do ya for, stranger?"

"Excuse me?"

"What'll ya have? Ta drank?"

"Oh, yes. I'll have a scotch and soda." I don't drink, but the order sounds reasonable in a place like this.

"Comin' up."

As I wait for my scotch and soda, I observe the rest of the patrons more closely—better described as "fixtures". They break from their zombie-like positions just long enough to let me know they're not part of the tacky mural along the top half of the paneled walls. The male "fixtures" have probably kept the place afloat, making it part of their pre-dinner routine after work. The few females, who've metamorphosized into the wallpaper of society, appear to have given up—in a world that's forgotten them, after the sparkle of youth's left a vacancy in their spirits.

Madge approaches with my drink. "Here ya go handsome. You from 'round here?"

Ah, small talk. I would normally ignore her, but this time, I have to put forth an effort. "Nah, I'm kind of mobile for the time being."

"Mobile? No place to call home? What kinda life's that?"

"Oh, it's on purpose. I'm doing a documentary on the last fifty years of our major cities in America—the highs, the lows, and the fascinating tales that fill in all the details. That's why I'm here now."

"Well, St. Louis has had some interesting times! I've lived through 'em, but this neighborhood . . . well, it's seen better days. It was something twenty, thirty years ago."

"Do tell." *I'm trying really hard at this "shooting-the-breeze" bullshit.* "You wouldn't know by the looks of it now."

"Sure wouldn't . . . it's sad really . . ."

Madge throws her bar towel over one shoulder and looks off, as if to be in another time. *I've got to keep her talking.*

"Can you describe it for me? Back then? Maybe it'll make my story. If I sell it to a network, it'll be televised, and they'll interview the people that I get my stories from—if that would be agreeable to you?"

"Well, sure it would be! I'd want some notice of course, so I could get my hair done." She gives me a smile of flirtation I doubt she's used in a while.

"Some of the more conservative folk may not have liked it, but those who lived and worked in it knew it was a *real* special time, and we did it with the most class you could want, with *all* kinds of entertainment."

"And by entertainment, you're referring to?" *Hurry up, Madge—reminisce faster.*

"Let's see . . . we had a couple of sports bars, a gay bar, a comedy store, live music venue, disco club, and the favorite of many who *still* remember it round here, the exotic bar."

"As in . . . a topless bar?"

"Oh yeah, topless! And in certain rooms full nude. But you had to be a VIP member, which meant a yearly membership that weren't cheap. Also, we had a bottle service of a hundred bucks, which was expensive in those days. That place made it hand over fist, and the girls weren't the kind you'd see at the nasty joints. Men had to be gentlemen, and the ladies had certain moves that were strictly off limits. Our owner believed that there should be some things, left to the imagination, even *with* nudity— yeah, a classy place."

"You said 'our owner'. Does that mean you were a dancer there, Madge?"

"Oh, heavens no! I started in the bar, but the boss quickly moved me up to the House Mother position. I took care of all the dancers personal needs, as well as keeping them in line. No doin' drugs or drankin' while they were at work. And they had to show up, on time—but most of all, no drama with each other. Now *that* was tough one to pull off!"

"By your smile, I can see that you really did love it. So what happened?"

"It went on long after I quit. I just got—well, I guess you could say—disheartened. Anyhow, after that I left and came here. I've worked at Rusty's since. I manage the place now that the owner is up in years. He knows he can trust me with the money—and to keep things runnin' smooth."

I'm writing on a small notepad for believability. "So Madge, what did you say the name of the topless place was?"

"I don't think I did say . . . it was called Peaches."

"And you left because you were 'disheartened'? Can you tell me more about that?"

"Well, let's see . . . a lot of heroin started pouring into the place at one point, *and* a few of the girls became junkies. For the most part, we survived that wave of drugs. But when the coke epidemic started, a lot of them started lookin' super skinny—that's when I knew they were gettin' hooked. It was a constant battle, but the worst of it still gets to me—talkin' 'bout it takes me back."

She's tearing up, and looking away with her hand over her mouth. "Take your time, Madge. I've got nowhere to be. I'm listening." *Spit it out Madge!*

"The worst of it—what did me in—was when Julia, one of our best girls, got beat . . . beat to death. *Whew!* That's hard to think 'bout."

Madge is fanning her face after using the bar towel to dry her cheeks . . . *yuck!*

"I can still see her purdy face, how sweet she was, and when I do think 'bout her, it always ends for me with that image of her bloodied, broken body on her kitchen floor—where I had the misfortune of findin' her."

I stop writing. I don't want Madge to think I'm doing a report on *this* part of the story. "Oh no, *you* found her?"

"Yep, found her *and* her little boy Lonnie."

Madge sucks down some snot and blows her nose—*revolting.* I have to control the disgusted look my face wants to display and keep her on track.

"Oh, so she had a child?"

"Yeah, she didn't have him all the time—shared custody with her ex—who wouldn't marry her because he said he'd never get hitched to a stripper. He married a librarian, of all things."

Good, her crying seems to be over, and her body language has taken on a more determined stance.

"He didn't have a problem with Julia's job—when he dated her and got her knocked up. Must have needed to prove something to himself or his family, doin' a one-eighty like that—a librarian, *really?* Julia called her an uptight bitch . . . *excuse my French.* Said she was mean to Lonnie—made him sleep in a sleepin' bag on the living room floor, 'cause they needed his bedroom for the little girl they was havin'. Poor kid, seein' a thing like that."

"Did they ever find the killer?"

"Well, there weren't no arrests. Everyone, includin' the cops, was sure it was this big-time drug dealer's doin'. He'd hired her for the naked room dance, four nights in a row, and he'd been known to beat on women. He was real powerful 'round here, and had lotsa cops in his back pocket so *no one* would touch him."

Somehow, Madge seems indifferent about the outcome. "So is that what *you* think happened? You must have been as close to her as anyone."

"Nah, I knew it was that no good, on-again, off-again boyfriend of hers, Nathan White."

"Really? What makes you so sure?"

"He'd gave her a few black eyes before. She always covered 'em with makeup, but I seen it, and I asked her 'bout it. She'd *lie* . . . and tell me excuses most abused women like to use. I'd heard him threaten her if she did

201

anymore naked room dances, so those four in a row pret
well set him off for sure."

"I'm surprised he was allowed in the club. Did the
owner know of his temper?"

"Sure, we all *knew* he was an asshole, but we kept our
noses outta each other's business in those days. Anyhow,
the owner couldn't kick him out legal-wise. Plus, he was no
trouble in the club. He drank a lot and paid his tab. That
bastard didn't give two shits about what happened to her
kid. There's a special place in hell for men like that, as far as
I'm concerned."

Madge is getting worked up again, *but mad this time*. I
need to keep her calm and engaged, so she doesn't storm
off.

"Do you know what happened to him after that?"

"Yeah . . . he's floated from job to job—think he's made
a full AA recovery, a few times. Rumor has it, some years
ago; he'd beat another girl nearly half to death. He'd tell you
a different story about Julia, if you asked him. He made up a
lie 'bout that night—where he was—and he's stuck to it . . .
convinced himself even that they were 'madly in love'."

Good, her attitude is flippant again. She's coming out of
her emotional turmoil. "So any idea where he might be
these days?"

"He does odd jobs 'cause he can't hold down a real one, and some handyman work on the side. Last I heard, he's been unloadin' cargo down at the shipyard. That's hard work for a man who ain't young no more. I'm sure nothin's changed—too stubborn and God-awful mean to admit any aches or pains, even if he's got 'em."

She appears to be getting antsy. Just a few more questions Madge, hang in there a little longer . . . "So, her son, Lonnie—did he and his new family stay in St. Louis?"

"Nah, they moved off to Chicago where the wife got a job as Head Librarian in a huge library. I guess them jobs pay *real* good. Lonnie's dad, Alfie, was a trash collector and he could do that anywhere. You know, stable union job."

I think she's good for one more. "You said he had a half-sister. Did you ever know her name?"

"*Umm . . .* it was Connie. Why do you ask?"

She's giving me a look of suspicion. I'd better tread lightly. "Just looking for more people from around here to talk to about the area. But she probably isn't here anyway since she grew up in Chicago."

Connie Baker, a good place to start—time to retreat.

"Well thanks, Madge!" Before she throws anymore of those good "bartender intuitions" my way, I'm halfway to the door.

"Hey, good lookin'! What'd you say your name was?"

Hmm, she's just *now* interested in my name.

"Joe. My name is Joe. Thanks again."

"Before you're outta my life forever, *Joe*, I just thought of one more part, 'bout Julia's story."

Is she helping me? *This isn't good.* "Yes, Madge?"

"Her stage name . . . I mean Julia's. They all used 'em. It was 'Lost Kitty'. I know, I know, it's odd. Never liked it fer her, but lookin' back, I guess it fit."

"Huh, it is odd. Well, thanks again, Madge!" *She's helped me in more ways than she knows.*

*****

Back at the hotel, I spread my map out on the bed to trace out where the next librarian *should be* pregnant with Lonnie's 'seed' by now. From the sequence of his victims, he seems to be choosing them using a reverse writing pattern. Instead of starting at the top of the "L", his first kill started at the bottom, from New Mexico, skipping across Arizona— *lucky librarians in Arizona*—to a victim in southern California, and then north with a librarian in Nevada, as well as in Northern Oregon.

How were the cops not catching on at this point? I guess a miscarriage by beating is easier to get out of, when a woman doesn't press charges, or even call the police for a domestic incident.

Next, he struck again in the heart of Texas, south of Dallas, headed all the way up to South Dakota, skipping over three states to form his first stroke of the "K". The trajectory of his next leg of the "K" *should* start in Missouri, Alabama, or even Georgia—but until there's a new report in the registry, I'm flying blind.

One thing is almost for certain. He'll be in Kansas after the current librarian has met with her tragedy. Judging by the timelines between each of the others, the current girlfriend could be getting the beating of her life any day now.

I'll watch the registry closely, but once he's struck, I may as well sit it out for a few weeks. He'll need a little time to set up shop for his next conquest, *and* I'll need to aim with accuracy in Kansas.

I begin researching blonde-haired, blue-eyed librarians, from ages twenty-six to thirty-four—his targeted age range. Women any older often take longer to impregnate because of fewer eggs—a practical strategy.

Ah . . . upon further reading, the age of his real mother at time of death was twenty-six, *and* at that time his stepmother, the librarian, was thirty-four. Rather than pragmatic, he's taking a more emotionally methodological approach.

I hate to go back to Merlot, empty-handed, but Lonnie's crimes practically span the country. One thing *is* eating at me. What next, when he's through with his "K"? His appetite is not going to just go away once he's avenged Lost Kitty. He will most certainly find a new purpose; create a new "killing puzzle" of innocents on which to exact his cravings. *I will give him that purpose,* upon his introduction to Nathan. However, he will *not* finish the "K" in his current puzzle.

He's Merlot's first request, and I do *not* intend to disappoint. Since I'm already in St. Louis, and have a few extra days, I'll take the time to find the illustrious Lost Kitty killer, Nathan White . . . after a good night's sleep.

FINDING THE BAIT

I wake feeling rested, forgetting for a moment where I am, until I inhale the scent of *old hotel room*—awash with lemon plug-in air freshener, which brings me back to reality.

The first thing on my mind is how eager I am to accomplish my recon; finding the Lost Kitty killer, Nathan White. As much as I believe in the old adage of "an eye for an eye", *and* I've been looking forward to doing that job myself—a matchup between Lonnie and Nathan could make for a great round of boxing . . . or should I say *street fighting*. The idea is intriguing to me and I believe it could be more entertaining for Merlot than simply watching me pulverize the cowardly librarian killer.

Now, Lonnie does have twenty plus years of youth on his side, which *could* go a long way to his favor. I'll see if Nathan appears to be strong, or resolved enough to counteract Lonnie's youth.

On that thought, I spring out of bed. After changing into the clothes I'd packed for a jog, including a hooded shirt and sunglasses, I step outside to stretch before my run—in time to appreciate the orange ball of sun, peeking just above a field of wheat across the street. The warped screen door creaks, bouncing off the frame as I release it.

My old roadside hotel consists of eleven rooms. It was either purposely built in the middle of nowhere, or its commercial neighbors have since been abandoned and torn down, giving way to low revenue crops. But, the old relic has survived, and with only two other cars in the parking lot—it too, is on limited time.

A five-room distance away, the full-figured front desk gal pops out of her small lobby, *already at work at seven*. She waves at me from fifty feet away, as if I'm across the football field at her high school, ten or so years ago—*I'm guessing*. I'm trying to look away, but her gaze is steadfastly on me, as she moves her hands to her hips, flashing a toothy grin. She's elated—as if she's just seen a movie star. *Geez!*

"Hi Joe!"

Next time, I'll think about staying somewhere busier where no one notices the tenants. "Hello! Just going for a run!" I wave back, pull up my hood, and begin to jog. Looking back a few times, she shamelessly stares as I disappear down the two-lane road.

I'm a few miles into my run, when I come upon a diner along the tree-barren road. It too, seems to have survived a commercial implosion. *Already,* several cars are parked in its lot. I'm not planning to stick around long enough for anyone to strike up a conversation with me, but I *am* looking forward to a coffee to go.

Before crossing the threshold, my nasal passages are assaulted by a stench—years of caked together odors, running the gamut from fats and sugars to cigarette smoke. Inside is the deafening sound of an older clamoring crowd—a byproduct of hearing loss, no doubt. *The "early bird" saying jumps to mind.* Some are reading the newspaper, while others congregate, debating different points of view. Many laugh as they reminisce. These rituals did not make their way into my gene pool.

The place is steamier on the inside than the morning dew outside. Smoking and hissing, the griddle hosts a variety of greasy breakfast meats, pancakes, and eggs—all being flipped by a cook in a sailor's cap with sweat pouring from his brow—adding to the flavors.

Its fragrance transports me to the days of slaughterhouse picnics growing up. Whole pigs were roasted over a spit, along with other varieties of carcass—events at which my attendance was expected. Awkward in groups, I despised how the gatherings made me feel "different". Now, I *embrace* my singularity.

Hood up and sunglasses on, I ignore the stares of a few of the single parties, eating at the bar facing the disgusting show playing through the opening over the grill, and order my coffee. Just then, I hear a familiar voice.

"Hi, Joe!" It's Madge, and she's stalking in my direction waving her bony, sun-damaged arm at me frantically.

"Good morning, Madge. What brings you in here today?" *Stupid, Abel! Why do you even try at small talk!*

"Well Joe, I live in these parts. I think that question is better directed at you, wouldn't you say?" *Great, bartender innuendos in the coffee shop already.*

"I apologize, Madge. I'm just not good at conversation before I've had my coffee. I didn't mean to be nosy."

"Oh, you weren't nosy, Joe, but really, why *are* you here?"

She's speaking with less of her easy drawl than yesterday, and her eyes reveal a suspicion lurking behind them, even though she's smiling as if to be flirting. I'm going to go with the "flirting" part of her expression.

"That'll be a dollar fifty, sir." The waitress behind the counter hands me my to-go cup. I hand her three dollars and tell her to keep the change.

"Why, I'm here for the coffee of course, Madge. Did anyone ever tell you what a gorgeous smile you have? It's the perfect way to start my morning, followed by this coffee. It was great to see you again."

At that, I excuse myself, as she watches me disappear out the door and up the road. I can't run with my coffee, so she gets a good, long look. I feel her eyes penetrating my intentions, or at least *trying to*. I'm not turning around to look this time.

Stopping at a diner wasn't the most prudent of decisions. I won't make this mistake on a road trip again. *No unnecessary stops Abel.*

After arriving back, I shower and pack the accoutrement for my trip to the shipyard—binoculars, a syringe, which I hope not to use, and sunglasses of course.

*****

Arriving at the docks of the Mississippi River, where Madge believes Nathan is currently employed, I know I'll need to exercise a great deal of stealth. It's not terribly large, as dockyards go, and the areas to hide, once out of the tree grove I've parked in, appear to be sparse. I'm making the assumption that it's the kind of place where everyone

211

knows each other, which could present another layer of complexity if I'm noticed.

I have a safe tunnel of vision between the trees, for now. From a distance, a nearly bald, burly built fellow, around six feet tall, has caught my attention. He's either filthy, or painted generously in tattoos. I raise my binoculars for a closer view. He looks to be in his fifties, and overweight, but definitely as strong as an ox.

He fits Madge's description, and those *are* tattoos. I'm searching for a specific inking, "LK" with a heart around it and a bow and arrow running through it on his neck. *How original.*

After opening crates with a crowbar, and examining their contents, he's nailing them shut again. I have a view of the back *and* right side of his thick neck, which is covered in roses, barbed wire, and two crossing picks. The picks implicate that he must have been in construction at some point. The barbed wire represents either nothing, *or possibly,* that he's served a year in prison.

As a byproduct of a study on sociopaths and psychopaths, I learned more than I cared to about the meaning of *particular* tattoos. The largest percentage of known *violent* psychopaths, are imprisoned and most have an affinity for the inked life. Much of the "artistry" on their skin may contain Mercury, especially present in the red hues, which is a neurotropic toxin, and has the potential to damage the brain and nervous system—if it were to make its journey through the blood brain-barrier. In an already challenged brain, *it could* contribute to further amplifying psychological disorders.

This fact led me to research the meaning behind said "tattoo art". *Perhaps red dyes have amplified the psychopath gene, passed from my imprisoned "bat-shit-crazy" birth father?* Interesting thought . . . a twist I doubt has been studied.

Until he turns, presenting the left side of his neck, I read the other stories he so willingly displays on the rest of his visible skin. His right shoulder has not one, but two triangles within circles, implicating going through Alcoholics Anonymous, twice, just as Madge had mentioned, if that *is him*. There are a myriad of nonsensical tattoos I can't quite make out down his arm.

And now that he's taking a rest—stretching his torso with his fingers interlocked against the back of his head, as if in an imaginary recliner—I'm getting a decent view of his knuckles. "E-W-M-N"—a poster proclaiming he's Evil, Wicked, Mean, and Nasty.

After he's done with his stretch, he moves to the other side of the crate to put in more nails. I still can't see the left side of his neck, *damn!*

I do see his face. A filled in tear drop is inked into crow's feet, under the left corner of his eye, implicating a death *or* murder has been completed. *My curiosity is piqued as to whether the "LK" is also on the left side.* On the right cheekbone, a teardrop outline is inked but *not* filled in. It seems Madge may have been right in her gossip about him beating another poor woman *nearly* to death.

Back to work. He's climbing aboard a forklift. I'll move in for a closer look. Making my way unnoticed, I relocate to a group of cargo cars, whose gold and green paint jobs are showing years of wear—via the rust on their corners and decaying edges. Though the cars doors are shut, wooden boxes, like those my suspect was examining the contents of, are piled high between them.

I climb up the stack of crates, and wedge myself into my new lookout, about fifty yards away from my *now moving* target. My binoculars are on him as he unloads a barge, placing its palettes into a semi-truck with his forklift.

Finally . . . something's caught his attention and he's turned to face the other side. Yes, there it is—the "LK" tattoo on the left side of his neck! *That's Nathan.*

What or *who* is he staring at? *Uh oh.* A freakishly huge, ex-convict of a man, with a deep voice, is yelling out to him and pointing right in my direction!

I slide and jump down from the crates I'm wedged between, pull my grey sweatshirt hood up, and dart behind a cargo car. A set of footsteps pounds the wet pavement a half dozen cars away. My heart is pounding just as hard in my chest! *It's a good thing he doesn't have the sensory abilities I do, or my cover would be blown.*

Seconds later, the thudding footsteps slow to a halt. Has he given up? Wait, there's more than one set now!

As lightly as my sneakers will carry me, I advance with wide strides to bridge the gap between the openings of two cars. Pausing to survey my surroundings as well as my next targeted spot—with the coast clear, I leap across an even wider opening.

Damn! A small rock camouflaged in the rough pavement is skipping audibly at its relief from my shoe. I duck down to look under the semi-trucks separating us. Nathan's Goliath-like cohort heard it and he's jerked his whole body around in my direction—they're stalking me again!

With nowhere to run that won't blow my cover, I crawl under the belly and behind the wheels of the nearest semi. Nathan, and his Amazonian sidekick, has stopped where I'd stood only moments ago. I watch their every move as they scan the area, up and down between rows of trucks—which

215

are beginning to start up—*no!* I must move again before my position is compromised.

It's too late. In lieu of a 'divide and conquer' strategy, they're both walking in my direction! I grab an axle under the semi and wedge my feet against another, pulling my body up tightly under the truck. I'll have to wait, silently choking down the backdraft of the truck's fumes.

Finally . . . after pacing a few full lengths, I hear their steps fading into the distance.

Phew! I release my white-knuckled grip, drop quietly under the truck, and roll out opposite the side of the two men's path. Ducking as I go, to keep an eye on their legs beneath the rows of semis—I serpentine through the grove of trees, where the rental car awaits, and my adventure ends.

Sliding down in my seat, I watch them patiently from a distance. They're hoping for a chance to deliver some vigilante whoop-ass, as they stand scratching their heads—a bizarre ritual of the "thinking Neanderthal". After wandering around the cargo yard a few more times, they make their way back toward the barge.

Nathan will not be an easy mark to apprehend—but I *do enjoy* a challenge. At least I know where to find him.

TRUTH BOMB

After three days alone, I'm not sure what state Merlot will be in. Her living needs have admittedly been left on the back burner, of the things on my to-do list. She'll have survived a little hunger and lack of hygiene products, but to make up for it, I've brought her a few offerings from St. Louis.

As I enter and raise her screen of foliage, I find her curled up in a ball on her bed. She doesn't roll over or spring up to see me. *Hmm . . .*

"Merlot? Hey there. I brought you some goodies. Are you ready to shoot your show?" She draws into the human ball more tightly except for the arm she uses to flip me the bird. *That's more like it.*

"Though not the greeting I'd hoped for, at least you're speaking to me." This response gets her to look over her shoulder, with an eye roll at the same time. I smile at her in an attempt to break the silence, a verbal "F-you", anything. But instead, she rolls right back to her fetal position.

"Look, yeah, I've been gone for three days but I've brought you a few goodies from my trip out of town. I know I've had you on somewhat of a restricted diet and, from what I've observed in your apartment's kitchen, you *do* have quite a sweet tooth. So . . . I thought the famous St. Louis Gooey Butter Cake might be a nice treat."

Still nothing . . .

"And, I know you'll look adorable in this Cardinals Jersey."

I pull it out of the bag, holding it up—tempting her to take a look. It's a tiny knit material that will cling to her body. "You're bound to gain some Petunias from that area wearing this." *I hope not.*

This ploy gets an instant response. She leaps out of bed, and plants her palms hard against the plexi glass—and glares at me. "You think your lame gifts are going to make me feel better? Well, you're more of an idiot that I'd thought! First you kidnap me, nearly rape me, and force me to do a show telling my Petunias my darkest secret. And then . . . you leave me here alone with a scant bit of diet food. I'm out of hair and shower supplies and wearing the same things over and over because the other items have not been cleaned! You haven't even brought my shaver, and I am turning into a hairy beast! What kind of animal are you trying to transform me into!"

She's evolving nicely. I will just need to refocus that anger. I decide to be congenial, at first. "I've brought you a month's supply of beauty and toiletry products, *and* taken care of your other laundry, which I'm sure is dry by now." *I had done her laundry before I left, but had not taken it out of the dryer.*

"As far as your other concerns . . ." I draw close to the plexi, and return her crazed expression. "I thought I told you *never* to use those two words with me, as the sexual assault part could not be further from the truth anyhow. This is the *last* warning. If you choose to use them again, you *will* lose privileges a lady should not."

I unlock her door and stand in the doorway. "Now, I honestly appreciate your passion, but it is misdirected—after we've taped your show, I will fill you in on some things that are nice developments in your first choice, Lonnie Baker." She dismisses me with the flip of her hand as she turns and walks away.

"You can go ahead. I don't feel like doing my show anyway."

"It doesn't work like that with your show, Merlot. *You* do not have a choice, as with the case of choosing Lonnie as your target. You're going to do the show, *and* you will do it as I tell you it will be done." She turns toward me red faced, and ready to spew, throwing her fists down at her sides.

"Or what!"

"Or you may find me investigating you, that's what! And after what I've told you today, you'll find just how apt I am at finding out everything there is to know about a person." I'm moving into her personal space. She takes a few steps back as I stare deeply into her eyes. "And something tells me that *you* do not want me investigating *your* past."

I leave it there and just continue to stare—jaw clenched, unblinking—waiting for her reaction, which will tell me how badly I *do* want to investigate her.

She blinks first. "Well then, go ahead! I've got nothing to hide. I'm just in a 'mood' from living like an animal."

She flops down, sitting on the bed with her arms crossed—*faking the submissive?*

"I would like a piece of that gooey cake, if you don't mind Doc. I *am* starving."

Nice recovery Merlot, but you've told me all I need to know. Investigation on.

"Normally, I would give it to you after you've finished filming, but since you're so hungry, it might help you focus." I take out a small slice of the cake as she moves to the desk. "Eat it slowly and savor it, because there are only two more slices. One a day for the next two days, before it's gone is all you get, or, you can get it over with and eat the whole thing now." *I'm testing which choice she'll make.* I've sliced the cake into thin pieces.

After she finishes a slice, and a bite of one more, she asks me to put the rest in her mini fridge. *Good choice*—she must like the ten pounds or so she appears to have lost being off her body.

"Today Merlot, we're going to start with your show, now that you have something in your stomach." I'm hoping the jolt of sugar will put her into 'filming mode'.

Before locking her into her room again, I give her a sexy ensemble to change into—a short red skirt and red blazer with a single button at the waist, like the purple one she'd worn for the last video, except this time, I tell her *not* to wear a shirt, so that she exposes the skin down to her navel and reveals plenty of cleavage. She seems fine with it.

Though I'm curious to see how she looks naked now with the weight loss, I don't think she'll want me to watch her change. Before dismissing myself to my viewing room, I hand over her shaver to take care of her leg hair that will make her self-conscious wearing this short of a skirt. *Watching her do it will provide a nice show for me as well.*

I put her foliage wall down so that she assumes she has privacy after closing her in. I then retreat to my viewing room and lower the foliage concealing it as well.

221

By the time I've tuned in to the cameras, she is already naked and shaving her legs, with a foot on the floor and one on the sink basin. She is careful not to nick herself, as I watch, wishing it were I doing the job.

Once she's finished, she takes the time to examine herself in the mirror, one side at a time. *Her body is perfection.* Does she even realize she's lost the weight? I can't tell from her expression. No smile or grimace—*nothing*. And I'm not close enough to her to get a scent of any possible reaction.

The low-cut look is going to rub her female viewers the wrong way, especially as their boyfriends start hanging around their computers when she's on. *Celeste has fine-tuned me to insecure female reactions.*

Announcing my presence before re-entering her room, I give her something else I've picked up—a choker, made of black leather, tied to a steel loop. Through the loop hangs a long silver chain with an arrow on its end, which purposely points to her lady parts. I tell her to tighten it around her neck so that the arrow hangs as low as possible, just an inch or so above her belly button. I love the look, *and* it makes her less relatable to her female followers, hanging against her bare skin—along with the message she'll be delivering.

She's delighted that I've directed her to wear makeup. I tell her to go heavy on the eyeliner, straighten her hair, and

222

top it off with a bright red lip. She looks club ready. I praise her to make her feel as confident as a woman who's been locked up for twenty-two days can possibly exude.

"Okay Merlot, the message today is honesty—*your* honesty this time—specifically that you've manipulated your numbers unfairly by seeing 'what' your followers react to and what they do not, in lieu of making 'authentic' choices when selecting your topics." She's feeling so pretty that I barely get a negative response from her—only a question.

"But Doc, h*ow,* am I going to even get a real show out of that? It will be so short to just go on and make some admission."

"Don't worry. I'll interject questions and prompts. My part will get edited out. Make sure you look at the camera during any admission of guilt. And remember, never apologize, and never look down."

She nods in agreement, takes a deep breath and exhales.

I give her the "go" signal.

"'Ello, my Petunias!"

I'm going to let her keep the stupid accent for now. That will be something else fake to reveal to her Petunias later.

"Three weeks of vacay! Like my new look?"

I let her get away with this one lie, given its circumstances. She's almost squealing in delight, pleased with herself, and already I anticipate the insecurity of females, furling their eyebrows in disapproval.

"*Loving* this new necklace!"

Good, point it out, you little sex bomb! I'm giving her a "thumbs up", so she thinks she's killing it.

"We will toast at the end of the show, just in case your glasses are out and ready to clink. Our show today is on honesty and . . . I have a bit of my own to confess—but first let's talk about yours. You *know* who you are!"

Not sure I like *how* she's presenting this.

"If you're sitting with your mate *or* your bestie, turn and look at each other. When's the last time you told a little white lie to each other, no matter what the reason or motivation . . . *hmm*? And did it really *help you* out of your situation? And if it did, how good do you feel about it now? Wouldn't it be better if you could just trust each other *not* to get mad, and take back that little lie—you know, just tell the truth? Why don't you try it? Wait—*wait*! I can't have a long pause, so do it after we've toasted at the end of the show in the privacy of your own homes. I'm not going to pass judgments and I don't want others doing it to you either, so do *not* leave your confessions on my feed below."

She's being so cute and relatable, those girls are getting less pissed off by the moment. I need to prod along "what" she is referring to. "Merlot, make them be specific about *what* they will be confessing. Give examples."

"I don't need to give examples of what goes on in their homes and lives . . ."

"Now, Merlot!"

"Okay . . . like if you've been, say, cheating on your diet, but telling your partner you've followed it to the letter. Anyway, you know the scale won't lie chickies!"

Ugh, cutesy again!

"More personal, more severe lies!"

"Or, if say . . . you've been thinking about some other guy, or girl, when you're in the bedroom with your partner?"

"Come on, Merlot—real life-changing lies!"

"*All right* . . . Even if—and this is just an *if*—you've maybe kissed someone, when you were drunk of course—so almost an accident . . . at a school function or work party? That's something that could've happened a long time ago and you just need to get it off your chest and be forgiven. Now wouldn't that feel good?"

"Right direction . . . go deeper."

"*Ugh*, okay! Say you're together now and everything is good, but you failed to tell your significant other that you slipped up, maybe at your bachelor or bachelorette party, but you love them more than anything else in the whole wide world and it didn't mean anything to you at the time."

"Really warm. Now go in for the jugular. *Do it now!*"

"We all need some pardon for something we've done, Petunias. Even if you *are* cheating on one another, but you want and *need* the other person to understand you're sorry and you want to stop . . . you just need to be honest with each other and work on you, as well as working together, to make things better."

Bingo! She's going to bust up some bad relationships and make fifty percent of them, at least, stop watching. Hell, they're going to *hate* her. "Tell them to talk about it now and toast. That's the end of this part." Merlot holds up her glass and performs her typical salutation.

"Now, how do you feel about that?" I don't actually care *how* she feels—just giving her a breather before we move on to her confession.

"Strangely, I feel like I may have actually *helped* some people with that, even though it was hard."

"Very nice, Merlot. Very honest, but you still haven't addressed your 'untruth'. So, let's hear it—on camera."

I'm cued up and ready to shoot again.

"But I thought you said we were done?"

226

"Oh we are—with *that* part. The next part, part B, airing next week, is going to be short and sweet. You're not asking them to get honest without showing you're human too. Now get on with it."

"Okay—fine!"

"Hi Petunias. About last week—hopefully that all went well. Let's toast to it now. To your happy relationships, true always! But now, I have my own confession of truth. Petunias, I have also been dishonest with you. In what way you may ask? Well, I know it is in your best interest. You see . . . I do have a little tendency to choose my topics, not just based on *what* is relevant, but on what I see happening in the ratings."

She's glossing over this. "What does *that* mean, Merlot? Be more specific."

"So, what that means is that if you respond to it, I know which direction to keep going, to gain more of you watching me."

"Because . . ."

"Because if you are watching me, I'm gaining more sponsors."

"And . . ."

"And that means I am getting paid more. So, I guess I am making my shows into what *you* want to see . . . so I'm paid more. More followers equal more endorsements."

She's bouncing a bit, trying to be cutesy with her delivery. "Which means what!"

"It means that money is or *has been* more important than my content—or what's necessarily . . . best for you Petunias."

"And what does that make you? Tell them you're a money-grubbing whore. Do it now!"

"*Ugh*, really? And that makes me a . . . a money-grubbing whore. I'm so sorr—"

"No, do not apologize! You're not sorry, not even now. Tell them without any remorse, not even in your tone."

"Okay! I value money, even more than you—and *that* makes me an opportunist, and it's what I'm good at—damn it! Are you happy!"

"Yes, well done. Let's see how *real* honesty goes over with your Petunias."

Plan B underway.

"That's a wrap—now on to Lonnie. You may be wondering why I haven't retrieved your 'chosen one' yet."

"Just like that? You expect me to jump from one thing to the next . . . as if, I haven't just been forced to royally screw myself on camera!"

"Oh, Merlot, cool your jets. Look around. You're no longer in control—and you're worried about your ratings? That's in my hands now. You're merely my mouthpiece for a revolution. Someday you may appreciate having been the star of it, *martyr or not.* Now, refocus. It's time to talk about your chosen lamb."

"*Ugh . . . my* sacrificial lamb? Really? You're going to kill the guy for me? Let's get something straight Doc, since you're the ambassador of truth. I'm picking *only the order* in which you kill them, because you're forcing me to! You're going to do it either way, so I have nothing to do with any of this!"

"Oh, Merlot, save the dramatics. We both know you have an ax to grind with this abuser. It was you who figured out part of his revenge, including spelling out initials on the kill map."

"Now, I've had an encounter with a lady who knew his birth mother quite well. At the end of said encounter, just as I was about to head in a different direction to seek out my answer, she divulged Lonnie's birth mother's stage name— 'Lost Kitty'." *Finally, Merlot seems engaged again.*

"Oh, that's *so* sad! Was she an actress?"

"Yes I guess, of sorts. Whatever, but the name was fitting. Thus, we have the initials going forward, 'LK'. The next girl should be knocked up and probably getting her beating any day now, based on the timing of all of the others. Lonnie is nothing if not methodical and timely about his mischief."

"Well, what are you doing here? Get out there and stop him! I can't believe you did all of that and you're not out there catching him."

"Though I appreciate your enthusiasm, Merlot, it's not quite that simple. Searching for blonde-haired, blue-eyed librarians, who, by the way are either twenty-six or thirty-four—the ages of his mom and stepmother when he witnessed the beating—is one thing. But the next arm of the 'K' could land in a couple of states. There is no way to know which one he has chosen his current girlfriend in, and I'm not able to be in two states at the same time."

"So you're just going to let the next one die . . . or her baby die—possibly both of them?"

"I have no choice. The registry will reveal the incident within a week of its occurrence, and from there, he is bound to start up his new conquest—this time in the heart of Kansas. That will narrow my search, *and* he will be courting her for a while before she's pregnant. Within a few months of the pregnancy news, she'll be quitting her job. This course gives me the best chance at getting our man."

"I can't believe you're letting 'your man' get away with it!"

"Again, admire the passion . . . but casualties happen, and Lonnie's next victim is unavoidable. Try to focus on the

230

positive. She's going to make the sacrifice to save the next few, if not more."

"There's no positive in any of this—wait, why do you say, 'if not more'?"

"Killing is in his blood now. He'll find a new crusade once the thrill of this one has found its happy ending. After he rewards himself, the angst to kill, with repetition, will nag at his soul, *if there is such a thing*. Soul or not, *this* is what gives him purpose."

Ah . . . purpose. I fill my lungs with a deep breath, and exhale slowly . . . euphorically—with the realization I've just spoken *his* truth *and* mine, to someone who can never understand it.

Merlot's facial expression is a twisted maze of raw emotion. She wants to speak, to protest, but she's unsure of what should come out of her mouth—especially to someone who's held her captive, and who's smiling about something she has *no* understanding of.

No matter. I close my eyes and suck down sweet air, letting *my purpose* wash over me. I'm transported to the exhilarating image of Lonnie's blood on my hands—upon exhaling, I open them again slowly, to Merlot's steadfast glare piercing *my thoughts* for once. For the first time, I think she actually *"sees me"*.

Her expression is one of terror.

AND ONE TO GO . . .

I try to engage Celeste, selectively, in what I've "seen" at the trade show. She doesn't seem particularly interested in it or its gadgetry, which I studied flying home from St. Louis. Getting a video feed from Las Vegas of different booths was not difficult, especially with techies putting the whole thing together.

She's looking lovely these days, Celeste—svelte, fit, and less proper. She seems to be benefiting, in more ways than one, from her boyfriend, now turned "trainer". *Good for her.*

Priya, studious as ever, hardly looks up from her books, and has at last begun calling Celeste "mother", but still not "mom" as Celeste has requested of her several times. She is doting over Priya less, which has given her more time with her muscle man.

Our daughter doesn't respond well to being showered with gifts or spoken love. She's a "show me, don't tell me" kind of person, which is going to serve her well in the future. The beautiful thing is that I didn't even have to teach it to her. If she were a normal kid, or below average, she'd be all kinds of messed up with me as a father—and Celeste would've turned her into a spoiled brat by now. Yes, Priya's a cut above on her own, with no help from anyone.

Now that checking in at home is checked off my list, I head to the hospital and complete my Sunday on-call duties—after which I'm free to hole up in my office for the work I *most* enjoy.

Settling into my chair, the first thing on my list is to check the national registry of suspicious deaths.

No dead, or beaten-to-the-point-of-miscarriage, blonde-haired librarians are showing up in the registry. Something tells me to check all of the morgues in the possible 'K' states for the same profile, in case the registry hasn't yet been updated.

After over an hour of research, my bad fortune rears its head. There are already two more blonde-haired, blue-eyed librarians—one seven months pregnant, and the other eight months pregnant—bludgeoned to death, babies gone too. *Damn!* Lonnie has accelerated his kills and dated two women at the same time—one in Michigan and another in Mississippi. *How did he pull it off?* I'm disappointed in my misstep.

However, this reveals a few important things. One is that he is already thinking about his new quest, after finishing his Lost Kitty retribution—and the other is that he is soon headed to Kansas.

I search the middle of the state first, for the profile of a librarian Lonnie is looking to date. There are only two that fit the bill and one of them will be twenty-six a few months from now. This would make for a longer dating period, and I doubt he'll wait that long before moving on to his next project, especially considering the latest developments—proving his impatience.

Another one is sixty days from being thirty-five when he'll have to take her out—and if he can't get the pregnancy to happen quickly enough, she'll be too old—ruining his perfect "LK". That points to the younger, Jessica Hartley. *It has to be her.*

Jessica works on the edge of Kansas City, in a smaller suburb. She's a tall girl, about five-foot-eleven, and medium-boned—a bigger girl than the others. I look up her online profile. She's a black belt in Taekwondo, as well as an instructor for a women's self-defense class at a gym where she frequents.

Hmm . . . I wonder if Lonnie has committed the time necessary in his research to find out Jessica seems like a woman not to be reckoned with. I could almost let this one

234

unfold, just to watch her tangle with him. It will also take some convincing to get this renaissance librarian to quit her job. I'll drop by and hang out when he should be making an appearance, just to see if he can actually interest her, or if he'll have to move on to the next, older candidate.

Based on the reports from the last two dead girls' employers, they were frequently showing up late to work before quitting—guessing he's a 'morning-sex-man'. His *less friendly* side comes out to play later at night. Around eleven thirty to two o'clock, are when his bludgeoned victims have been found.

I look up Jessica's library's activities, including school visits. It appears Tuesdays are the only days *not booked* with activities in the mornings. If she were to leave early, he couldn't count on catching her in the late afternoon. Her self-defense classes don't permit her to stay later than three o'clock on Tuesdays, so Tuesday morning it is. I've no doubt Lonnie has figured out her calendar as well.

I call the airline and book a flight to Kansas for a quick trip to the library before heading back to St. Louis on Tuesday. Celeste will think I'm in surgery, and Bella will block off my schedule, at my direction. If anyone tries to check on my whereabouts, they won't get past her.

*****

The last twenty-four hours caught me off guard. With an emergency surgery, surprise staff meeting that lasted for three hours and my normal Monday duties, I hadn't time to drop in on Merlot. Her physical needs are in order. She'll be fine.

After my flight lands in Kansas, I arrive, catch a cab a block from the library, and walk the rest of the way. Just after the doors open, I head to my section. People tend to leave you alone when you camp out in "self-help". I'm watching as I pretend to read.

Ah, there she is . . . a tall beauty, *and* she walks with confidence—not as shy looking as the rest of his victims. Lonnie is in for a challenge. I keep my head in the self-help book as she passes me. *Irony is comical.*

After twenty minutes of dodging glances, I see a square-jawed, blonde-haired guy walk in. He's wearing a blue jean jacket, fitted flat front pants, and a grey t-shirt revealing he's in great shape. Acting as if he's looking for a particular section—he scans for Jessica, when no eyes are on him. *Your tall, blonde beauty is two aisles away, you nitwit—now go to her!*

Getting warmer and . . . *there* she is! Yes, he's a pro. He plays the bookworm well. Pretending to be engrossed in the one he's ripped open, he reads using his finger to scan the page. *He's gotten her attention.* About three or four inches taller than her, I'm guessing she doesn't run into many guys looking like him around here.

He looks up, holds the finger he's been reading with like a revolver, blows the top of his barrel finger, as if it's smoking, and then holsters it—*cute.* She laughs and smooth's the hair on one side of her head behind her ear.

Pretending to be shy for just a few more seconds, he practically trips over his own feet as he moves toward her with his hand out to shake hers. They've officially met. He's done his homework to know he should treat her with as much respect, as with any man he meets.

If I weren't planning to kill him, I'd be sickened by the obvious display, which she fell for. I almost hate that I needed for him to do this to win her over.

She seems like a "kill or be killed" kind of girl, one who would go down in a bloody brawl. I wonder if he's considered his pretty boy face getting scarred?

I've seen enough. I'm heading out to retrieve Lonnie's nemesis, *the one responsible for his demons.*

*****

After taking an hour-and-a-half flight, I arrive in St. Louis. I've found a used work van for sale, that I'm paying cash for, near the airport. It's outfitted with a steel cage and tethers, used for hanging tools.

I'm dressed in a navy jumpsuit with a black baseball cap, and a rag hanging out of my back pocket. Aside from the clean hands and nails, no one would figure me for a white-collar guy. I've even let some stubble grow in.

I drive to the docks for surveillance. My grey van sinks into the pavement, *as though it belongs there*. It's after lunch, and Nathan is working. I shouldn't have to wait more than a few hours before he calls it quits. Loading work starts at the break of dawn, so they knock off by three—but it's too dangerous to take him out in the open, when the place is crawling with heavy-handed dock guys.

Two forty-five rolls around, and he's headed into a small office with windows too grungy to see through. Guessing he's punching out for the day. At least he appears to have made *something* in his life work out—too little too late. You just never know when beating a girl to death, in front of her son, is going to reach out from the grave.

Nathan pulls away in his old pickup—a rust bucket with flaking white paint and a metal box locked up in the back. *Oh yeah, Madge said he was a handyman too.*

After a fifteen-minute drive, he eases into the parking lot of a block, one level watering hole.

There are tacky beer signs in the front window, and no other windows down its side. *Tsk, tsk, Nathan—through AA twice and you're back to the well—once a drunk always a drunk.* Hopefully, this diversion will be nothing more than a few happy hour brewskies or shots.

Five thirty rolls around, and the parking lot has filled up. *This place is popular*, littered with pickup trucks and work vans. I've parked near the back of the building, on the row closest to it. *Come on Nathan—we've got a twelve-hour ride ahead of us.*

Finally! My luck has changed, and at last, Nathan makes an appearance. I think he's going to his truck, but instead, he staggers in my direction. He's had about three too many drinks by the looks of his lax facial muscles. *Did he see me following him? Has he worked up the nerve in his drunken state to approach me?*

I'm crouching a bit, with my hand on my unlicensed gun, silencer engaged. Just as I think I'm about to be confronted, he doesn't even look up. Instead, Mr. Glassy-Eyes walks right past the front of the van, and cuts around the back of the building. *Ideal.* There's no parking lot—only grass, and a few tall trees—making for a private pissing spot. *Thank you, Nathan.*

I was planning to follow him home, but I've got to take advantage of this moment—a gutsy move in the daylight.

239

Quietly, with a roll of duct tape on the arm of my gun hand, I creep around the back edge of the bar. He's got his back to me. Drowning out any possible noise I could be making is the thumping beat of eighties rock 'n' roll reverberating from inside.

I'm ready for swift action, carrying a large pre-torn piece of tape, with another strip handily stuck to my jumpsuit. On my approach, I see he's holding his "Johnson", as he hums "Sweet Home Alabama"—*fitting*.

I carefully balance my weight, planting one foot firmly in the soft grass, as I use my other leg to thrust a hard kick against the backs of his knees. *Timber!* Two dirty hands fly in the air as he goes down . . . knees crashing first, landing a belly flop onto the ground. *It's a good thing for his unit that he's got a beer gut.*

I grab him by both wrists, pulling his arms behind his back, and lean into his neck with my knee, which maintains a good face-to-grass plant. *Ugh!* What's that smell?

Oh yeah, it's his urine. *Nice.*

Clearly drunk and confused, he manages to spew out, "I'm in my piss! Get me the fuck up!" It's taken me seconds to tape his wrists, just in time to hush his second retort of "Hey" . . . with a strip of tape. Last, I secure his ankles. *This stuff really does work for just about anything.*

Reality may be setting in as he goes limp with a good blow to the back of his head. I take a moment to scan my surroundings, listening for any others who may have gotten impatient with the bathroom line. Satisfied that we're still alone, I quickly retrieve the van and back it up onto the grass—out of the parking lot's view. It takes less than a minute but already, I see Nathan in my rear-view mirror, on his feet, up and hopping. *I've got no time for this!*

I throw it into reverse, until a big *thud* stops me, and I jump out. Oops, half of Nathan's body is under the van, facedown. *Yes, even drunk this one's a fighter.* I drag him out, roll him onto his back, and throw him over my shoulder and then into the van. He's a heavy guy, but no match for my adrenaline.

Doing the humane thing, I give him a dose of the sedative Derick had enjoyed, but only enough to last *most* if not all of our drive. Between it and the liquor, he'll sleep it off like a bear.

At less than a four-hour drive away, I'd like to pick up Lonnie and let them ride together—*how sweet, a reunion for old times.* Unfortunately, my schedule doesn't permit it. I'll have to pick up the Librarian-Killer on another trip.

Merlot *will not* be happy. I certainly didn't intend for her to have a burly roommate, who frankly stinks. I'll be sure he is well confined.

241

In the wee hours, the van I've purchased hauls ass down the lightly traveled wet pavement. One stop on the side of the road to relieve myself—hours of radio stations coming and going through the old crackling speakers, as small towns become little more than a blur in my path—I arrive at five thirty-five in the morning. Normally, I don't park near the cave, as I wouldn't want to give its existence away; however, it's still dark out. *I'll have to make this quick.*

Merlot is startled as I swing the door open. "What the hell! Why are you here so early?"

Tired and slaphappy, I make an attempt at humor—something new for me. "Honey, I'm home!"

"Seriously, Doc. What is going on?"

I lift the foliage in front of her room so that she isn't in the dark, and explain I have no time for conversation—just yet.

I wheel the surgeon's table to the back of the van and open its doors. Nathan looks at me with bewilderment and narrowed groggy eyes, which tells me he's deciphering his surroundings, *already beginning to think of an escape plan in his still-altered befuddlement.*

"Hello, Nathan. We can do this the hard way or the easy way." I pull out a syringe, and he makes a two-syllable sound—so apparently, he wants to cooperate. I roll his body, with duct-taped appendages, onto the table and wheel him over to Merlot's patio, the room with the handy hanging cuffs and ankle braces bolted to the floor. *Her patio furniture will only be brought in for special occasions.* His temporary bed fits, just barely. After testing the space, I roll him back out, in front of Merlot's room this time for an introduction.

"Merlot, this is Nathan White." I sit him up and pull the tape off his mouth and ask him to say hello to Merlot.

"Fuck you, man! What the hell is this all about? Where am I!"

"So . . . you brought me some charming company *and* a 'wreaking' bonafide lady-killer to boot?"

"Yes, a killer of one lady, or—is there more than one you've killed, Mr. White?"

"No! I mean—I don't know what you're talking about. I ain't never killed nobody. Sure, I've been in a few scrapes, but not with no lady. What kinda man would do that?"

"Oh Nathan, I do *not* have time for this. I'm sorry I asked. You and Lonnie will have time to talk this over. We'll get to hear your side of it then. Merlot, I do apologize for the inconvenience. He's big, smelly, and obviously foul-mouthed. Though you've been without human contact for over three weeks, aside from myself, I am warning you before making any rash decision—he is obviously lacking any sort of couth, so odds are, *not* a great conversationalist.

243

You're going to be roomies for a few days though, so I will let you choose . . . tape the mouth or *do not* tape the mouth?"

"Come on, pretty Negro lady, let me keep my mouth free!"

"I am not African American, for your information. I vote tape him, Doc."

"Before you decide, he will be shackled too. Are you sure that you want me to tape his mouth?"

"Whatever. If you ain't white, you're black, yellar, a Jew, or one of them brown terrorist bastards in the makin'."

"I think you are right, Merlot. I will tape this racist's mouth shut. You should not be subjected to his slander."

My surgeon's table has handy straps for the unruly patient, who may insist on pulling out his or her drip lines. They work nicely on Nathan. I roll him back into Merlot's patio, and secure both wrists overhead first. With his ankles still taped, I cuff one and connect it to a metal floor restraint. I then cut the tape and secure the other—spreading his feet with just enough chain attached to the cuffs to keep the blood flowing as he changes his stance. Performing the same exercise, I secure both wrists overhead. He's got enough slack to move them around a bit, so that they don't lose all blood flow.

For the sake of Merlot's sanity, I decide to clean him up. I rip the tape from his mouth, so that I am able to enjoy the response his bath is *sure* to deliver. Though the waste of water is a brief consideration, its frigidity will create a reaction worth its entertainment value.

Merlot watches with curiosity, as I step outside to the tee to fill the bucket. A minute or so later, I give her a sly grin as I disappear from her sight, into Nathan's room with my five-gallon pale of icy cold water. I could do this nice and fast, like yanking off the tape, but slow and steady will provide more satisfaction.

With precision, I hold the bucket high at first, allowing the icy liquid to flow through his shirt, and down through his pants, *where the real fun begins*. Targeting below the belt is far more effective, so the king's ransom makes its way onto his privates as I pull his trousers forward. He yells and curses, threatening what he'll do to me when he's free— even spitting at me, which I dodged. *The luggy came with a snort of a warning.* Truly, this is the most fun I've had in a few days. Thanks to the drain, his odor will roll away.

Before taping his mouth shut again, I offer him a sedative, but warn that it may damage his joints if he were to hang by his wrists for the amount of time I intend to be gone. *I prefer him in top fighting form.* He shakes his head to confirm a "no".

Realizing at some point he will begin to moan and yell under the tape I've reset, I put on twelve hours of classical

245

music to play on a loop, so that Merlot does not have to suffer too greatly through his rants.

I fill her small refrigerator with the healthy groceries I've picked up at a farmer's market, on the way to the dock I followed Nathan from. Fresh fruit, smoked jerky, and nut cheeses I'd packed on ice—healthy snacks I knew she would appreciate. She gave me a little grin when I handed them to her, and I apologized for the gap between this and the next visit. *I hate apologies, but women love them.*

Promising that it will be worth the wait, I decide to break the bad news to her about the other two victims, so that she will look forward to Lonnie getting what's coming to him. The impatient sociopath broke his regime, with no regard to any consequences. I suspect he has a new plan for the next phase of his debauchery, so it seems he just couldn't wait to finish this one.

She's so invested with the development of the two recently dead women that a tear runs down both cheeks. I break rank with what I know is best, and hesitantly, give her a hug—which she seems to appreciate.

Hmm, didn't mind the touching . . . or is she faking it?

SMOOTH SAILING

The sun has been up for almost an hour when I arrive home and park my bike in the separate one-car garage, reserved for my sporting goods. *Celeste never comes in here.*

Entering through the front door, I'm greeted by the aroma of a dark roast, and the gurgling of the coffee pot percolating at the end of its cycle—perfect timing.

Once in the kitchen, the refrigerator door separates Celeste and me, as she stands foraging for something to eat. Perhaps her insecurities will have awakened again? I wait patiently. *Does she really not realize I'm standing here?*

"Good morning, Celeste."

She closes the door, empty-handed, and I'm ready for a good old-fashioned lambasting. "Good morning, Abel."

No such luck. I'm ready to tell her I pulled an all-nighter at the office—*anything*—but she whisks past me with a lighthearted smile as if I've been there the whole time, which is both reassuring *and* disconcerting.

Now that the coffee pot has exhaled its final groan, the house is silent—no creaks, sounds of running water, or footsteps upstairs.

"Celeste, has Priya gone to school, already? It doesn't start for over an hour."

"I think she may have gone down to the casita. She likes to study there. Anyway, her friends at school carpool now—she gets picked up by one of them most mornings."

Celeste seems to have let go of her "re-mothering", now that there's a boyfriend in town. I find this . . . unsettling.

"And you're not bothered, even a little, by not seeing her off?"

"No, it's really come in handy. My time is filled up now with the Children's Hospital events. The planning meetings are quite demanding. I'm grateful that you insisted I take it on though. It *has* been incredibly rewarding, so thank you."

Huh. She actually kisses me, on the cheek. I look her directly in the eyes as if to say, *I don't believe a damn thing coming out of your mouth*—except the part about not caring if she gets to spend time with Priya.

"I didn't actually insist Celeste, but I'm glad you're *filled* on a regular basis, with what makes you happy." I'm planting a seed that I'm on to her, in case she has ideas about doing anything other than just screwing the idiot boyfriend.

She's uncomfortable and dismisses herself promptly. I pour a second cup, and turn around to face the window to the backyard. Priya is standing at the casita door dressed in her school uniform—a pleated plaid skirt, cotton button-up shirt, and knee socks. She takes a moment to scan her perimeter and then pulls a key from her shirt pocket to let herself in—*suspicious behavior*. I'll enjoy my coffee in the kitchen while I wait to see what happens next.

After several minutes, the door to the casita opens and she sticks her head out, looking left to right twice before stepping out. Once she's locked up, she briskly walks back toward the house. How is she getting to school? I'm fully expecting her to come inside and lie to her mother about missing the carpool ride with her friends. A few more minutes go by, but *nothing.*

Finally, I head upstairs for a better view from the landing, out of a high window over the living room—only to catch her walking up the block, wearing her backpack and carrying her lunch pail. *She must have left them outside the back door before going into the casita.* At the corner, a car pulls beside her and the door opens. She nods her head in a *yes* motion and hops in. It's a large black SUV . . . *hmm.* This is more troubling than Celeste having sex without protection—*I hope she's using protection!*

I've been so busy enjoying the life I've earned, as well as keeping my work at the hospital and lab running smoothly, that it's just now hitting me—holes are springing open in my 'cover life', like a sponge soaking up water. For the first time, I'm considering the fact that Celeste *thinks* she is barren, when it's actually me who is 'fixed'.

Now sex with her is definitely out of the question! If she gets pregnant, I can't have her claiming it's mine. And *if* she does, she'll have to make a decision; either keep me in the dark and get an abortion, or tell me and face a divorce. Both are messy, and messy does not work in my life—*ever*. I don't leave loose ends that have the potential to implode. I will need to come up with a plan to counteract this possible debacle. However, the most vulnerable powder keg at the moment, which needs diffusing, is Lonnie.

*****

A short day at the office, gives me a chance to visit the cave to give Nathan a glucose drip and steroids, as well as an IV to prevent dehydration.

When I placed a catheter on him ending in the grate below, Merlot was disgusted—until I reminded her that I *am* a Doctor, and thus body parts do not make me squeamish.

250

Any other deposits, *should he not hold them*, will be washed away by another bucket of frigid water. Nathan's discomfort should have him in the right *agitated* state of mind, without rendering him *too* weak.

With no surgeries until early next week, I give Celeste a convenient work-related excuse to leave town for a few days, *as if she'll give a damn anyhow*—and I'm off to Kansas.

This time, there's truth in it. I'm taking sensitive samples from our lab to be shared with researchers out of state for a breakthrough drug. If approved, the trial is set to begin in two weeks. One of our scientists, or even a senior resident *could* do it, but I've convinced them that I want to speak with the committee who makes the funding decisions. It's a one-day commitment, but three to four days as far as the senior staff, my lab rats, and Celeste are concerned.

*****

It's been a whirlwind of a day, ending in an eight-and-a-half-hour drive. If I weren't so eager to apprehend my formidable prey, I would probably be exhausted. After I flew to deliver the samples and make a compelling presentation to the Funding Committee—I hopped on another flight home, took a cab to the storage facility where I'd left the van and headed to Kansas.

251

The fellow, who sold it to me for cash with no title in St. Louis, left the old license plates on—making its connection to me impossible. I'm fortunate to have dealt with people possessing fewer brain cells than frogs.

I'm running mean and lean on this trip. I've brought bedding, water, and essential snacks—*no café visits this time.* On the edge of town, I find a pit stop devoid of any other vehicles, and back into a bare spot with ample tree coverage to camouflage the van. *Yes, this will do fine.*

After a decent night's sleep and a breakfast of jerky, trail mix, and an apple, I shower in the rest stop and I'm on my way. *My pugilist awaits.*

I've got one day to apprehend Lonnie, before Merlot loses her mind, and Nathan is too far gone for good fighting recovery.

*****

It's eight-thirty in the morning, and the library is buzzing. I find Jessica reading to a kindergarten class in a group circle. With no sign of Lonnie, I head to the *do-it-yourself area* . . . books for "Dummies" and "How-To's". I stay away from the deep topics—no need to alert a nosy librarian who may have spotted me in that section last time.

There's a loud-mouthed woman engaging strangers a few aisles over. I suspect she's woken up and hit her "hair of the dog" already. She's telling some poor transgender kid how fabulous she is, despite her twenty-five-pound weight gain, and in the next breath that she has a fashion line. The clothes are not *actually* her designs, but she sells them by getting kids around his age to post while wearing them on social media.

His payment would be a promised boat for a weekend, another of her ventures where she rents and docks them at the nearby lake. Says he only needs to get her clothes lots of "likes". *Ugh!* It seems there is no respite from this shallow minutia!

I head to the opposite end of the room to escape her harsh tone. *Where is the peace a library once provided?* It's a good time to go, just as she belts out a macaw-like cackle, splitting eardrums within two rows of books. I see a librarian rushing toward her aisle, f*inally*.

There's a light *ding* at the front door when suddenly, I'm nearly face-to-face with Lonnie! I veer as inconspicuously as possible, turning to head into the men's room, as he continues walking toward the kindergarten circle.

Doing an about face, I duck around the back of the aisles, tracking barely behind him with only the bookshelves between us. Stopping two rows short of the children's circle, I advance near the front, and spy through a gap on a shelf to my right.

Once he arrives, he says something to make the kids laugh, and then borrows Jessica away from the group.

I assume he's making dinner plans with her—until he goes down on one knee and pulls something out of his pocket. *No—it's a ring box!* How could he be asking for her hand in marriage *already*? There must have been some earth-shattering sex in the last few days for him to think he can get away with this!

I race as quietly as possible around the back of the row, and advance again near the front, with only one aisle between us to get within earshot. My head is visible above the books, *so I turn my face away from Lonnie and Jessica's view.*

Jessica speaks in a loud whisper, as I strain to hear her. "Lonnie, I don't know what to say. I mean, you've caught me completely off guard with this. I know we've been talking online for a few months but still, this is *so* fast."

Of course! He's getting into relationships with them online and over the phone before meeting them face-to-face!

Lonnie's plan now hinges on a thin axle at her rebuttal. He's doing his best to remain cool and collected, but I hear the tinge of panic in his vocal cords as he delivers his response in a slightly higher volume *and* faster pace than her whisper. "I don't understand, Jess. I thought you wanted this as much as I do?"

Ah . . . the guilt trip response—to put her off guard. He masters his prey like a true salesman.

"I do . . . I'm just, well . . . afraid of making another mistake—that's all."

"Oh Jess, you poor baby. I'm sorry you had to go through such an awful experience with that—that *monster*. But I'm here now, and I'm going to protect you and our little guy, or girl. In fact, I'm getting my boat delivered tomorrow morning. I was hoping we could spend some time sailing to celebrate. What do you say?"

Ugh! Sailboat? Baby? How did he impregnate her so fast? He's pulling out all the stops on her! At this pace, he'll have her quitting her job in no time—not waiting for her to get nice and round before he strikes. He's in too big a hurry!

"Well . . . that *does* sound romantic. I don't know what I did to deserve you, Lonnie. I'm the luckiest girl in the world. Of course I'll marry you!"

No! She's buying into his bullshit romance!

"There's one other thing Jess, and it's a tough thing to ask, but I really *need* you and our baby to myself. Sharing you with a job and all of your obligations is difficult with my schedule. I want to shower you with everything you deserve

255

in life—which means the crazy number of hours you work is well, out of the question. Would you consider taking the pregnancy time off work to see how it suits you? If you are dying to go back once you've had our baby, then I guess I'll just have to live with that decision."

There's no "getting back" Jessica . . . he's planning to "shower you" with gut punches!

"That *is* asking a lot—but time off, especially now, does sound appealing. I could always ask for a leave of absence, just for a few months to start, and decide from there?"

"There's my girl. I love you so much, Jess! Now pack some bags after work, at least a few weeks' worth, and let your friends know you won't be seeing them for a while. You can celebrate our engagement when we get back into town. Just no traditional 'girls' night out', with our little bun in the oven."

Argh! Shift of plans—I'm going have to take care of this before she gets on that boat!

"Wow, I've never been on a boat for that long. I'm so excited! But I don't plan to tell my friends anything until we're back. I want to tell them in person, and since you've never met them, I don't want to get the third degree over the phone. You can come with me to tell them. They'll melt when they see you—so that's the plan. I only wish my parents were still around . . . they'd be *so* happy."

"I know, Jess. Me too. We're starting our own family now though—two orphans of the world, beginning our own era . . . our own family. That's all we need."

Orphans? He's so convincing! If I didn't know his background, I might wonder if he's changed. He's tied up the loose ends before they sail away. *Hmm, no one will find her body if they're out in deep waters.* With this "leave of absence", and no family, she won't be missed—not for possibly a few months.

Following a kiss and hug, Lonnie has the gall to wave to the class. After three dead women and six unborn infants, I'm going to enjoy making this bastard disappear!

GOTCHA!

I've parked around the corner from Jessica's home, in front of a vacant lot.

The giant shrubbery between her and her neighbor's home is making for the perfect stakeout spot. People really should trim for safety. Her centurion era, canary-yellow bungalow has a screened-in front porch, with its door on the side. *Ideal entry.* It's after eight o'clock. What's taking Lonnie so long?

The TV's sound is blaring, in what I assume is the living room just off the porch. From the shrubbery, I hear her let out a gasp, louder than the program she's turned up, while moving about in the house. *Did Lonnie park in the alley and come in through the back?*

Advancing quietly onto the front porch from its side door, I crouch under the window looking into the petite living room. She's watching a news program with her back to me.

She's got one hand over her mouth, while rewinding the news story with the other. Upon hitting play, she turns the volume down—freezing the screen on a hand-drawn picture of a man that looks almost identical to Lonnie. She hits play again, viewing images of one woman, and now another. Both are blonde, with blood-soaked hair and clothing, lying either unconscious or dead. The announcer says they were both pregnant librarians and believed to be engaged to their attacker, one from Michigan and the other Mississippi—but that they don't know the identity of the assailant yet. *Damn!* Now that the two have been linked together, the file may soon be taken out of the morgue's unknown registry. This is not part of my plan!

Jessica begins to pace. *Is she going to run?* After a few laps around her living room, she disappears, dropping to the floor—I hear her grunting. I crouch further out of view. Through the few inches of clearance between the back edge of the sofa and corner of the window, I see her bottom half on the floor, and she seems to be reaching underneath the couch, obviously looking for something.

Without warning, exhibiting cat-like reflexes, she springs to her feet with a gun at her side! *Great, now I have an armed—and highly hormonal—six-foot Black Belt to deal with too.*

I don't want to kill her. That would make me the same as Lonnie. But I won't let her do it either, or worse, let him be arrested and get out of it, due to bad investigative work or a legal loophole. Once his identity is uncovered, all will be lost, and I'm *not* backing out now—not when I've already got an additional surprise for him. *Think fast Abel.*

Jessica raises the gun with both hands clenched tightly around the shaft, squinting down the barrel with one eye shut. *Oh boy* . . . she turns a fast circle, and I duck before she points it in my direction—then whips around once more, and advances toward the back of her house.

Seconds later, I hear a door slam. She must be in the backyard—*perfect.* I slip into the side yard cramming myself into the shrubbery again. With the help of a dingy-lensed streetlight in the ally—peering through branches slightly baron of leaves in their centers this time of year, I've got a clear view. She's stalking around the yard, with the gun hanging by her side—probably thinking Lonnie will pull up from the alleyway to her house. *She's definitely ready for him.*

Uh oh, change of plans. I'm not sure where she *thinks* she's going, but she's on a mission—advancing again, this time toward the front of the house, up the side yard I'm hidden in!

It's completely dark without star or moonlight, but the yellowed glow from the streetlamp in back, is illuminating the side yard just enough. Holding my breath, I wait until she's one step past—and with careful precision, I lunge my arm through the bush and clench the wrist of her gun hand—squeezing it with the force of a vice grip. *"Ow!"* she cries out, as the pistol thuds into the grass.

Emerging in the same instant, I rapidly cover her mouth and nose with a rag pre-soaked with chloroform, which I'd readied for Lonnie. It will only make her temporarily dizzy. I don't intend to damage her *or* the baby.

To be sure she won't be able to ID my face at a later time, I stay behind her, and kick the gun away, then whisper; "I'm only here to help." She makes a muffled growl as she raises her elbows with intentions of slamming them into my gut—a self-defense tactic she's taught in her classes. I promise it could get much worse if she doesn't remain quiet *and* still. At the sound of my voice, she cranes her head to the side to get a look at my face, but her eyes dart back and forth too rapidly for her brain to register my features. "Relax, Jessica—don't make me hurt you", I whisper, and at this she rethinks her tactic.

Her accelerated heart rate and panicking breaths, force her to suck down the fumes from my rag. As her torso melts along with her limbs, I catch her so that she doesn't hurt herself falling to the ground. Her dazed eyes roll around fighting the short sleep the chloroform will deliver. Instead, I lay her next to the shrubs, pull a syringe out of my pocket and give her a gentle sleepy-drug shot—assuring she'll be out until morning. *I've got to move swiftly now.*

Scooping her back up, I make haste down toward the back yard, imagining what fun it could've been to watch her give Lonnie hell. With a baby on board, the entertainment value would not justify all its possible outcomes.

Inside her back door and down the hall to a bedroom off the living room we go. With a pillow to fall back on, I get her into bed and under the covers. There's no evidence of a bump, scrape, or bruise, so she may not recall *exactly* what happened in the morning.

Knowing Lonnie will arrive at any minute, I turn off most of the lights, and change the channel away from the news station. If he's on his way, he may not have seen or heard it.

I move to the back of the shot-gun-style house, and squat down in the kitchen. I'm ready and waiting with a clear view to the front. Just moments later—I hear the thunk of a car door closing. He didn't park in the alley— good thing the porch is unlocked. Its screen door creaks as it opens, and slams bouncing against the frame a few times. *He's in a hurry.*

"Jess! Hey babe, the boat arrived late. It required some preparations before we took off, but now we need to get going . . . Jess?"

When she doesn't answer, Lonnie looks around and appears a bit . . . *pensive*. His first instinct takes him toward the bedroom, where there's a faint lamp light streaming out of the cracked-open door. He senses something is *off*, and pauses to check his surroundings before pushing it open.

Go on Lonnie—step inside.

"Jess? What are you doing?" He enters moving toward her. "I thought you'd be excited and ready to go."

Good, he thinks she's sleeping. On bare feet, I rush the door, practically holding my breath—needle in one hand and Jessica's gun in the other—peering into the crack between the door and its frame.

"Jessica . . . baby? Are you okay?"

He puts his hand on her arm. *Shit!* He's going to roll her over. He'll know that 'this' isn't a *normal* sleep. Lunging inside the room, with only a large step to reach him—my needle is in his neck, plunging a heavy dose of what put both Derick and Nathan out cold. It should last long enough for most of our drive.

"Ouch! Mother! Who the hell are you?" He spins around to find me—needle up, shaft empty. "You're mine, you son of a bitch!"

I drop it and cold cock him square in the nose, sending him backwards. He catches himself on the bed and bounces up in one motion, aiming at me for a tackle. I dodge his flying attempt, and a few more slugging past me. Within seconds, his wild air-punches subside—as his eyes begin glazing over.

"Give it up, Lonnie. She's not going to complete your 'K'!" His shoulders begin to hunch, as he plops his butt onto the edge of the bed next to Jessica's feet.

"What the—what the hell are you talking about!"

"Oh, Lonnie. Poor sociopath, Lonnie—too busy patting yourself on the back for all you've gotten away with to think someday your sloppiness could catch up with you."

"You're crazy! I don't know *who* . . . you think I am, but you've got the wrong guy!" His words are beginning to slur, and he's fighting hard to stay coherent.

At seeing my gun, he begins to beg—*or is that negotiating?* Either way, he has no idea what I'm capable of or how disgusting his rhetoric falls on my ears. "If you want to live, you'll shut your mouth! You've got seconds before passing out, so take this opportunity to put your narcissistic nature aside and listen."

His eyes roll up to meet mine, staring at me as Jessica begins to snore lightly.

"Good, that's much better. I have an old friend of yours I'm reuniting you with. Does the name *Nathan White* mean anything to you? No? Go way back . . . back to the night, that *last* night 'Lost Kitty' lay at his feet, in a pool of her own blood." An optic reflex, though ever so slight, tells me he's never forgotten. "Ah, I see you're recollecting him now. Well then, as you fall asleep, think about vengeance because I'm going to give you the chance to exact it."

There would be no more conversation between us for several hours, as the drug finally reduced him to a puddle, lying over from the waist up atop Jessica's legs. The corner of what appears to be a plastic sandwich bag is poking out of his right pocket. My curiosity gets the better of me, and I go for it. It doesn't budge, so I roll him onto his back and slide out the bag holding a stiff object. Immediately recognizing it—a pregnancy test stick, with a negative result in its miniscule window . . . *hmm.*

How did he convince "Jess" that she was pregnant with this? Obviously, he was planning to kill her anyway. I decide to search her bathroom to see if I can find a positive stick anywhere.

After rummaging through her drawers, medicine cabinet, along with every nook and cranny, I find nothing . . . *wait,* there's her purse on the table in the small dining room off the hall outside the bathroom. I've got to get out of here, but this is eating at me! I plow through the contents of her purse, and in the outside pocket is an even smaller plastic bag. There's another pregnancy stick inside this one, and it has a positive reading—*I guess he did knock her up after all.*

I want to keep this one as well, but she'll expect it to be where she left it. I don't want to leave my fingerprint *or* Lonnie's behind, so I search her kitchen for cleaning agents and find alcohol wipes. Covering my fingers with them, I clean the baggy and put it back where I'd found it. Mystery solved—time to get going.

Starting out through the back door to get my van and pull it in through the alleyway, I look down through side yard all the way to the front. *Damn!* I'd forgotten about Lonnie's truck with the trailered boat!

Now that he's rushed *his* plans—I'll have to get rid of this beastly piece of evidence! If Jessica finds it here, after seeing what she did on the news, her memory of me will certainly be "jogged". I head back inside, and once again dig through her purse for keys to lock them in tight, while I take care of this "snag". They get at least one more hour together—how nice.

In his haste, Lonnie left the keys to his truck in the ignition, *thank you.* I start it up and head out the way I had come—down a backroad less travelled. I'd driven over an old wood plank bridge just a mile or so away, on the way to her house. There should be a good hiding spot near it.

Hmm . . . who else might know where he was headed? The mechanic who readied the boat will know when he took it, but with Lonnie's plans of treachery, it's doubtful he spoke a word to anyone about *where* he was headed. Jess will not remember his arrival—so I just need to get rid of this giant spectacle of evidence.

As I approach the bridge I'd driven over, I slow to a crawl. There's a one-lane dirt path just after a small grove of trees on the other side of the bridge.

With no headlights in sight, I stop in the road and back the boat down the path. The trees hide both the truck and the boat, as the path dead-ends in a hurry. It appears to have been cleared in the first place for a fishing spot—*yes!* Backing the boat's trailer close to the water, I leave the driver's door cracked open with the keys in the front seat—after cleaning my fingerprints from every surface I've touched.

Why did Lonnie stop here and leave his truck with the boat behind? Perhaps he heard the news . . . saw the sketch of his face? The truck and boat parked randomly *here*, another part of the mystery for Jess and the cops to figure out later.

Running at a fast pace back to Jessica's place, I arrive almost an hour after leaving. The short distance took longer as I was forced to stay inside the tree line along the road, where the earthy was lumpy, but I was hidden.

Two sets of snores greet me as I come through the back door. Catching my breath, I use Jessica's bathroom and then double-check the front door lock. This time it really is time to get going!

After pulling my van into the alley with the lights off, I manhandle Lonnie into the back of it. The thought of duct taping *only* his appendages is appealing to me—in case I am able to speak with him about his quest and what drove him to it after the drug wears off. It won't last the full distance of our drive, and even though I'd figured out his motivation— it's the first time I have the opportunity to speak with a fellow serial killer one on one.

Hmm, on second thought he's *not* one that I respect, *and* he may start begging or attempting to negotiate as he comes to. I'm going to tape it to save myself the aggravation.

After seven and a half hours of the old van rambling us toward Lonnie's final destination, I hear him stirring—he's managed to sit himself upright.

"Hey there, sunshine! Hope you had a good rest. You're going to need it . . . Huh, what's that?" I laugh at my bad humor. *I'm getting delirious at this point.*

"Look, I don't know if you remember your bedtime story, so I'll tell it to you again. You remember, Nathan, the jealous boyfriend of your *real* mom, who beat her to death?"

He looks in my direction with consciously narrowed eyes.

"Yes, I know all about that. Well, Nathan is waiting, but he's got no idea *you're* on the way—or anything about you, I'm guessing. The thing is, I don't care for you *at all.* However, he is the beast who made you 'what' you are, from my research. I don't believe you weren't born this way—so that fateful episode is what I strongly suspect has turned you into the sociopath you've become. Unlike myself, who possesses these tendencies naturally—you, my friend, were *created.* Now, I'm *not* giving you a hall pass because of it—no, no, no! You've left quite a bloody trail, and one of the worst kinds, what with the innocent women and their unborn infants. Jessica's should be fine, by the way, and definitely better off without the likes of you in her *or* your kid's life."

"So, back on topic—where was I? Oh, yes . . . you and Nathan are reuniting. What a happy occasion, *for me anyhow*! The story between the two of you needs

269

closure. Therefore, I've decided to bring it back to life so that it can play out—comprehend?"

He looks puzzled, *still*.

"Well, that's all for now. It's only fair you and he hear the rules at the same time. We'll be there to meet him in just under an hour. Sleep, stay awake . . . it's your call—but if I were you, I'd reflect on what he did to me *so* many years ago. It seems you've been taking out vengeance on victims against your 'mother figures' instead of your rightful maker!"

REUNION

Where the hell *is* Doc? *Ugh . . .* I'm sick of this fool's grunting and yelling through the tape on his mouth. The foul odor of his shit has wafted through the air and permeated my room. I have to stay underneath my covers completely to try and block it out.

It was working until he woke me, blurting out an abrupt obscenity—and now I'm unable to ignore that my bladder has become a balloon. Might as well get this over with.

Holding my breath, as if I'll be able to do it for long, I rip the covers away, and slide out of the warmth of my bed. *Brr!* The slab floor is frigid!

After relieving myself, I wipe and stand in front of the sink. My legs look thinner than ever. I pull up the Cardinals jersey Doc had brought me from St. Louis to look at my torso—I've still got most of my curves, but the outline of my ribs is beginning to show . . . *uh oh.* The Petunias will think

I'm dieting. This may not fare well for my numbers. I've practically preached accepting one's body 'as is' to them. I'll need to wear something a bit baggy in my next video.

I've been doing push-ups, planks, lunges, and crunches so that when the time to escape presents itself, I'll have a shot at success. Doc hasn't said anything about my weight loss. I doubt he's even noticed.

Normally, my week's activities include video content, filming, editing, and answering posted questions from my followers. I gauge the success of each day, depending on how much of these tasks I've completed. Now *those* "tasks" seem, well . . . trivial.

My focus has shifted to what most people take for granted—*survival. Think, Merlot* . . . how or *what* can you do to escape? There has to be a way to maneuver out of this jam.

Objects heavy enough to crack the shell of my prison are bolted *so tightly* into the ground. There's no amount of working out that will render me strong enough to loosen them.

What if anything, has he overlooked . . . forgotten—the cameras? Huh, there's a thought. I know something that he *thinks* I don't know. How can I use it to my advantage? What are *his* weaknesses—yes! His fetishes. No. No, I couldn't . . . *could I?*

The tiny bumps spreading up my legs are turning my skin into that of a plucked chicken. Spotting a pair of jeans I'd thrown over the side of the tub, I slide them on and crawl back into bed.

Ah . . . the warmth I'd left behind in the sheets is still partially there. I snuggle under them, along with a quilt Doc had brought from my apartment. I imagine I'm back there—comfy and free, in my *real* bedroom. My eyelids are relaxing.

"Merlot! I'm here!" I raise her foliage wall for a clear view. She's under her covers, leaning up on her elbows. "Did I wake you? "

"Why the hell are you here *so* early?" *I really wanted to drift off with my happy thoughts.*

"I've got a real treat for you. You're going to want to get up for this!"

"Okay—I'm up! I give . . . what *treat* do you have at this early hour?"

"Now that's the spirit! I'll be right back."

I back the van up to the cave, as with Nathan's delivery. Using a dolly that came with it, I strap Lonnie in around his arms and legs. Rolling him down a short ramp, I position him in front of Merlot's room for viewing.

"Here he is! Your prize, Lonnie Baker!"

"What do you mean, my *prize*? He impregnates and kills librarians and babies! You're not turning him loose in

273

here, are you?" This guy is blonde, blue-eyed, and handsome—in a bad boy "model" sort of way. I may have fallen for him in their shoes too, but I know his history.

"Not to worry, Merlot. You're *not* his type. You know Nathan, the racist next door?"

"You mean the one who's crapped his pants, and stunk up the place?"

"Oh . . . yes—well, nothing a five-gallon bucket of water won't fix. I see I need to put introductions on hold for a few minutes." I wheel Lonnie out of the view of Nathan's room and fill up my bucket. *I really haven't time for this*, but it does serve to get Nathan charged up, when I pull his trousers away from his body and pour an entire pail of icy cold water down his backside—washing his excrement out, and through the grates.

Next, I wheel Lonnie into full sight . . . *the circus freak for all to see,* and continue. "Now, where was I? Yes, you only asked for Lonnie's demise, but as a special treat—I'm exceeding expectations, by reuniting both men! To recap the story, so that it is clear to all; Nathan here, killed Lonnie's mom by way of beating her to death, while Lonnie watched at only four years of age. So, now you know where his nasty habits originated. However, before you go feeling sorry for him, remember the monster he's become, *and* that he would do it again."

274

His eyes are narrowed at me, his hair disheveled. *The demon inside him drools . . . longing to strike me down.* I inhale to enjoy the scent of my captive beast's rage. Hell, I *relate* to this reaction—m*y own beast is charged!* It is an exercise in control *not* to release it and let it take Lonnie apart.

Nathan glares at me too with the same determined expression—then squints at Lonnie for a better look. I decide to rip the tape off both of their mouths. It's only fair each has ample opportunity for trash talk, before the big fight. They remain silent—so I continue.

"Yes, Nathan, this is the kid who curled up in the corner, watching, while you beat his mother to death. *What a mess you've left behind.* Now that he's all grown up, his beatings are every bit as lethal—and frankly, far more methodical than your jealous outrage toward his mother. Why, if what you say about her being the *only one* is true, it was merely a crime of passion. But Lonnie here has taken a page from your book and raised it to an art form."

Nathan's eyes have widened, but still, he remains silent.

"Speechless? This *is* a first."

"What the hell does any of this have to do with me? That bitch did exactly what I asked her *not* to do! She was a lousy mother anyway, stripping for men every day. If you ask me, I did that little snot-nose mama's boy here a favor. Bet you grew up nice and safe with that garbage man of a dad and his uptight librarian . . . *huh, pretty boy*—you poor baby!"

"Careful, Nathan. What's the saying . . . *poking the bear?* If you know what's good for you, you'll be more guarded with him. Now, you both seem to be tough guys when it comes to beating women to death. Let's see how you do mano a mano."

"Doc, what are you suggesting?" *Is he going to fight them? What if he loses? I know way too much of their pasts, thanks to him. They'll never let me out of here in one piece.*

"I'll answer your *real* question, Merlot. I'm not going to fight them; however, I'm touched if you're concerned for *my* safety—these hands need to be in top form for surgery tomorrow. No, they are going to fight one another."

Lonnie is shaking his head profusely. "I'm not fighting him! You've got the wrong guy. I don't even know this man! Let me out of here!"

"Oh, Lonnie. Your cowardice is *such* a disappointment! My money was on you. You're younger, appear to be in better shape, but your mind . . . well, the 'flight' seems to be mightier than the 'fight'—and you *will* fight."

I place the tape back over his mouth. *I can't take the whining.*

276

"Now, here are the rules. Because you're both tired, I'm giving you each a highly caffeinated drink. I want you both hungry for victory. I could induce a drug that would put you at your most aggressive and, though that *would* be entertaining, I am nothing if not a purist—so I prefer to watch your *true* natures at their most terrifying of states.

Lonnie, you will get yours after Nathan. He's been in that uncomfortable position for quite some time now. I'm going to free him, at gunpoint of course—then lock him in again to enjoy his energy drink. He'll have twenty minutes to stretch and get the blood flowing to his extremities.

Lonnie, you'll be given yours to fully recover from the earlier drug, as Nathan stretches. Finally, you'll both enter the arena, where you'll be surrounded by an electrical force field, which I will engage from behind that booth. If you try breaking through into any of the rooms, it will engage and by way of electrocution, you will forfeit the fight to your opponent. That threat means Ms. Merlot remains safe, as do I." *I hold up my remote as exhibit A.* "I control the electrical force field, but you control your destiny. Yes, Nathan?"

"What exactly do you mean by 'we' control our destiny?"

"Another tasty detail. So glad you've asked. This, boys, is a fight to the death—or didn't I mention that? After all, what is more fitting an ending than this? You get to enjoy

277

your sport *and* live or die by the punishment you've inflicted upon others. Rather poignant, wouldn't you say? I said . . . 'poignant', *isn't it!*" Wide eyed, they both nod in agreement.

"Doc?"

"Yes Merlot, what is it?"

"Um, I hate to cut in here but—" *I've never seen him this incensed, crazy-wild expression and a voice of thunder.*

"Speak . . . up!"

"Well, what happens to the last man standing? Why I ask is, they both killed women, or at least one woman. Are you just going to let the one who wins *go free*?"

"That's very insightful and really, none of your concern. Let's just say I will evaluate the living participant's life expectancy after the fight. One thing *is* certain. There *will* be a fight, or they will both die, and in any creative way that I see fit."

Hmm . . . their expressions are that of fear. I see it in the twisted muscles under their skin—smell it seeping from their pores. It seems trepidation about their own destinies has taken over the beasts' natural aggression—*this won't do.* These two men *should* abhor one another, especially Lonnie for Nathan—yet he shows an obvious lack of disdain. In fact, *neither* man seems riled yet. *I need to sweeten the pot.*

After they've finished their drinks, I place them in front of Merlot in their restraints.

"Merlot."

"Yes, Doc?"

"I've decided to incentivize our fighters. Guess what the prize is?"

"I'm *enthralled*—what?"

"You are my dear—that's right gentlemen! Merlot has a tasty little body under that t-shirt. She's been exercising to get in shape for you. *It hasn't gone unnoticed my dear.* Shed the shirt and show them your body."

"No Doc! No way! I'm not—"

*"No . . . i*sn't an option. Now do as I say!"

His voice is scaring me . . .

"I'm not doing anything with either of these two animals—do you hear me!"

"You see gentlemen? She's got a lot of fight in her, just how you like your women. Not only will one of you go free, but you'll also get to do anything you like with Merlot here—short of beating her to death. I won't allow that. Now Merlot—take it off!"

"Yeah Merlot—take off that damn shirt. I ain't messin' round with no black lady unless I check out the goods!"

"Nathan, I give the orders here. Merlot, I'm not asking again."

I'm not sure what he's up to, but for some reason I trust him. "Okay!" Reluctantly, I disrobe from the waist up. The cold air hits my nipples and instantly they stand at attention. Both stare as though they've never seen brown perky breasts in their lives. Doc is smiling, in what seems like an approving way, and I get an idea. I don't stop with the shirt.

He sees me going for my top jean button and picks up the music remote. He chooses the song "American Woman"—so crafty. *I know we're thinking the same thing.*

I jump onto my bed and roll my round butt out of the jeans I'd put on slowly, so that all three men have a full view of everything. *I'm not wearing panties.* Though this feels painfully wrong, I've not had this kind of attention in such a long time.

I believe he will keep me safe. He doesn't mind that I am performing for other men, other . . . monsters. I realize I've missed the attention—*any* attention. I feel pathetic for a fleeting second, but decide not to let it spoil my show. *I need this.*

All three men watch, eyes glued, pants bulging, mouths dropped open—*Nathan actually drools.* The song ends with my legs facing them, knees spread eagle, while leaned up on my elbows. I've practiced this routine by myself before, hoping to use it on a man I love, *not this crew*. But, here it is. My erotic performance used on the likes of animals.

"And that, gentlemen, aside from your lives, is what you are fighting for. What do you think? Ready to live *and* have your way with Merlot?"

"Hell yeah! I ain't never seen brown sugar before, but I got a *real big* sweet tooth now!"

"How about you, Lonnie? It's obvious you're also 'excited'. Why so quiet?"

"I, I don't know how to . . ."

"How to *what*, mama's boy? You ain't never been with a woman before? Are you *queer*?"

"Now Nathan, we won't have you disparaging homosexuals or any other group of people. Besides, Lonnie here has gotten several women pregnant, so he is well-versed in sexual activity with females."

"It's not that. I just haven't had sex . . . *without,* a purpose. It's against my rules."

"Ah, I see. The 'no beating to death' part is ruining it for you? And perhaps the fact that Merlot is far from your type? This 'type' was soon to change anyhow, once your 'K' was complete. Oh, I've ruined that for you, haven't I? Well, if you can't get past your 'rules', then perhaps fighting for your life, as well as being freed to complete your 'K' is incentive enough?"

"Okay, I don't know what the hell you just said, but wow! Little mama's boy really is screwed in the head! Hey Lonnie, I can't wait to beat some sense into it, just like I beat it into your mama's! Oh yeah . . . that's right! She never got any sense—she just got dead. *Hah!* You're next, pretty boy!"

At this, the veins in Lonnie's temples begin to bulge—his jaw clenches. The whites of his eyes turn blood red, and the scent of his rage is beginning to seep from his pores. *It's show time!*

"Now *that* is the fighting spirit boys!"

"Merlot . . . please put your clothing back on." She's wriggling around with her pants off. "It wouldn't be a fair fight for Nathan. He doesn't need a distraction."

I *really* want Doc—want him right now! I wish he'd put these two in another room to duke it out; come into my room so we could go at it. And when we're finished, I'd lock *him* in here and escape. I would visit to feed *him* nuts and berries. He'd get red meat, only when I'm in the mood for play. I'd watch him on the cameras and do my show the way *I* want to do it. I'm sick of being the victim—*what did I ever do to deserve any of this!*

I should hate him. I kind of hate myself for *not* hating him. Instead, I want him, want him to pleasure me . . . *oh, how much I crave it! Ugh* . . . stop it Merlot! You're damaged goods—bound up inside from your past . . . *like Lonnie.* My thoughts are all over the place. I need to get the hell out of here!

"Merlot! Your clothes—put them on—now!"

WHAT NIGHTMARES ARE MADE OF

Doc is actually whistling. *What's that song?* It sounds like the tune "Whistle While You Work" from . . . *Snow White?* He's wearing a hazmat-looking suit, wiping down the walls and scrubbing the floors. A mixture of cleaning agent and blood is running down the drain of my patio floor. At least it's a fresh-scented one.

Now that it's been cleaned, I may ask to sit inside and soak in some sunlight. I'm trying *not* to remember *or* dwell on the side of him that I've just witnessed. It'll ruin my fantasies. *The ones of my rock star are gone from my dreams.* Though warped, my tête-à-têtes with the Doc are all I have left.

As I watch him clean, all I can think of are the day's events. They're reeling over and over in my head, like an anthem I want to stop singing. Perhaps if I let them play out just once, from beginning to end, I'll be able to deal with their aftermath and forget them forever—instead of the trauma I'm experiencing now. *Holy hell was unleashed in here today!*

First, Lonnie saw red after Nathan resurrected the memory of his dead mother; however, in a controlled fashion, he let Nathan throw the first punch. Easily dodging it, Lonnie landed a "nut-cracker" jab to the nose, causing an audible crunch and blood pouring out of two tiny faucets.

Blinking it off—now Nathan saw red!

Like a fastball pitch, Lonnie once again aimed for the nose, but Nathan interfered catching the fist in midair, and then brutally bending it backwards.

Unfazed by the pain, Lonnie didn't flinch. He kicked Nathan's shin so hard I could hear the sound of a bone snap. Naturally, Nathan grabbed for his leg, which left him standing on one—giving Lonnie the advantage as he kicked out the good leg. Landing flat and hard on his back, Nathan gurgled to breathe, until Lonnie's first stomp to the gut, brought him back with a huge audible inhale.

Stomping Nathan over and over like putting out a fire—first to the groin, and then to the face—I could barely stomach to watch as I swallowed the impending bile ganging up on my throat. A voice inside wanted to convince me that this was merely a movie, but I needed to be present in case the gory action scene invaded my space.

Nathan, the old warrior too stubborn to die, grabbed Lonnie's foot as he aimed for his gut again—and with a twist and a jerk, he brought Lonnie down on his face.

The action was interrupted by a sudden loud gasp and a caw. It was Doc unabashedly laughing and clapping like a seal. I was stuck in a house of horrors at a circus of death. Doc's "act" played out on the stage he had set—his role; the happiest spectator on earth.

When Lonnie's head hit the floor, he quickly flipped on his back, but to no avail—as Nathan straddled him into a leg-lock pinning him to the ground. Unleashing a symphony of damage, Nathan's fists knew no pain of their own as he pummeled Lonnie's face . . . *pretty boy no more!*

A pang of anxiety rose in my stomach. *What if the Doc was really going to allow this savage to have his way with me?* I knew he had to be mentally unstable, but for the first time, I sat front row and center to the "crazy town" inside of Doc's head.

Lonnie appeared to be out cold after a few sledgehammer punches, but Nathan kept going. Each contact was accompanied by the sound of force against human sludge, followed by flying blood, making me jump backwards when a wad of it smacked the clear wall in my vision! It was all I could do not to burst into tears.

I must have screamed because Doc finally snapped out of his childlike trance, looking up at me with an expression, which I'd never imagined seeing from him—almost of *concern*? That was the *only* thing I took comfort in through all of this. *Maybe he wasn't going to feed me to the winner of this bloody brawl.*

Looking away from the fight, he gathered a vial and a syringe, and began drawing liquid into it. Nathan must have noticed the cheering had stopped. He paused long enough to turn and see Doc armed with the syringe in one hand, and picking up a gun with the other.

In an effort that only a *huge* rush of adrenaline could *possibly* deliver, Nathan shot up, leaving Lonnie's lifeless body behind, and lunged full speed ahead toward the Doc.

"Doc!" I yelled out, "Shoot him!" But he only stood . . . smiling. What happened in the next few moments was a recipe for an eternity of nightmares.

Blue craggily streaks surrounded the arena, with Nathan as the point of contact! Sparks bounced off him—a human roman candle—as he began to smoke from underneath his clothing, until finally, he was burning from the inside out!

The stench in the air could not be contained outside of my walls. I ran to my bathroom and vomited profusely.

After a few minutes of recovery, I peered out of my bath to see Doc clad in gloves and a hazmat helmet, wielding a fire extinguisher as he put out what had been one very racist and angry asshole of a man.

He looked up and paused just long enough to say, "I warned him."

Speechless and horrified, I watched the disintegration of charred flesh cooking and bubbling until completely extinguished.

Once Nathan's remains stopped smoking, Doc shoved them into a bag with a zipper. I couldn't help but wonder . . . *Was Lonnie dead too?* This thought unfroze my tongue.

"Hey Doc, what are you going to do with Lonnie's body?"

He didn't even look up. Instead, he took Lonnie's wrist in one hand and studied the watch on his own. *Taking his pulse?* Next, he slipped into a room, *that I believe houses supplies*—one I had not been allowed to enter—and reappeared a few minutes later wearing hospital scrubs, while wheeling the steel table next to Lonnie's body. He stopped only to pull surgical tools out of the white credenza in the room *meant* to interview other doctors. Something told me *not* to ask questions.

He hoisted Lonnie up and onto the table, cleaning the caked blood off his face, and hooked him up to a few IVs he had readied. Last, he administered a shot of something.

A minute or so later, as Lonnie came to . . . groaning and coughing, Doc lifted his head onto a pillow and gave him a sip of water. I couldn't believe the care he's giving this . . . *killer!* Ignited by anger—*I needed answers.*

"Hey, Doc! I thought this was our guy? You made me pick from your 'bunch', and what? Now you're going to treat him like a patient? Have you forgotten all of the women and babies he's brutalized?"

I thought for sure he would answer my inquiry this time, but instead, he shot me a glare as if to say, "*shut the hell up*"! I can't read the Doc's other looks, but this one was pretty clear, so pushing the matter was not an option.

Lonnie seemed to be well awake, and as refreshed as a man who took a beating like Nathan had given him could possibly be. Doc strapped him to the table at three different points. If Lonnie had been able to move before, he couldn't now.

"Good . . . you're awake. You're probably wondering *why* you're still alive? No need to ask, as I do not appreciate the value of small talk—so I'll get right to it. Your former foe Nathan, decided to charge into the electrical current, and as I had assured, the outcome of this action left him fried from the inside out—a painful and hideous way to die . . . but, his choice.

This *does* leave me in a bit of a quandary, as I was sure that you would no longer be with us as a result of Nathan's rage. He was actually quite close to giving you a brain hemorrhage, which by now would have rendered you lifeless. Because I had *no* use for Nathan alive, I would have ended him quickly and cleanly had he not done himself in. Instead, he's made a colossal mess of my lab *and* Merlot's forever home. Oh, I'm off track . . . small talk. *Huh . . . w*ho knew I could do it? You look as though you have something to say Lonnie."

"*Um* . . . look Doc, whoever you are—you promised that the man who won would get their way with that woman over there, *and* be set free. I don't want anything to do with her. I'll just go instead. Deal?"

"Oh, *Lonnie*. Normally, I am a man of my word, but given all of the lies you so freely spewed, I do not feel bound to keep any of my promises. I *had* hoped you'd be the survivor in order to harvest a few healthy organs for someone more worthy of them. However, with the punishment they've taken from Nathan, well . . . their condition would be questionable *and* unexplainable, so what I have in mind instead is quite interesting, now that your demise has been extended."

I watched and listened to the conversation, taking place between the two of them. Lonnie's eyes were darting back and forth. He was thinking as prey would, scheming about how to escape. It wasn't lost on Doc.

"Trust me, Lonnie. There *is* no escape. Examining the details of what I know to be true, you show emotion only in specific cases. An example is that of your mother's beating, which brought out by Nathan's taunting, revealed it. Though your behavior *is* anti-social, your narcissistic side forces you to garner attention when you do socialize—albeit for a short time—until your victims are tidily out of your life. This brings me to your killings."

"Had I not discovered your mother's stage name, 'Lost Kitty', I would have believed your victims' deaths to be crimes of passion or simply sloppy murders, thereby almost random in nature. However, the forming of 'LK' across America—along with the victims' ages being that of your natural and adopted mothers, *and* fitting the physical description of your birth mother—my diagnosis of you as a sociopath seems, well, incorrect. No sociopath that I have ever come across in my studies has had the discipline of planning, execution, and especially patience, as in your meticulously calculated homicides."

"No, these acts were premeditated, carried out with exactness in order to fulfill one final goal—which smacks of psychopathy. Being that only one percent of humans present with the brain abnormality that assuredly creates a *violent* psychopath, this is still highly unlikely as your diagnosis."

"Now, you surely understand why this is a quandary I *must* solve? And given a brain scan is not possible under these circumstances, there's only one way for me to unravel the mystery."

Holy shit! What was he planning to do . . . to Lonnie? I wanted him dead, only because I didn't want him going free to kill other women and babies. But this was taking a turn I never wanted *anything* to do with. I fear it will haunt me for the rest of my life.

"I have a treat for you, Lonnie. It's a 'block', which will numb the nerves in your scalp. While I couldn't care less what you *feel* during our 'procedure', I need you to lie still so that you do not disrupt your motor skills, as well as other functions as I go cutting into your scalp. You see, jerking your head could be detrimental. I also think you may *enjoy* being able to hear *and understand* what's going on inside your brain as I discover it for myself. Merlot?"

"*Ugh* . . . what?"

"You don't seem to be upset by the sight of blood, which we have established in the most pleasant of circumstances."

292

"What's your point Doc?" *He was actually flirting with me in the middle of this?*

"I will turn Lonnie's table to allow you a better view if you would like. The brain is a fascinating 'computer', *and* it is rare that the average person gets a good look inside. What do you say? Care to view my work?"

My wheels were turning. "Only if it means you'll let me join you out there, so I'm able to observe close up?"

"Oh Merlot, do you really think you'll be able to trick me? Remember the last time you made a run for it and how well that ended?"

"Of course I wouldn't try to run. Besides, you've got that electrical force field thingy . . . I don't want to fry." *I forgot he has a way of reading my thoughts.* I had to be convincing, now that he was on to my intentions—so I sat on the edge of my bed, uncrossed my legs, unzipped my jeans, and put my hand inside. I gave him a moan as I pleasured myself . . . *ah! This had to be real.*

"It's just . . . my performance, from earlier, reminded me we never got to finish, back when you took my blood. I know you have a 'thing' for blood Doc. Maybe you could get some of that blood you drew from me, and use it all over my body—you know, as an aphrodisiac. You've been *so* busy. I'll bet you haven't been 'satisfied' in a *long* time. This could be a reward for the both of us. We should celebrate getting our man, shouldn't we?" *I could see he was in agreement by the bulge forming in the crotch of his surgical pants.*

"Well Merlot, since you put it in those terms, I will allow it. I'll open your door after I get your blood."

When he left, I took the opportunity to spy out the remote he had used for the electric fence. I wasn't sure which button to use to disarm it—if he remembered to turn it on again. He almost caught me staring in its direction when he returned.

"Hey *um* . . . Doc? Merlot? What if . . . if I confess? Would that count for anything? I mean, can't a guy who's dealt with the trauma of his mother's murder get a second chance? I could serve time, if that's what it takes. Of course, I would rather just confess and be on my way but I'll do whatever it takes . . . *please!*"

"Oh, Lonnie. Shallow apologies, *or any at all*, have no bearing. Besides, if not you then someone else would be paying the price—and since you were the winner by choice, *Merlot's choice*, it is you who shall pay. I deplore apologies and your confession means nothing more to me than telling me I was right."

He unlocked my door, and I smiled at him as genuinely as I could manage. "Thanks, Doc." I positioned myself behind Lonnie's head on the table, far enough back to give him room to work. He picked up the remote and engaged the electrical force field—*damn!*

"Put on this surgical gown and helmet with face guard. You're going to need it, as there will be splatter. Would you like to help me shave his head?"

I looked at the floor, doing my best not to cry.

"Okay, have it your way."

"What exactly are you looking for Doc? I assume you're going to look inside his head?"

"Yes. You see, if Lonnie *is* a psychopath, there will be less grey matter in the ventromedial prefrontal cortex, which is a marker distinguishing the psychopath from the sociopath. In order to fully confirm it, there will be lack of the connections from this area of the brain to the amygdala."

"I didn't understand any of that, but does it mean that he's a 'psycho' if he's missing some of the um, grey matter, and there's nothing connecting it to the 'amy' thing?"

"Amygdala—and yes, but 'psycho', as it is commonly used to refer to eminent violence, is not necessarily the outcome of a psychopath. They're not all violent. What it *does* mean is that this area of his brain, responsible for sentiments of empathy, guilt, and even embarrassment, are not present. You see, Merlot, the amygdala processes emotions like fear and anxiety. Without the connection,

295

there is no fear, and thus no concern for his actions or their consequences. Combined with what he's gone through in his formative years, the recipe for violence is highly present."

"What if he doesn't have missing grey matter? Does that mean he *can't be* a psychopath?"

"There is also the possibility of physical damage to that part of his brain by blunt force trauma, which would mean he wasn't born a psychopath, but is at a loss for empathy and guilt by way of the damage. This *could* create a sociopath, especially when mixed with the traumatic experience Nathan brought to his childhood."

"Um . . . *hello*! You are both talking as if I don't exist. I'm right here, and I'm no nut job! I'm guessing by now, you're a brain surgeon? Or at least, I hope so? Be careful with my head. Do not mess me up forever, please, *you God-complex asshole*! Just get it over with and put me back together in one piece!"

"You see, Merlot? He has little, if any, concept of consequence following his actions and no real fear is present, despite his begging. No tears, trembling, sweating, or any other bodily reactions to something so terrifying as this—all physiological reactions, which I enjoy *so* much in a normal human."

"I do see what you're saying! If I were in his shoes, I would've soiled myself by now or at the very least, be blubbering like a baby."

"Yes Merlot, a normal response."

Doc tapped on Lonnie's skull with a small surgical hammer. He didn't blink. "Okay, we are ready to begin. I'm marking his skull in the frontal lobe region first. Next, using a surgical blade, I'll cut away the skin. His nerves are blocked, so he remains nice and still. After peeling back the scalp, I'll use my surgical saw to make a clean cut."

Ugh! Blood was spurting everywhere! Doc was as cool as a cucumber and looked as if he was having the time of his life. I just couldn't believe he was doing this, and I really couldn't believe I was watching it *so closely*. I had to remember the real reason I was there with him and not in my bedroom *cage*. I had to hold it together—*ugh*, even though the bone sawing was smoking and making me woozy. *Do-not-pass-out Merlot!*

"I'm lifting the square of his skull now. Do you know what you *are*, or rather *aren't*, seeing here?"

"What? What do you see, Doc?"

"Shut up, Lonnie. I am speaking to Merlot."

"I—I don't know? Is there something missing or damaged? I've never looked at this before."

"No, there is nothing missing or damaged. His frontal lobe shows no abnormality or trauma. All is perfectly typical with this area of Lonnie's brain."

"Yes! I told you. I'm not nuts!"

"Lonnie, you obviously have a lack of consequential cognition; therefore, I would warn you to keep your mouth shut, as it fails you at every turn."

"So, what does this mean? That he's *not* a psychopath?"

"He could merely be lacking activity here and *that,* without a real scan, we cannot detect. There is only one last thing to do. We will see if there are normal connections to the amygdala. Pull your mask back down."

Doc shaved the side of Lonnie's head and gave him another numbing shot, but he didn't give it enough time to kick in. Lonnie yelled out in pain, and I couldn't help but to squint and grimace as the blood splattered my facemask. I tried not to watch the gruesome act so emphatically this go-around. *Instead, I was thinking about how I could get that remote.* It was in Doc's pocket. There was no way to snatch it, especially with him holding sharp instruments. I wouldn't be able to retrieve it just yet.

With a more determined look on his face, rather than the one of a boy catching a frog, like during the first cut—he pulled the skull piece off and began prying Lonnie's brain apart, where there appeared to be a natural crack. I could hardly bear the screaming, and my stomach was flopping. I swallowed repetitively so I wouldn't throw up, until I couldn't stand it any longer!

"Doc! What are you looking for?"

Finally, he straightened up and let go of Lonnie's brain—who appeared to have passed out. "Unbelievable! It's missing."

"What's missing?"

"The amygdala. Do you know what this means?"

"*Um* . . . no."

"People *can* live without them. In severe cases of epilepsy, where medications have not worked, surgeons have removed them, but it appears as though Lonnie was born *without* one. I have no answer as to what effect this may have had on him, combined with his childhood trauma. There are no studies of this that I am aware of. It *does mean* that he has a complete absence of fear, thus his begging episodes have *purely* been negotiations! "

"So does that mean you'll spare him?"

"Of course not. But that was never the plan. It does complicate *how* I will completely end him. I was to enjoy a merciless death, had there been an attachment to a normal prefrontal cortex."

"I've had enough, Doc. Dead is dead—why so many rules? Shouldn't you just put him out of his misery at this point?"

"Merlot, you do not understand 'justness', or this example would not be lost on you. We will work on that—soon."

He was freaking me out, but I had to keep my wits. "I was the one who chose him Doc, so no 'justness' is lost on me. Just end it, please!"

"*Hmm* . . . he *has* gotten his beating and I've gotten some answers about his physiology. I suppose there's no use in dragging it out any further—besides, we've got our reward to attend to." He held up the bag of blood—*my blood*. I wanted to take it and run, but I wouldn't get far.

He took off his rubber gloves and jammed them into Lonnie's throat, gripping his nostrils tightly until there was no sign of life.

Doc must have read the uncontrollably distraught expression on my face. He escorted me back to my room and took off my bloody garments, as I stood there—a zombie.

"Some time in a bath to relax and unwind before we celebrate as I clean up the space will help you release any trauma you may be 'feeling'. I, on the other hand, have had a *stupendous* day. It isn't often one enjoys an accomplishment

300

of this proportion, not to mention finding a true medical rarity. If I haven't already said it . . . *thank you,* Merlot, for choosing Lonnie."

SPELLBOUND

I've replayed the whole scene while taking a bubble bath, but I have to stop. I need to get him off guard in order to make an attempt at escape. The act I perform next must be convincing. Letting it go in the tub has its benefits.

To get in the mood for Doc, I play with myself under the water. It takes some time to become *barely* effective. The bubbles are a good hiding place for my hand. I'm sure to stop before I orgasm. I must remain "hungry".

There's sensual music playing. *Oh*, if only he weren't, well, *whatever* he is, he would be perfect—but he is *and* he's dangerous. In the heat of our encounters, I seem to forget this fact, but now, discipline is paramount. I must keep my main goal as my first priority, but I cannot allow him to sense it—which means . . . I *do* have to let my guard down, *ugh!* He'll suspect foul play otherwise. His sensory abilities are unexplainable. It's as if he reaches into my thoughts and pulls out my intentions. I must subside my desire to escape, *for now . . .*

After drying off, I enter the bedroom wearing only my towel. Doc has lit candles in the newly sparkling arena. The cave walls of the other rooms are down, with greenery and little white lights twinkling everywhere. I haven't seen it this magical looking since I first arrived.

Doc appears out of a dark shadow in the arena, and I let my towel drop to the floor. It was an involuntary reaction . . . *not one I had planned.* I've dropped my guard along with the towel . . . *good*—I guess. I hadn't realized he was there, watching my reaction to his pre-game seduction. *Use measured control Merlot.*

"You're looking lovely. I see the exercises and new diet are paying off."

"So you don't think I'm too . . . *skinny?*"

"Do not question me. I rarely give compliments, for they are almost never warranted. Come out of your bedroom. I have the treat we talked about."

The door pushes open easily, and it appears I have free reign in the cave. I can't help but gaze, starry-eyed at my surroundings, like a naked prisoner who's been set free. "It is lovely Doc. Amazing what you've done in here. Really."

"You're right. It is amazing. If only you knew the trouble I've gone to make this place special . . . for you. It's good to see you appreciate it, for once."

"Oh, I do. Can I . . . touch you?"

"No, not yet. It's my turn to disrobe. Stay where you are." For once, I'm going to give Merlot a show I know *she'll* enjoy.

I slide my black linen shirt off, and next my trousers. Merlot's eyes rest on my half erection.

"Now we are both naked, but there's something I need. I haven't had it as *fully* as I'm going to have it with you." I present her blood. I've put it in a wine glass. Merlot's thoughts scream loud and clear to me.

My blood! Is he going to drink it?

"The look on your face reveals your question. You must know by now that I not only know what you're thinking by your scent, but also by your expression. I do not intend to drink your blood. I'm not a vampire. I enjoy the blood of a sexual partner, but only in a consensual way, during acts of lascivious nature. Your idea of this 'celebration' makes it far more tantalizing than if I had asked, as before. You've awakened the carnal monster inside me Merlot, and now I've uncaged you . . . my *prey*."

Oh! I can't keep it together! I want him more than I want to escape right now. I know my expression is giving

304

me away. I stand quietly, with no particular pose, just . . . *waiting*.

"That's better. Now spread your legs."

I go to my knees and put my nose in her sweet spot. Drawing in a deep breath. I taste her slowly while gently stroking her buttocks along its crevice with my fingertips. Her pulse is throbbing on my tongue. She can't hide this response. She's longing for a deeper dive.

"*Oh!*"

"Oh *what*, Merlot?"

"*Oh, please*, Doc! I'm so, so ready . . ."

A beautiful stream, like a drizzle from a faucet, weeps from her.

"That is a *true* talent, Merlot. It will make for a nice cocktail." I place the wine glass in its path, forming the new elixir until the glass is full to its brim. I stand, and tell her to keep her legs spread.

"Are you going to pour that on me Doc?" I don't know if I'm going to like this or be freaked out by it, but I'm under his spell. I find myself searching his face for any feelings at all. I know I shouldn't care—escape should be all that I care about when this is over. I'm so conflicted!

"Lie down on the floor, Merlot."

Reluctantly, I do as he says. The raging heat inside me welcomes the coolness of the smooth floor and I ready myself, not knowing *what* to expect. I relinquish my trepidations and give in to his game. No more double-talk inside my head—*the lusting animal inside takes me over.*

Standing over her, I pour the mixture from the glass, creating my work of art—from the nape of her neck, down between her beasts, and filling her naval cavity. It cascades down her inner thighs, transforming into a deep crimson against her smooth brown skin. I kneel and straddle her body, as I trace my fingers through it, swirling, as I pour more over each breast at the nipple.

"What do you think of my art piece, Merlot?"

"It is sort of pretty . . . on me."

"It's more than *pretty*!" While admiring my work, I slide into her, just once. She cries out from a guttural place of deep satisfaction. I pull out of her slowly and stand again.

"Get up, Merlot. Go to your room!" She does exactly as I say. "Get on the bed, on all fours."

I know she likes this position. I want to make her buttocks red and I don't want her to see me climax. Women tend to fall in love during face-to-face sex. I'm unequipped to reciprocate, *and* I have more work to do with her, before I decide *what* to do with her . . . in the end.

She looks back at me. "You're going to spill blood on my bed? Won't it stain?"

"Don't worry about the mattress. There's a layer over it that no liquid can penetrate. I'll burn the sheets later. I have new ones for you. Now stop breaking our pleasure with your worries!" I smack her ass on both sides, *hard*.

"Ouch!"

"That's your punishment. Now here comes your reward. I tease her erogenous zones, making her beg for it once more—*and she does*.

"*Please Doc, please!*"

I drizzle a small stream of my "Merlot cocktail", from the sloping curve of her back all the way just past her tailbone. Tantalizing me as it ventures further, all the way down to its calla lily-like destination—pooling around her sweet spot, and then drip-drip-drips onto the sheet.

Oh . . . what an invitation!

The rest I pour across her shoulders, and over her ass loaves—*red mounds of beauty!* Sliding inside her again, I discover a greedily insatiable pull—she's pleading me, "Oh Doc, don't stop!" I grip a handful of her hair as we thrust our bodies in equal and opposite motions . . . until we've wrung out every drop of pleasure within us.

"Oh Doc . . . *yes!*"

"Yeah, I'm right there with you."

RUN

Several minutes pass as I lay here waiting, waiting for him to get up—and *go clean up*. This could be my opportunity to escape. His eyes are closing shut . . . now open—repetitively, as though he's going to take a nap, but I'm not falling for that.

My bed is a bloody mess, and we're just lying here in it, *ick*! He probably enjoys it—no wonder he's not jumping up to go clean himself off. I would do almost anything to spring out of bed and bathe, but as soon as I do, he'd lock me in nice and tight—*I just know it*. Now that I'm fulfilled like a bulimic after Thanksgiving dinner, I'm thinking more clearly. *I must mask my thoughts and reactions somehow.*

Rolling onto my side facing away from him, I let out a satisfied sigh—followed by a yawn. Yes, that should throw him off my thoughts. I'll bet he's wondering when he'll be able to indulge in this "blood play" again. *Snap out of it,*

Merlot! What he's thinking is only important if it's about locking you in at any moment.

Now that he can't see my face, I look around within my peripheral. *What garment can I throw on quickly?* I spot his black button-down shirt outside the room on the floor. *Perfect.* I've got a pair of slip-on flats under the edge of my desk—without much tread, but at least I could run in them. The front door appears to have an electronic handle. *He must operate it from an app.* There's also a small screen with letters and numbers for a manual code. *Hmm*, I need to think like him in order to decode it . . . *he's stirring!*

My heart is pounding, and I'm certain he'll detect it. Deep quiet breaths Merlot—g*et u Doc . . . get up and go to the bathroom!*

"*Hmm* . . . I see someone is a deeply satisfied, sleepy girl." His voice has a boastful tone—he, a successful hunter, who's seduced and, by appearances, slain his conquest. Lying in my blood may scramble his perceptions and save me in this moment.

Seconds later, as he draws in a deep audible breath—I sense him at the foot of my bed, staring at me. My eyes *appear* closed, and are only opened enough to see his ominous shadow through my lashes. Thankfully, they are long and thick, so that he's not able to see the slits of my eyes.

His image is replaced by purple silk, as I feel a waft of air settle over my body . . . a cool cloud. The bed sheet hovers above me, falling first at my feet and shoulders, and last, settling like a bubble bursting in slow motion over my torso—finally covering my face.

He's whistling again . . . *what is that tune? It's lovely.*

"Do you recognize it, Merlot? I told you, I am able to read your thoughts. You don't have to answer. I'll tell you anyway. Your generation wouldn't appreciate a violin piece. It's called *The Song of the Caged Bird.*"

He thinks his irony is clever and probably lost on me, but I'm quicker than he thinks. I still pretend to be asleep. He's not buying it—*so far.* I snuggle deep into my pillow and curl up in the fetal position. What else can I do aside from a fake snoring? *Go to the bathroom!* "Okay, sleeping beauty. You're obviously too *drained* for conversation."

Yes, finally! I hear his nearly silent footsteps as he ventures toward the bath. *Turn on the water Doc . . . make some noise.*

"You know Merlot, now that we've taken care of your first 'worthy' target—well, excuse me, *two* worthy targets—it's time for an intermission."

"Intermission you say Doc?"

"Why yes, Merlot—*intermission,* where we work on *why* you were brought here to begin with. The ending of

310

Lonnie was a lesson in 'justice' for you—of the most severe nature albeit—but nonetheless, a fine example of perfect 'justness'. Lonnie got a heavy dose of what he's exacted upon his battered and slain victims, and in the process was given the opportunity to exact *his* vengeance on the very monster who'd created him. Now *that* is poetic justice, wouldn't you agree? Oh, still playing possum, are we? Fine." I assume the carnal encounter she's fully enjoyed contradicts with her lack of freedom—*a confusing angst I've caused . . . delicious!* I will leave her to her quandary for now.

At last, the water is running! Now that Doc's "pontification" is over, I dare to sneak a look. He's by my tub, running water—and it's loud. I reach over and inch his pillow along the bed, trudging it through the battleground of the concoction he'd exhumed from me—and continue its journey underneath the sheet. Tiny suction points from my skin to the silk that I lie on, break free of the caking that's begun to set up, as I roll over his pillows cleaner top, leaving my bloody DNA stamp behind. A tinge of relief, barring a bath, lasts for a second until I plop back down into more of the crimson sticky well he'd poured—now pooled in the middle of the bed.

I place his pillow where my shoulder should be, at the base of my head's pillow. After pulling the sheet over that pillow too, and scrunching it into a tight ball—it now

311

mimics my head. This is a shallow disguise no doubt, but I only need seconds to get away.

It's time to go Merlot. You may not get this chance again!

If not for the force of the water against the cast iron tub, I'm sure he would hear my heart's thumping beat. I'm close to my shoes, but rather than risking any noise against the floor by putting them on, I make a grab for them *and* the shirt in my bare feet.

Surging adrenaline hurdles me through space like a gazelle, *shoes and shirt in hand*. I glance over my shoulder, fully expecting to find the Doc ready to punish me—but he is nowhere in sight. The water is still roaring against the tub. *I can't believe my luck so far!*

At the front door, I slip on my shoes and tie the arms of the shirt around my waist. Still naked and coated in my own blood, I punch in a code. B-L-O-O-D. *Failure.*

Ugh! I just knew it would work. Think, Merlot! What describes him? Hmm ...

C-O-N-T-R-O-L.

No! If not his fetish, or his personality, then what does he value? Yes! I'll try that ...

J-U-S-T-I-C-E.

Click! The door lock's sweet surrender, and I'm able to push it open! *Yet, why are my senses so eerily heightened?* I pause for the longest few seconds in history . . . *the water is*

312

still thundering from my bathroom—there's nothing to do now but run.

Though it *will* make a thud, my instincts tell me to make a dramatic exit. *There's no time for second-guessing.* Stepping back into a squat, using the full weight of my body, I throw my shoulder against the door in one hard jumping motion.

"Humph!" It's the Doc's voice! His weight on the other side of the door has thrown me off balance—but my wild force has sent him to the ground backwards! I catch myself on one knee and quickly recover. I'm up and into a full sprint!

He was waiting for me—just as I had sensed, *but how*? There's no time to think, only run. It's pitch-black and this doesn't feel like the path I remember from when we were filming the intro to the *'supposed* series' he used to entrap me.

The ground is uneven, and the slaps of tall weeds are stinging my legs . . . *faster, Merlot!* My breath is shallow and sharp in my throat, but my adrenaline carries me like a razor cutting the wind.

I hear thunderous footsteps—attached to a body of steel—and they're closing in on me! Bloody and desperate, my solitary focus is autonomous freedom. There is no other acceptable outcome to this race—only win . . . or *I lose!*

CHOICES

"Merlot! Look out—the cliff!"

I don't look back, but I hear *honesty* in his voice. It's too late. I am in full flight. As my arms spin, in what feels like slow motion, something lands against my right palm.

Instinctually, I close my grip around it, a thick root—grown out over the cliff's edge. Hanging on with every ounce of strength I possess, my body is in free fall, as it crashes against the rocky cliffside!

"Hang on, Merlot! I'm bracing my feet under the tree's roots anchored in the cliff you went over. You're grasping near the end of the same tree's root growing out of the hill! They're extremely strong . . . do *not* let go!"

"Yes, but it's also smooth! I don't think I'll be able to hold on much longer!" My feet are kicking wildly as though I'm riding an invisible bike, attempting to find a solid surface on which to land.

As my swing slows, I'm alerted by the intense decibels of rushing water below. My body's weight is too great a burden for my grip, but I dig deep, finding determination greater than my pain—*for now*.

"That's it, Merlot! Steady your swing. I'm reaching for you. Do you see my hand? It's only inches away from yours."

"I see you hanging over the cliff! Do you want to fall too? Get back Doc!"

"I'm secure enough in the roots of this giant tree for both our weights! Now . . . there's a slight protrusion on the side of the cliff. You'll have to swing toward it, in a controlled motion. Once you've made good contact with it, push off in a leaping motion. At the top of your jump, reach out for my hand and let go of the root. There are only inches between us. I will pull you up from there!"

"I . . . I don't know!" I'm looking down—it's so dark, but I think I see a cliff wide enough to land on, about ten or twelve feet below. From there, I may be able to get down the steady but steep slope, and escape.

"Don't even consider it, Merlot. Even if you land without breaking or spraining anything, the hillside is rough terrain, and you'll end up in the frigid water below. You're naked for God's sake! Hypothermia is inevitable in the river. You'll have little time to get to warmth—warmth that I can provide!"

"What if I don't end up in the water? You think you're the only alternative? I've been in a cage of sorts before, and I think I'd rather take my chances! Nothing is worth being your caged bird!"

"Even if you *don't* end up in the water Merlot, you're coated in blood. You're a mark for a bear *or* any carnivorous animal in these woods. You only outran *me* by a step or two *with* a lead—and I'm barefoot. Come on, Merlot! You're no match for a hungry predator!"

My fingers are beginning to slide on the fat root—I have a decision to make. Take my chances against nature's odds . . . *or* be a caged bird, with "who knows what" penance to pay.

In a flash of memory, I think back to my real past, before "Merlot" existed. It's been so long, but I have the same resolve within me as back then. Doc thinks I will unveil his secrets . . . jeopardize his world. Little does he know, my own "world" is in jeopardy—a world outside of "Merlot", *which must remain buried*. I have come *so* far, but I won't risk its discovery—and I cannot live within the confines of a cage!

"No, Merlot! You foolish child!"

I risk life and limb. I do push off, *hard*, but instead of dropping to the cliff two body lengths below—I let go at the peak of my swing, and risk the depths of the chilling water that lies below.

ABRUPT PIVOT

"Merlot . . . Merlot!"

I didn't hear her land, not even a splash. *I must find her.* She knows everything—well, *most* everything—about me, and the *justice* of late I have exacted. She has played a role in it as well, but no jury would convict her, a captive, as an accessory. *I'm not going to give in to these asinine thoughts of fear!* I will find her, and when I do, she *will* pay.

The cliff is too steep to scale in the darkness. I decide to follow the path of the flowing water below. When I first explored this place at summer's beginning, it was a stream—but with heavy rains, it has become quite a waterway. She won't last in it for long, which means I should find her shivering on its banks somewhere—*if* she's still alive by then.

The trees along the cliff are getting thicker, the terrain rougher, as I move along its edge. Before long, the cliffs stretch out past the shoreline, making it impossible to see anything but water below. If she *did* survive, she could remain in hiding on a small stretch of land out of sight, but not long before she is forced out from the cold, or caught by bears hunting for fish.

More likely than any scenario, she will be washed over the waterfall not too far away, crash onto rocks hiding in shallow waters at its base, killing her or breaking her bones too badly to swim any farther. The fall there is roaring with force and speed. Her broken body will get sucked under its current and washed away, for miles before being discovered.

After searching until almost dawn, I'm confident that Merlot has been transported by nature—a naked drowning victim to be mysteriously washed up—whom a kayaker, or an adventurous hiker will eventually discover.

What a waste of my perfect intent, my hours of planning and execution. I *am furious* with myself for the miscalculation of her prowess. Her longing, moaning, and screams of sexual satisfaction were *so real*, yet she still ran at the first opportunity. It wasn't as if I believed she wouldn't try at some point—but I never conceived that she would get past me at the door. Her instincts were my *true* miscalculation.

Now I will need a new "Captain". However, knowing for certain that Merlot is dead *is paramount* before taking on this endeavor again. I couldn't risk her outing me. I will lie low, once again abstaining from my *justice-inflicting* activities, until I am certain of her demise.

It does occur to me that she hasn't my real name, *and* that she was blindfolded on the trip to her lovely new home. Getting here again may prove next to impossible, *if* she happens to survive. Likewise, if she were to attempt to unveil me to the authorities—she'd risk being thought of as a lunatic.

Talk about losing her Petunias—this would surely do it. Even *they* couldn't follow a drama queen of that epic a proportion—an obvious attention-seeking liar. No, I don't think she would take the risk. She loves her "fame" too much. After exposing her to them for her manipulating ways a few days ago online, she's sure to be hanging by a *virtual* thread, as well as being discredited for at least one of her 'go-to' statuses.

Soon the sun will rise and the long night of pleasure, angst, and searching will finally be over. Having gathered the remnants of Lonnie and Nathan, before the delicious blood play with Merlot, I have little to accomplish upon my arrival back to the cave. Soon, it will be time to depart my sanctuary, for probably some time to come.

I clean up the beautiful trail of Merlot's blood from the arena into her bedroom, collect the sheets for burning, and remove the plastic from an otherwise pristine mattress. I've bathed and sanitized the tub in such a way that no forensic master could possibly detect an inkling of blood splatter.

Now, what to do with what remains of Nathan and Lonnie? I'd not been able to bear the thought of giving Derick away. He's made such a nice stone. Two hundred and fifty pounds with heavy bones, specially crushed into an Asscher cut diamond, which fitting with Derick's blockheaded intelligence, has served as the piece *de' la resistance* to our truth game. It makes me smile to pull him out of my pocket and reminisce.

Perhaps a body *is* a horrible thing to waste when I am able to reflect fondly on the special thing I've done for the world by removing it—instead transforming it into something that is a nearly flawless part of nature.

Yes, a collection of these would be quite nice. I will choose a different cut of stone for each, so that I recognize each one of them later—pay a tribute to our special "time" together.

Nathan, I will transform into a Princess cut stone. Just the thought of knowing I've turned this racist S.O.B. into a "Princess" is going to give me a chuckle when I most need an escape from the mundane. It isn't often I laugh, and honestly, watching the brute turn pretty boy Lonnie into a pulverized pansy was quite enjoyable. Had he not gotten caught up in his terrible rage of jealousy so many years ago—*such a strange human trait*—he would never have had to become a Princess now . . . *yes, this cut is right for Nathan.*

Lonnie, well . . . pretty boy or not, this is a complex stone I will pay homage to—though he will *not* make me smile. He has wrecked a code, one he should have figured out long ago. One, which all psychologically challenged individuals, has a duty to control and shape into a useful life—*as have I.*

I've got it! The emerald cut diamond will become Lonnie's new identity. Its halls of mirrors, of both light and darkness, create a mystical beauty. These "mirrors" are a simple metaphor, which he could not see himself introspectively in—the potential mirrors of "light" he squandered. Instead, he capitalized on his reflection of darkness. This stone's cut is terribly unforgiving of flaws— and whatever flaws happen to appear in my precious stone, once condensed, will serve to remind me of his.

Good-bye sweet sanctuary . . . *for now.* I will tie up loose ends and pause long enough to see no repercussions arise. I will not, however, deny myself of this life that I've *earned* forever.

In the doorway, prepared to tear myself away, there is a pull at my insides. I know it's time to depart and re-group, yet something feels, *undone* . . . except, I do not *feel.*

No—*this* is an intuition.

The cave walls are down. I've undressed the lights and tulle, *touches added to lure Merlot.* To any onlooker who could unlikely discover it, it's a cave of moss and ivy. I've even thrown rock and dirt onto the main floor, a gut-wrenching assault to my cleanliness, and a task to clean later.

I check the chamber of truth where Derick awaited his S & M Mistress and Nathan had been captive—nothing, not even a detergent odor. One by one, I re-check each room, and lower its green wall again.

Only the storage room is left. There's no sign of food or drink in the refrigerator, which I will remove soon if my return takes longer than expected. I've cleared out my surgeons' supplies. No hazmat suit, not even my five-gallon pail used to harness a hornet's nest, and wash Nathan with—twice. *What then?*

The pang in my gut isn't leaving me.

I open the freezer one more time, and there it is—a crack along one side of the back panel, slightly ajar and larger than the seam on the other side by about an eighth of an inch. I take a screwdriver out of my tools and pry it apart.

I'd hidden half a bag of Merlot's blood! The one I had greedily started that rendered her out cold. The sweet, savory-scent of her beckons me now. I recall the video that

323

finally won her the spot as my Captain—the one about her "rare blood". *We shall see about that.* I will thaw a small chunk and put it to the test soon. The rest will stay frozen, for posterity's sake, and can remain so for up to ten years. Re-freezing it is not an option—if it is to stay useful.

Though I shouldn't care at this point, I would like to know if her instincts, *which I'd underestimated*, were validly 'special'—or if she merely took me by surprise of my own miscalculation. I admit that this exercise is mired in ego and probably nothing more, but I *must* know.

I'd backed the van down to the cave's entrance, in case I couldn't beat the sunrise. With all of my sanctuary's accouterments loaded and everything locked, its door blends seamlessly, once again into the hillside. I place heavy vines I've released from above, over it for safe measure. Their variety is akin to that of the brain-occupied end of a worm, which regenerates with a cut—instead of dying.

A dense fog has rolled into the forest, compelling me to use my headlights. Beseeching the heavy blanket to illuminate the air—dawn has arrived, if only to a slight glow. As I round the top of the trail, a continuous flashing of light through the gray, alerts me to caution. *Hmm . . .* what is that off to the right? *I'm heading left.*

It looks like some jackass took the curve in the road for granted, *in this fog?* Both the cars headlights *and* hazards are on, which means he or she probably hasn't passed out completely.

The physician in me says to check on the car's occupants, or at least call for help—but the psychopath doesn't give a damn. *I'm going to listen to him.* Besides, this is not an event I want on anyone's radar *if* there were ever to be an investigation. *I'm going left.*

Just as I begin to step on the gas, a siren sounds in the distance. *Damn!* Turning my headlights off, I back behind the brush I'd hidden my bike in countless times, crunching more overgrowth under the truck's tires than I'd have preferred.

The emergency vehicle arrives at the scene, and though I should wait it out, this could take a while. The fog won't hold out much longer, and no one has exited the ambulance yet. Its occupants are most likely gathering things they'll need approaching the scene, which means they're not looking in my direction. *Time to go.*

The rev of the old beast's engine would grab their attention, so I pull out onto the pavement with my headlights off as I gently accelerate out of sight. I've got to get to the warehouse, hide the van, and cycle home as expediently as possible.

My cadence of pedaling, an unconscious act as I ride— plays backup to the chorus of conscious "what ifs" I need to flush out. How did she get past me? Did she survive? If so, where is she now? And will she attempt to reveal my Sanctuary—my deeds? *No! I will not give in to this trepidation!* Shake it off Abe. All will work out.

As I approach my neighborhood, the sun has just begun to shine through—which I find *no* comfort in. Waving, as he opens the automatic gate, the guard acts as if he thinks himself a friend to all the "rich people" he keeps safe. *I might end myself if I had to stay in that little box for eight hours every day.*

Once again, the clouds roll together, snuffing out streams of light, as my front tire hits the drive's curb, leading down to our estate. The abrupt jolt clanks my jaw shut—and it occurs to me that I haven't slept for over twenty-four hours. *You've got a long day ahead, Abel . . . wake up!*

I slip my bike into the empty spot, in the rack of four others I've collected. Celeste last saw me taking a cab to the airport a few days ago. *She'd never notice if one bike were missing. Hell, I'm not sure she knows how many I have.*

She *does know* I don't want to be bothered on business trips—and that *I despise* phone conversations—says it's like calling to converse with herself, so she's given up on the effort. I've left it off on the trips retrieving my prey—

ensuring it wouldn't ring with a random call at the wrong moment.

The last few days' events are in my rear-view mirror. Lack of sleep and layers of sweat are the only detriments weighing on my fortitude, as I approach the front door. *Huh?* The house is completely lit up. That's odd for this time of morning.

TYING UP LOOSE ENDS

"Abel! Finally! Where have you been? You were supposed to be back a day ago."

She cares? I'm surprised she noticed.

"The trip ran a little long, Celeste. Calm yourself. It wouldn't be the first time."

"Well, it *is* the first time we're set to take a big vacation *and* you're not here . . . with barely more than an hour before our flight leaves!"

"Vacation? What are you talking about?"

"Abel Dorian Rhodes. Are you *serious* right now? Our trip with Priya to India! She planned it months ago. Didn't you put it on your calendar? It is *really* important to her!"

"Oh . . . yeah. Sorry, Celeste. I just can't make it this time. Aren't you going with Priya's little friend and her family anyway? They're from India, right? They should know their way around. Work is just *too* intense right now. If you'd like, I'll break it to Priya."

"No worries, Dad . . ."

"Oh, Priya honey, we didn't see you standing there. Are you okay?"

"Yes mother. Dad's work *is* more important than this trip. And he's correct—the Guptas know the area, even though they grew up in California, *Dad.* They go to India to visit their parents. It is Bhanu's first trip though."

"Well, sweetie, I guess if it doesn't bother you, we will make it a mommy-daughter trip with the Guptas. Abel, get her suitcase please, and bring it to the foyer. The driver will be here any minute. I still can't believe you didn't answer my calls or texts—you're not out of the woods with me yet, Mr. Rhodes!"

Though she waxes dramatic, there is no accelerated heartbeat, dilated pupils, or even a change of expression. No, I think she likes the idea of their trip without me. Better this way—I deplored India the first time, and I have other pressing things to attend to.

Priya's demure manner on the other hand, though true of her nature, may be worth analyzing. I do appreciate how little trouble she's been in my life, but something is definitely off. I sense it through her little stone-like exterior. I follow her up to her bedroom where I confront her.

"Priya, now that it's just you and me, is there something you want to tell your dad about? Something perhaps, you can't trust anyone else with?"

"*Why* would I want to do anything of the sort father? You have made it clear what our arrangement is. I am good with it. I appreciate your support, and if I truly need to confide in someone, I will think of you first. Is that all?"

Stupendous. She's realistic, displays gratitude, and dismisses me all at the same time in the most diplomatic of ways. Maybe she *is* learning something from her dad. *If only this had the heartwarming effect it should have.*

"That is all, Priya. Have a good time and be safe."

Awkwardly, I kiss the top of her head and roll her luggage downstairs and into the foyer. Celeste is waiting with two large suitcases and a smaller one at the front door.

"How long are you ladies gone for again?"

"As if you remember being told. We will be back in two weeks. Now give me a kiss and get showered so you can head back to work. You smell as if you've been running in the woods."

"That's funny, Celeste. I'll see you ladies in two weeks. Have fun!"

I do have a long surgery in a few hours and rounds to complete first, so Celeste was right. After cleaning up, I grab a fruit cup on the way out the door.

Five hours later, when most are headed home from a long day of work, I have *other* business to attend to. Merlot's tracks need to be erased. She had a large online presence, but thankfully a very private real life.

On my way out of the hospital, it hits me that a slide of Merlot's blood, packed in a small cooler with dry ice—which I had planned to test once the coast was clear in the lab, is still in my office. I'm circling back.

After I take care of Merlot's apartment, I'll bring the boys, Lonnie and Nathan, to the incinerator where I'll enjoy a *very* late-night fire. They're currently in the storage shed.

If even one overly eager lab rat decides to put in some overtime tomorrow, time of death for my future diamonds would be over twenty-four hours. Though the bodies will keep for a few days, I prefer the ashes be as pure as possible. I haven't studied the effects that further natural erosion would have on any of my trophies. Nathan is half charred as it is—so I'll not risk more flaws over going without rest for one more night. Merlot's blood can be tested while the guys are cooking.

It had been just a month with my caged bird—now flown away, only to hit her "windshield" of sorts. And with all of the work it took to the point when I lured her into her new cage . . . *it's over now Abel*—let it go! I despise regrets. There is nothing that can be done about the last thirty-six hours. I would change nothing up to the point of her escape anyhow. *I must look forward.*

Arriving to her apartment at dusk—so meticulously have I handled her affairs that no one would ever guess she's been gone. My disguise is weak—a pair of sunglasses, but as always, I take the stairs to avoid any elevator conversations.

It's been a few days since emptying her mailbox, but I decide it's better to leave dated advertisements on her countertop to skew the real time of her departure—in case an investigation were ever to take place.

What to do with the bulky furniture? A girl skipping out on rent wouldn't move it, so neither shall I—not to mention doing so would be quite conspicuous.

Though I'd gone through her desk before, once more wouldn't hurt. She doesn't appear to have a car—so no car payment or insurance. I had taken a photo of her checkbook, which, is nowhere to be found. I didn't insert funds into its account for her bills, given it has *only* been a month. Luckily, I hadn't had time to tend to it in the last few days. Had I done so, it may have raised suspicion. Given her lack of organization, she'd probably lost it since the first time I was here.

After cleaning out personal effects, I stand back and look for anything I've missed. I hadn't noticed before, but there are no photos of any kind . . . *anywhere*. This seems odd for such a gregarious type as she.

As for her clothes I had not taken to the cave, *if left behind*, could raise an eyebrow. Women treasure their wardrobes, *also known as their identities*. I would throw them in the trash, but they might actually be harder to track if I donate them. I wouldn't put it past the cops to go dumpster diving for remains if anyone were to go looking for her anytime soon.

On my last trip of packing my SUV with bags and boxes, nearing the bottom of the stairs, it occurs to me that I hadn't come across the silk-braided ropes she'd tied me up with . . . *hmm?*

I didn't notice them when I cleaned out her drawers, or in the leftover clothes in the closet. She must have gotten rid of them before my introduction to the cave—however, she did tie me up with them on *that same day*. I must have thrown them in with the other clothes and mistaken them for girly paraphernalia, perhaps lingerie? *Oh well.*

"Hey man, moving in or out?"

"Huh?" *Shit! I've been noticed.*

"I mean, I take the stairs to stay fit too, but that's some serious dedication lugging that heavy looking box along. Can I help you with it?" A tall young man, tall enough to look me

333

in the eyes—which are now exposed, given the sun set over an hour ago—has confronted me.

I have to stay cool.

"No, neither. Just taking some things my sister is donating off her hands to a charity."

Why did I say that!

"Oh, cool man. I'm Bryce, if you ever want to work out some time, or go biking. You look like you could keep up."

His hand is stuck out for me to shake. I just nod and look at my hands around the box as if to say, "My hands are full . . . *man.*"

"Oh, cool, cool. I get it. Let me get out of your way. What did you say your name was?"

"Javier. See ya Bryce."

He pushes the door open for me, and smiles as I make my *nearly* clean escape.

ACKNOWLEDGMENTS

Anonymity was born out of the question, "What would happen if a stalker, or worse, were to target someone on the internet who so freely opens their lives up to everyone?" It snowballed from there . . .

This book began years ago and was put on hold in the midst of dealing with my mother's illness, but I wouldn't change anything about how I spent the last few years of her life. When I decided to warn her of a few of the more scintillating scenes in my book, she only had two things to say, "Oh Rachel, I wasn't born yesterday," and "If it's your inspiration, write it. Don't worry about what others think or say". That was the final gift she gave me, and I am truly thankful for it.

I am grateful for all of the loved ones in my life, but I want to acknowledge and thank those who have truly encouraged and supported me along this journey.

To my husband Ed, thank you for believing in me. You are my rock and the love of my life.

To my brother Alex, thank you for willingly engaging in 'rough draft' conversation about my book and offering your perspectives. You are one of the most intelligent people I know.

To Tara my niece, thank you for cheering me on with your infectious optimism, and trying to lend a 'social media' helping hand. There is no one else like you!

To Charles and David, my two partners in crime, for both fun and support, from the time we were teens. We've celebrated in good times and leaned on one another through stormy times. I couldn't love two friends more!

To Rachael, a girl couldn't ask for a better friend! Thank you for offering your services as my first reader, and for initiating 'book night' meetings with me over the phone where you described every detail you loved! Your willingness to share your thoughts and enthusiastic reactions feed my writer's soul.

To Mitzi, my lifelong friend and reader number two, thank you for offering and sharing my upcoming book release with your multitude of followers as well as expressing your appreciation for its characters. Also, thank you for telling me to stop daydreaming long enough to make good grades, and telling me now that I am doing exactly what I was meant to do.

To the talented designers at Damonza for my book cover. You nailed every detail with your artistry. Working with Robynne has been a pleasure!

To Kristen, both family and one of the most gifted writers and teachers I will ever know, thank you for taking the time to help guide me through this publishing and marketing process. Without your help, I'm not sure I would *ever* have gotten this far, but with it, I see the spark at the end of a daunting tunnel where my work will see the light of day. More than anything, thank you for offering an olive branch when I tearfully admitted that I felt as though my time had passed on my dream of becoming a published writer. You immediately looked up and read to me multiple peoples' stories who had fulfilled their dreams in their forties and later. That was the beginning of my hope on this journey!

Keep reading for a sneak peek of the
second installment in the
Anonymity Series...